Op Oloop

First edition published in Spanish (privately) in 1934
Copyright © Heirs of Juan Filloy
c/o Guillermo Schavelzon & Asoc., Literary Agency
Translation copyright © Lisa Dillman, 2009
First English translation, 2009

Library of Congress Cataloging-in-Publication Data

Filloy, Juan.
 Op Oloop / by Juan Filloy ; translated by Lisa Dillman.
   p. cm.
 "First edition published in Spanish (privately) in 1934."
 ISBN 978-1-56478-434-6 (pbk. : acid-free paper)
 1. Finns--Argentina--Fiction. I. Dillman, Lisa. II. Title.
 PQ7797.F535O6 2009
 863'.62--dc22
                    2009014806

Partially funded by a grant from the Illinois Arts Council, a state agency, and by
the University of Illinois at Urbana-Champaign

This work was published within the framework of the Sur Translation Support Program
of the Ministry of Foreign Affairs, International Trade and Worship of the Argentine
Republic

www.dalkeyarchive.com

Cover: design and composition by Danielle Dutton, illustration by Nicholas Motte
Printed on permanent/durable acid-free paper and bound in the United States of America

Op Oloop
Juan Filloy

Translated by Lisa Dillman

Dalkey Archive Press
Champaign and London

10:00 A.M. The clock struck ten.

He'd taken great care writing the invitations. Now all he had to do was address the last envelope, to his closest friend, Piet Van Saal. But he couldn't. He felt as though two heavy talons grasped him by the shoulders, determined to wrench him from his task.

He sat there for quite some time, his head lolling against the headrest of his swivel chair. Laxity suited him. Then, slowly, demurely, he opened his eyes. And once again leaned toward the desk, trying to fool fate. He looked left and right, furtively—like a common criminal—and took up his pen. But he could get no further than the *S* of Señor. A fine, elegant capital *S*, like a meat hook. And on it he hung what remained of his body (fatigue) and soul (exasperation).

Thus, Op Oloop was convinced yet again that it was simply impossible for him to act contrary to his nature. "SUNDAY: WRITING, BETWEEN 7:00 AND 10:00 A.M." That was the rule. When life is as ordered as a mathematical equation, you can't just skip a digit whenever you feel like it. Op Oloop was entirely incapable of any impromptu act that might violate the pre-established norms of his routine, even such a trivial, graphical act as addressing an envelope he'd already begun while still within the allotted time.

"Oh well. I'll see him in person," he consoled himself. Op Oloop was method personified—an accomplished executioner of spontaneity: method made word; all his hopes, desires, feelings channeled into the vessel of method. He was method incarnate: undisturbed by even the tiniest rogue impulse, the littlest leap or bound—be it spiritual or carnal. How could he break that rhythm? How could he alter that flow?

"It's no use. I'll never break free. Force of habit has forced my hand. All I ever wanted was to mold myself from something small and insignificant into something great, like a little Renaissance jewel, patiently chiseled, sparkling with intuition, shimmering with wisdom. Alas, idiotically, I chose to enroll myself in the bitter school of constraint. I've turned my psyche into a stopwatch of perfect and ineluctable exactitude—complete with alarm and glow-in-the-dark numerals . . . I hear and see my failure at all times, and with absolute accuracy. And I suffer, unable to defeat my undignified genius, strangling everything from the tiniest whims to the most overwhelming urges. And yet . . . I find that a new insurrection, timid yesterday, implacable today, is trying to create chaos in the already crowded house of my mind. To no avail. Constraint has long since castrated my need to *be something* in the eyes of the world. Instead I've only managed to be some *thing*."

He wasn't actually speaking. His voice was directed inwards, towards a *daimon* curled up in his mind.

Just then his manservant walked in.

"Sir. Allow me to remind you that today, Sunday, at ten-thirty, you are scheduled to have your Turkish bath. You have only a few minutes if you still want to arrive on time. Shall I call for the car?"

"Unbelievable! I've told you before, I never forget anything: the car has already been called for. Now, please see that you deliver this correspondence to the corresponding addresses. Today."

The mechanical nod of his manservant's close-cropped head caused his chin to tap his chest. Then he bowed to hand Op Oloop hat, cane and gloves.

Some people measure out their lives in streetcar transfers, or overdue notices from the bank, or calendars hanging on the walls of the offices where they illicitly refill their fountain pens. Op Oloop was not one of those. His entire house was a living ledger, a meticulous archive, a veritable emporium of mementos. Each wall displayed a profusion of synoptic tables, statistical maps, and polychromatic diagrams. Each piece of furniture was a warehouse of data, of old reports, of studies and experiences. Each drawer, a file folder safeguarding the reliability of Op Oloop's memory. Even his pockets held remnants of his profound lucubration.

Thus, being the only begotten son of method and resolve, Op Oloop was the most perfect of human machines, the most notable object of self-discipline that Buenos Aires had ever seen. When everything in life from the important universal phenomena to one's own trivial, individual failures has been recorded and annotated since puberty, it's fair to say that one's systems of classification will have been honed, condensed to their most perfect quintessence. Or else deified into a great, overarching, methodological hierarchy. Method's very greatness, of course, is revealed in its sovereignty over the trivial!

He left the room.

The picture of savoir faire and distinction.

Standing in front of the mirror in the foyer, he put the finishing touches to his toilet, readjusting the angle of his hat for maximum jauntiness and confirming the pulchritude of his lapels. Two accents offset the shade of brown he wore: his matte-white face and his tobacco-colored eyes. Three sharp points provided the requisite contrast to the overall effect: the clairvoyant sparkle of his pupils, and the pearl stud twinkling like a star in his crimson tie.

From this vantage point, he contemplated his office. A breeze filtered in through the wide pointed arch of the open balcony. A calm morning. Curious, festive sun. His eyes fixed on the solid or-der of his bookshelves, the columns of bound folders, the straight plinths of adding machines and hole-punchers, standing out against the sedate gray walls, curtains, and carpets. The whole of it gave him a feeling of assurance, of self-possession, of fitting squarely into the balance of the world. He nodded. Everything was in order. The inscrutability of his labors could never have withstood the incur-sion into his sanctum of any fashionable decor, feeble and vapid, demanding orthopedic armchairs on which the indolent prefer to perch, facing luxurious bookbindings (containing no text), Brandt wrought-iron fixtures (vain, superfluous), and Lalique glass bowls (brimming over with thorns).

Once in the car, these ideas took off in search of higher ground. And before he knew it, Op Oloop began to sermonize to himself:

"Alas, the great princes, heirs, and priests of today—jaded by court favors, idleness, and easy women—have never truly worked, never toiled to the point of exhaustion, have never truly made a noble effort! They know nothing of the heroic, nothing of violence or the harshness of life—they live lives of sloth, privilege, wealth, and pride, receiving these gifts both from above (from God! silver spoons and embossed plates!) and from below (servants wiggling their coccyges! lackeys with bulging muscles! girls offering up fleshy caresses, cottony sweetnesses, and silken Christmases!)."

People squandered their lives tracing useless patterns in the air, on the ground, in the water, and onto objects: trails, furrows, wakes, text. Freeloaders blowing smoke rings, choreographing dance steps, contorting their bodies to play sports, all filled him with the great-est indifference. If instead of producing these inconclusive patterns they diligently counted the number of umbrellas lost in cafés, the number of cases of bigamy and appendicitis, the number of com-mas obstructing the clarity of local laws, then at least they would have proven themselves of some use, helping to establish indices of normative probability in the causal links between these disparate elements. Alas, not everyone is born with a calling, infused with a divine fervor. Some people know no duty beyond tracing their own pathetic patterns in nothingness. Op Oloop was not one of those people. Wearing a raincoat, he knew exactly the number of umbrellas lost; being single, he knew every line of the national jurisprudence with respect to bigamy; enjoying good health, he could quote at length the ancient and modern theories with regard to appendicitis; and abhorring lawyers, he could tally the precise number of commas speculated over in this or that tangle of Latin and hermeneutics.

The car pulled up in front of the bathhouse.

Yes, incredible as it may seem, the lonely lives of some of the most evolved specimens of our species have always swung on the well-oiled hinges of routine. Poor Kant's imperatives never let him get past the beer halls of his own hometown; poor Pasteur's microbes forced him to steep in a pure and pasteurized milk of solitude; poor Edison's inventions kept him wired all day and night, insomniac and deaf. As the spirit expands, so the flesh is subjected to ineludible clichés. Imagination, fornication, and inebriation become mathematical habits—all the hours of the day become irrevocably allocated to pleasures, functions, familiar events . . . become as ingrained as duty itself. Whenever the mind tries to ascend into realms of new and sublime abstraction, matter persists and confines it in the cellar of habit.

10:40 A.M. At precisely 10:40 in the morning, Op Oloop was just emerging from a changing booth and heading for the bathing establishment's *sudatorium*, a small percale sheet covering his sex.

Ever-smiling, ever-flexible—thinking of their tips—the employees bowed as he passed: the attendants, like xylographers, worked their clients' woods thinking only of the final cut. Op Oloop appreciated them—truly, he did. The moment he crossed the threshold, his thoughts in the *apodyterium* focused on their concerns. And he sought to enlighten them.

"Some day, when I build a decent house, like Pliny the Younger in Laurentum, I'll construct the most perfect facilities. And then I'll take one of you as my assistant: I'll have a masseur from the Maison de Bain on Rue Cadet in Paris, a *parfumier* from the *hammam* I frequented in Istanbul on that boulevard in the Pera district, and the Yankee engineer who built the great bathhouse in Valparaíso. Much as modern mansions boast an arsenal of bottles behind their bars with which to intoxicate their guests, I hope instead to have heavenly, hot thermal baths—a miniature Caracalla—for the heartfelt happiness of my friends."

"And, of course, your girlfriends . . ."

"Never! Clearly you've never seen that Ingres painting . . . There's nothing more repulsive than a group of academically obese women melting in the *tepidarium*. Forget all the perfume and music floating in the air—no exorcism in the world could free us of the ill humors of women! They're a pain in the nose—that's their greatest shortcoming."

He'd reached the first room. His robust physique hadn't diminished in the least in the heat. No. His five-foot eleven-inch frame bore his pre-dehydrated one hundred and ninety pounds perfectly. Yes, Op Oloop loved Turkish-Roman baths for several reasons. To begin with, because after nearly two decades living outside of Finland, he'd finally completed his process of Argentinification. Secondly, because baths like the ones he'd grown up with—such as those at Helsingfors—were *a priori* doomed to fail in Buenos Aires. Thirdly, therefore, because these local baths awoke within him a long-vanished feeling of nationalism, incompatible with his usual hatreds; here, in these Argentinean Turkish-Roman baths, he found he was able to love his homeland, and in a much different way than the Finnish masses: with a sort of meaty patriotism, achieved synthetically after decanting his great universal love. But the most important reason might have borne some relation to his flat feet and plantar corns. To the remarkable physical aberration that were his flat feet and plantar corns!

"Have you ever reflected," he often asked, "on the network, the web, the pattern that your feet weave and tangle in their diurnal maneuvers, over the long canvas of the years of your life? Well, of course not. Normal people are so unaware of their own normality."

But Op Oloop often pondered said theme. When one suffers from a deformation such as his, the brain naturally rocks back on its heels. All roads seem to lead to a steep precipice. And one builds up stores of tears and prescriptions—both entirely useless.

The Statistician knew perfectly well, for instance, that pains in the feet could be caused by an infection of the dental alveoli, or of the tonsils. So, just in case, after having removed the latter, he replaced most of his teeth with dentures. Likewise, he knew that inadequate footwear led to bad posture and that the resulting foot deformations could lead to a whole host of maladies, including: poor circulation, indigestion, anemia, back pain, rheumatism, renal dysfunction, insomnia, and weak legs. And so, again, likewise just-in-physiotherapeutical-case, he spent most days at home, barefoot. Like certain democracies, his problem was constitutional in nature. And he saw it transcribed onto a collection of plantar molds that a specialist in podiatric deformities had made under the pretext of lumbering Op Oloop with a whole series of useless apparatuses.

"Orthopedy," he consoled himself, rubbing his feet in the 48°C heat, "is an old dodge unworthy of our internal perfection. What difference does being paralyzed make if the brain cells corresponding to our absent feelings aren't active anyway? Lazarus was perfectly happy when he was stock-still and silent, but does anyone know how things turned out for him post-miracle? And orthopedic thaumaturgy would certainly count as a miracle. What matters is avoiding *spiritual* crippledom, which mildews the entire psychology of one's life into resignation. Desires are made lame—designs, handicapped . . . No matter what canes and crutches hope and the wise men of the world might extend to you, all your decisions become abridged before coming to fruition. And the vital problem remains unresolved throughout our lives."

The profuse perspiration provoked by the first room of the bathhouse triggered a languorous, abulic sensuality that tended to put most novices under. Op Oloop placed a cold, damp cloth on the nape of his neck and lowered his eyelids, like two rattan blinds, in repose. In doing so, he hoped to stave off the evidence that his feet had spliced the prime of his life into a premature decrepitude. Because, he thought, culture ages individuals. It reins in juvenile exuberance, compresses adulthood, and compels one to live by its own strict principles. No one is more a slave—which is precisely what culture turns us all into—than he who worships freedom. Thus, Op Oloop's sensual sensibilities, sick at their roots—in his physical form—resented his intellectualism, since everything is, after all, related . . . and it all ends at the brain. Unless, that is, you're some kind of brute—a soccer player or marathoner—whose feet are in demand precisely because of their terrible vigor . . .

By the time he reopened his eyes, this latest outburst of his had run its course. But he rose resolutely, nonetheless. He wanted to assert the glories of exudation in the 65°C *caldarium*. What a bitter failure! His movements were awkward and halting. Sweat poured off him—he looked like a small-town fireman's leaky hose, or a weak old man, riddled with woes.

For an athlete or stevedore, thirty-nine isn't a difficult age: prodigies, both, in mercenary, dispassionate professions. But for a yogi who's remained passive, saving up a lifetime of psychic energy, or else a phlegmatic gentleman trying at all times to economize on any potentially futile gestures, it can be quite a lugubrious time. As in Op Oloop's case. As far as he was concerned, everyone who tries to economize—whether internally (that is, emotionally) or externally (that is, monetarily)—lives inundated by ghosts. While he knew from his own experience that spending one's time analyzing the sentiments of others tends to eclipse one's own feelings of foreboding, this same property allows one's skepticism to mature to the point that—rather than simply tempting one away from the path of righteousness—it begins to populate the inner peace one had been seeking . . . with specters.

He was right not to enter the *laconicum*, the petite, maximum-temperature enclosure. Three emaciated jockeys were within, rubbing themselves down exhaustedly. Their faces, wasted away to begin with, wore bitter, sneering expressions. Perhaps they were thinking of all the little friends who had wheedled hot racing tips out of them and were now sitting pretty in the city's bars, spilling the hows and wheres at tables laden with aperitifs and hors d'oeuvres. Perhaps they were dreaming of mayonnaise and noodles, the fattening foods and the fragrances that tend to fill family homes on a typical Sunday. And obsessed by the lurid contrast between their lives and these dreams, they went on rubbing themselves down, exhaustedly, in order to keep themselves at the starting gate, at the proper weight, atop the sinews of a thoroughbred, themselves just one more long sinew, beginning at the spur and ending with the whip.

Op Oloop shot furious, sidelong glances at them all. When one's head sits a little more than five feet eleven inches off the ground, and that distance is filled by a sturdy architectural mass, then the procedure of observing these kinds of fellow—bony, aristiform, their skin sallow and saggy—is necessarily carried out with the dogmatic superiority felt by a MAN confronted by three sacks of kindling.

Besides, he detested betting, detested turfmen. When one has "systematically" gone broke in every casino in the world by following supposedly infallible methods for winning; when one has invested thousands of insomniacal nights obeying Napoleon's postulate, "*Le calcul vaincra le jeu*"; when one has subscribed to *La Revue de Monte Carlo* for fifteen years in order to assess the probabilities of risk from the eternal verities of the roulette wheel; when one has waded through the "Six Hundred Fifty-four Habits of the Perfect Gambler" in order to compare the success of Marigny's system (irrefutably logical) to the predictions of "Madame Cassandre, *Voyante*" (random and improvable); when one has placed bets following the theories of Theo d'Alost, d'Alembert, Gaston Vessillier, Professor Alyett, and Ching-Ling-Wu, and lost one's time, money, and patience on each and every occasion, be it in differential games of chance, equilibrium, intermittent progressions, etc. . . . one reaches the irrefragable conclusion that, in the end, chance is something that's rather hard to grasp, like an eel slipping through a child's fingers.

Just at that moment, a fellow so obese he'd need a whole harem around him to get a hug, pushed past Op Oloop with the protruding prow of his paunch.

"Please, sir! Do watch where you're going!"

Grunting was the only reply. Strange, ventriloquial grunting. Almost *flatus vocis*.

Op Oloop suddenly forgot his tirade against jockeys and gamblers and redirected his vitriol onto this big brazen bather:

"What on earth does this fellow think? *Does* he think? No! Individuals like this suffer from a sort of animalistic regression. They're only capable of 'thinking' about whatever it is they happen to desire. The more they stuff down, the more they gobble up, the more their stores of fat act as levees, holding back real ideas. To the point that their actually conceiving of anything of substance borders on the impossible. The ideas just seize up in their corporeal prison! And the few that do break free, after daring and no doubt hair-raising escapes, meet their demise when they make it to the mouth— where they're strangled by such curious sounds . . . It's rather difficult to make head or tail of these people. Their skinny legs and disproportionately diminutive derrieres speak to the enormous pains they take, trying to assimilate. But their paunches grow and grow, regardless of how much they fast—because flab is born of a shortage of ideas, growing in inverse proportion to cogitation. It brings forth a flaccid rotundity as soon as the mouth stops articulating thoughts in favor of gobbling meats and sweets. When one reaches that stage, the cerebral lobes abandon the skull and sink down into the buttocks . . ."

Hypothesizing thus, Op Oloop returned to the *tepidarium* in order to shower and then get soaped up. He ambled sadly, with a low-flying *tristesse* that hovered around his feet—that he trudged through like a man ankle-deep in sand, or a man scaring toads in a ditch.

He'd never before made this journey wearing such a profound expression of bitterness. His mind was still boiling over with new diatribes against the jockeys and the fatso. But the instant the shower's cool streams hit him, a new, somewhat tepid smile welled up, more in his eyes than on his lips. He'd just managed to convince himself that, yet again, he'd successfully fought off—silent Quixote of equilibrium that he was—the forces of evil, on this occasion embodied by the emaciation of some and the corpulence of others. Then, along with the shower's cold water, he too released a spray—a spray of pure thoughts regarding his health and coenesthesia. And then he rang the bell.

An attendant, on tiptoe, wrapped him in two towels, tied as robe and turban.

"Shall I call the masseur?" he inquired.

"No. I'll take a swim first. Followed by a Scottish shower, salt scrub, pedicure, and a sherry cream cocktail made with three egg yolks."

With that, stepping lightly and gingerly, and before even reaching the edge of the pool, he dove naked into the tourmaline salt water.

Op Oloop knew that nudity was strictly forbidden. But being a man respectful of all prohibitions, he had previously alerted the attendant to his intentions, offering a hefty tip in exchange for his turning a blind eye to this infraction, which would allow Op Oloop's own naturophysiocratic naiveté the pleasure of swimming nude and guilt-free.

"Ah, to swim! To swim! What a fine, graceful kind of joy, to dive into the water from atop a quivering board! A man in the water seems as though he's flying in the sky. The economy of one's strokes is borne out by the rhythm of the waves. And in the depths—utter delight. One's body surrenders, transported in a mystical union. To swim! To swim!"

Agile, golden, strong, his body forged its way towards the *frigidarium*, the final room in the bathhouse. Humming. *Andante. Allegro vivace. Presto* . . . The magnificent statue of his flesh withstood the alternating assault of hot and cold blasts from the Scottish shower; he delighted in the nickel tub, the cunning of a thousand tiny jets penetrating his pores; and finally, swathed and draped in towels and reclining in a chaise longue, he let his blood and his fantasies run free with delicious nonchalance.

He'd been reposing thus for ten minutes.

"Your cocktail, Sir . . ."

"Your pedicure, Sir . . ."

The physical and psychic relaxation was so utter and perfect that opening his eyes at the intrusion of the two voices represented quite an unpleasant effort. But there was nothing to be done. He extended his arm to accept the golden glass from one and stretched out the physical aberrations that were his flat feet and plantar corns to the other.

"Take as many precautions against happiness as against the plague," he thought to himself. "Getting carried away causes bloating, and happiness quickly turns to misfortune. If only people were cautious and employed a bit of strategy—savoring the stuff in tiny sips, in little swallows, we wouldn't have such an abundance of unhappy idiots about."

And with that he downed his sherry cream cocktail in one gulp, caressing the liquid with his tongue.

All at once, his thoughts sunk then into an almost atmospheric depression.

A sharp, hostile feeling, the result of a brusque maneuver on the part of his pedicurist, had cut short his flight of fancy. His sense of self had been impregnated by one of anxiety. He felt the futile flutterings of his soul as it tried in vain to recapture its former gaiety. And then, apathetically, he plunged down, down, down—that is, inside himself—until he butted up against the soulless soles of his feet.

Op Oloop said nothing. He had trained his sentiments so well that, in emergencies such as this, the gravest of admonishments and the harshest of reprimands—if well delivered—could be condensed into a single grimace of displeasure.

"Please, sir, a tad gentler. I'm well aware that my plantar corns are many and rough. That they resemble rubber-soled shoes. Yes, to a T. But I beg you not to be intimidated, not to rush. You have precisely half an hour in which to perform your task."

"Sorry, sir . . . I won't rush . . . Your feet will feel fine when I'm finished. What's more, I'm going to give you a home remedy that'll work wonders. Three grams of collodion, three and a half of salicylic acid. Soak your feet every night . . ."

"Mind your own business. I have not got a single night to spare."

His words, weighty with solemnity, sank the pedicurist in his place, and he bent back over his work as though he'd been shot in the back of the head.

An equally weighty silence engulfed them both.

Op Oloop's riposte no doubt upset him more than it had its target. His was an *anima symphonialis*, and any sharp remark was enough to shatter the intimate rhythms of his decorum, to destroy the great harmony of his methodology. But something even more upsetting lay ahead.

Sometimes impatience boils over in even the most phlegmatic of creatures. Op Oloop suffered from this fundamental weakness. It was surfacing. He couldn't bear having let slip, and spontaneously, a belief he ought to have guillotined with his two lips the moment it strayed into his mouth. And now he burst out again, this time to and for himself:

"I have not got a single night to spare!"

"I HAVE NOT GOT A SINGLE NIGHT TO SPARE!"

"I HAVE NOT GOT A SINGLE NIGHT TO SPARE!"

Indeed, he now felt hounded from within by a ferocious, uncontainable compulsion. The retort he'd issued so naturally, a dictate from his subconscious, had now been rekindled and multiplied in every corner of his mind. It bounced off the walls of his soul, shattering into yelps and titters. It wove itself into the boulevards of his nerves, echoed, spelled out in sonorous, synesthetic, Neolux script. Strident and sparkling, it bubbled over in a veritable pandemonium:

"ERAPS OT THGIN ELGNIS A TOG TON EVAH I!"

"I SIN HAVE GLE NOT NIGHT GOT TO A SPARE!"

"ERAPS A OT TOG THGIN TON ELG EVAH NIS I!"

There was a moment when he believed chaos had entirely conquered his mind. The words tumbled about capriciously like a troupe of acrobats at a dress rehearsal. Never in his life had he endured such a sickening sensation. Accustomed as he was to an orderly calm—indeed, verging on the spiritual tranquility often ascribed to your garden-variety beggar—he could abide neither life's *grand mals* nor their accompanying din.

A lucid interval brought on by the sound of the jockeys' high-pitched voices nearby briefly armed Op Oloop with just enough good sense to try and free his mind of this chaos. All in vain. His entire self was being subjected to a kind of insurrection, and it rolled in a maelstrom of anxieties while an ill wind blew through his heart.

Thus—he'd been left with no other choice!—Op Oloop took up the age-old position of his ancestors, the stance of those who'd come before him, when they came upon hard times. The stance, that is, of Soren Oloop, the most illustrious of the Oloops, in that Van Ostade painting. The stance of defense, of buttressing oneself! The stance that closes off all points of entry and affirms the supremacy of silence! He straightened up slightly in his chaise lounge. Thrust his left elbow down onto the armrest. Wedged his cupped hand under the tip of his chin. Stretched his index finger the length of his nose, so as to be pointing at his baleful eyes. Barred, with the triple lock of his remaining fingers, the embrasure of his mouth. And placed his thumb beneath his jaw as a final indication of his new disposition.

He kept this up for a quarter of an hour. Immobile.

Anyone who's managed to tame their passions, urges, and desires knows that a peremptory tone can subdue any impulse: once the peak of rebellion is past, insurgency will always obey the command to surrender arms, to allow discipline to be reestablished. This was a phenomenon well known to Op Oloop. On many occasions, the rigors of his method had led to coarse pronouncements of his entelechy, ideas, desires; but, each time, the pull of familiar comforts, and his familiar tranquility—ruled, admittedly, by an excessive implacability—finally rendered them docile before returning them, chastised, to his mental barracks.

He was still shaking, upset. All his hastily repressed protestations could be seen in the twitching of his eyes. This particular rebellion had been profound. It was a rebellion of instinct itself, with the most intrepid representatives of his consciousness—intellect and will—standing guard as *meneurs, condottieri, patrones.*

The pedicurist had finished. Holding Op Oloop's talons in the palms of his hands, he admired his work, highly pleased, satisfied with these *objets d'art.* When one achieves this sort of ecstasy in so lowly an occupation, this ecstasy tends to denote a certain mystical quality, even an outright psychopathology. But the pedicurist was blissfully unaware of this—he sat, absorbed, Op Oloop's feet in the palms of his hands like two cracked porcelain statuettes.

The cry Op Oloop let out on seeing this was imprecise in nature, but entirely dismantled the buttressed ancestral stance he'd assumed. Seeing this adoration of his semi-handicapped feet, the intellectual and psychological regiments that had been struggling to beat back the guerrillas of his unease collapsed entirely.

"What aberration! Absurd! Get this fetishist away from me!"

And he ran, nude, towel in hand, toward the changing booths in the *apodyterium*.

Again, that obese fellow blocked his way, his colossal jelly-belly quivering like some jury-rigged shock absorber.

"Please, sir, do watch where you're going!"

This time the elephant stopped. The grunts he'd emitted on their previous encounter were now clarified, expressed as completely comprehensible commentary:

"Look here, sir. This is the second time you've said that to me, but I'm not the one who's running around crashing into people. If you're not crazy already, you must be most of the way there . . ."

Op Oloop froze. His lips curled into a blasphemous sneer. His eyes, intent on rebutting this accusation, squinted and nearly crossed. His comeback, however, was somewhat less than spectacular. The abuse his contorted rictus had intended to hurl at the fat man dissolved into panic-stricken jibbering:

"Crazy? Crazy? Crazy . . . 'Crazy.' Crazy! Crazy. Crazy! Crazy? 'Crazy!' Crazy . . . Crazy? Crazy!?"

The word went through every possible nuance of expression. It traversed the inverse staircase of his psyche, up and down, adding entirely unprecedented steps to the route. And suddenly recovering his vanished fury, he escorted it from the point of its initial feverish intensity until finally it overflowed once more in stentorian desperation:

"Crazy? Crazy? Crazy . . . 'Crazy.' Crazy! Crazy. Crazy! Crazy? 'Crazy!' Crazy . . . Crazy? Crazy!?"

This ballyhoo was short-lived. The other bathers' *Calm Downs* acted as a balm, blunting his obsession, helping him attribute the insanity in question to others. An admirable procedure! Out of inertia, however, the word had now become an ineradicable concept in his consciousness, and continued to lurch around his skull.

He tried to calm down. A look of serenity returned to his wild eyes as a towel was returned to his heretofore-exposed member. And entering his changing booth, Op Oloop said, "Thank you, boys. No call for alarm. It's nothing . . . It's all over now. What a disgraceful elephant! Please excuse me. My head is a pocket-sized edition of hell!"

Omne individuum ineffabile! That old adage from his school days finally applied to him. Op Oloop, method and order personified, perfect picture of sophrosyne—as he used to characterize himself privately, the better to accentuate the apparent instability of others—had cracked, and over nothing, crashing from the peak where his personality sloped down into the pit of dementia.

As he was dressing, his brain engaged in its usual unconquerable inclination to cerebrate. Op Oloop looked on the mishaps of the morning as minor traffic accidents in the proper flow of his ideas. And noting the external barricades imposed upon this flow by the occurrences in the bathhouse—as well as his resulting internal persecution by incomprehensible forces—he tried coquettishly to hide this new flaw in his metaphysical mirror.

Nothing but a fallacy! You can have a supreme command of reason, understanding, morality: all that which man has achieved or inherited through contact with other men; but your biology, the exclusively biological, cannot be controlled mathematically. Yes, it's quite absurd, this determination to conquer oneself every single day, to be wholly worthy in one's wishes and wants! This ever-so-distinguished desire to disdain the scruples and edicts issued by the flesh and its passions! This unhealthy hierarchical desire to be an emperor of discipline, never bending to whim or fancy!

During the aforementioned emergency, Op Oloop should have taken psychoanalytic inventory, insightfully and solemnly: that is, methodically. Sadly, however, method is of no use when one is dealing with the stratagems of chance. The man of method may channel all his spiritual currents towards productive ends, be relentless in his suppression of predilection and propensity, but when accident upsets the flow of his life, he finds himself drowning in a sea of tedium, hatred, and rage. Op Oloop, strong swimmer that he was, felt the profound sadness of his situation—the premature exhaustion of a shipwrecked seaman with no shore in sight.

Achieving sovereignty over one's external actions and the internal psychic processes that allow them to occur is of little use if—the moment a risky situation arises—every effort aimed at assuring control is thwarted by some quirk of natural instinct.

Indeed, as he well knew, every scrap of sequential thought—acting to abolish that cardinal sin, error, as well as emulation and syllogism—and every drop of logical comportment—meant to tame base matter, to subjugate the flesh and restrain the blood—lay prostrate, enfeebled, before the image—the mere image!—of a woman.

11:45 A.M. The clock struck eleven forty-five. At that moment, Op Oloop was staring pensively at himself, a morose monster of melancholy and self-pity. The three thumps on the door reverberated within him. After dressing absentmindedly, mechanically, he took his gloves, hat, and cane. And then his leave.

The bathhouse attendants awaited him, feigning new duties in his vicinity to disguise their desire for a *pourboire*.

With mathematical austerity, as on every other identical occasion for the past several years, the Statistician handed a tip of thirty-five centavos to each of the four men, comprised of coins in the denomination of twenty, ten, and five centavos, respectively.

The employees jabbered their thanks and winked at one another.

There was always a tip. And it was always the same: thirty-five centavos each, comprised of coins in the denomination of twenty, ten, and five centavos. Routines are unyielding. They take hold like lice. They multiply, teeming over each new encounter, as on hair follicles. Only fever or insanity can wipe them out.

Op Oloop was glowing. The bath had appled up his face. Like a confidant eager to confide.

"Come," he bade the attendants mysteriously.

They were surprised by this sudden change in his conduct. They presumed his "attack" had passed. And they came.

"I'm going to give you a bit of useful advice. But, take heed! I feel the whisper of a pygmy filling my mouth—thus, let the discretion of giants fill your chests!"

The pedicurist drew in close.

All of them looked Op Oloop up and down.

There was a horrible silence.

The others, glancing at one another, cocked their heads mockingly. And nearly in unison, without a clue as to what he'd meant, they babbled, "The whisper of a pygmy! The discretion of giants!"

They were overcome by a gnawing perplexity. Op Oloop stepped forward, resolute. His reputation demanded that he eradicate the poor impression left by his earlier conduct. He was conscientious. He knew that the unconventional stuck far more readily than the normative in the pea-brains of humble folk. He knew that the blather of the masses spread like wildfire and quickly set the wood of infamy alight. And so, to keep his name untarnished, and erase any memories that might have been created by his behavior that morning, he explained, "Yes, boys, I'm going to give you some useful advice. Free legal advice! Mussolini banned tipping in 1920. On October 1, 1930, the Spaniards did the same. Since 1882, when Von Jhering undertook a critical, psychological study of tipping, to the publication of Pierre Mazoires's work, *Usage et evolution du pourboire*, Paris, 1931, people have been interested in the topic. It's my duty to know these things, and many others. I'm a statistician, after all! And I've come up with a jurisprudential file on the subject for use by seminarians, academics, and other intellectual types. Don't let your boss pull one over on you! I know you earn only fifty pesos a month. But, as you yourselves know: your salaries are compensated by tips. If you have an accident at work tomorrow, don't accept any indemnity based on your salaries—include your clients' tips, just as your employer depends on them to supplement your pay. That's the theory upheld by Sachet and all French jurisprudence. Don't be fools! Unite! No one can live on fifty pesos. By giving you, collectively, a one-peso forty-centavo tip each time I visit, my generosity compensates the injustice of your employer. Which is why I have the right to call out: Unite! Create a Tipping Control Office in every establishment, in every city, in every country. Don't be fools! Band together; found a Gratuity International!"

Op Oloop's voice had now reached the majestic heights of the prophets. He made a sweeping gesture. And then stepped out onto the street.

Everyone in his wake was pensive. Even his corn-ridden strides were sprightlier than usual. Effusion, vehemence—attitudes he'd never before had recourse to—now sprang from his lips, fresh and candid, like artesian well-water bubbling in a wasteland. His goal had been reasonable enough: to exonerate himself. But he had fallen victim to extremity, having awkwardly misjudged his audience's limits. A difficult boundary to gauge, but failure to do so causes offense. Op Oloop proved to be in excess of said limits. Sophistication can seem grotesque to the uncultured. Even bonhomie, when it transgresses certain limits, becomes suspect. What a shame, the distaste caused by such honest intentions!

Comments sprang up all around.

"What the hell is wrong with that guy? I've never seen anything like it!"

"I feel the whisper of a pygmy filling my mouth! Did you hear that? And all that nonsense about tipping!"

"Maybe his brain melted in the steam room."

"What I don't understand is why he flew off the handle at me for looking at his feet. It doesn't make sense! I've been doing his feet for four years!"

"He can't fool me. He's got bugs in his blood. It's syphilis. Why else would he say, 'My head is a pocket-sized edition of hell'?"

The jockeys offered their opinions as well, having suffered the insolence with which Op Oloop had stared at them.

The elephant, hearing his bathhouse peers concur as to Op Oloop's state of mind barely two feet from his belly, rounded it all off by once again proclaiming phlegmatically, "There's no doubt about it. If he's not already crazy, then he's got to be most of the way there . . ."

How arduous to elucidate, to illuminate all the whys and wherefores of a disturbed soul! Psychiatry—the geography of pathology—

attempts to locate, via its formulas, the many varieties of alienation experienced by *Homo sapiens*. Lurching heroically towards these terrains of obscure, atavistic aboriginality, the psychiatrist—plotting the coordinates of health—maps these temperamental and hereditary troubles in his treatises. But sometimes this is impossible: the cerebral hemispheres, intricate labyrinths even when they fill the cranial cavity, are all the more impenetrable when they fill both cheeks of the posterior. As has already been stated: some people's brains border their anal regions. Thus, their senses are dulled, and the psychopathological pestilence is such that the intrepid scholar-explorer inevitably butts up against a dead end.

In no time at all, Op Oloop reached the corner of Avenida de Mayo, thoughtlessly turning west.

He strode along merrily, audaciously, waving grandly to whomever happened to see him, proffering gestures that brimmed over with his new euphoria.

Dementia has a tendency to lend a certain nimbleness to its subjects. It can help throw off abulia and lubricate joints otherwise stiff with apathy and melancholy. But in Op Oloop, this display escaped all such simple classification. In effect, all men systematically distill themselves throughout their lives, increasing their internal extravagance while decreasing their external luminosity. How, then, are we to explain this manifest failure on the part of a thoroughly proper man to balance his humors? How to justify these oscillations, be they brusque or subtle, when in Op Oloop the equilibrium and tranquility of equinoctial well-being had always, to this point, reigned supreme?

A bus driver saw Op Oloop's expansive gesticulations and pulled over, assuming he wanted to board. Op Oloop was so shocked at this that he did, with a little hop worthy of a newsboy. His body swayed with the sudden lurching of the bus. He climbed the stairs to the second level and made for the empty seats. There were several basketball players aboard. He didn't notice. He saw them as something else. And as they were passing Rodin's so-called *Thinker*, extending an arm like a *cicerone* in front of the Parliament Bulding, he proclaimed, "Gentlemen! Before you stands Rodin's *Thinker*. Originally a part of his *Gates of Hell*. But it doesn't belong here! It resembles a traffic warden. I protest. Yes: with all my might, I protest!"

The boys went downstairs and informed the conductor. And when he in turn climbed up the stairs to ask Op Oloop to please alight, the man in question simply responded, disconsolate, "How tawdry is the *Thinker*, seen from the window of a bus!"

Across from the Parliament, there in the middle of the road, he concentrated all of his attention on the two-way traffic, his powerful physique leaping hither and thither, stalked by tooting horns, sudden screeching brakes, and careless drivers. A sorry sight! He, so proper, so free from all things common, looked like a broken mechanical toy. Finally, he registered the danger of this siege. Stunned, and sure one superhuman effort would solve his dilemma, he leapt into a taxi.

"Just drive. Drive round and round the roundabout."

He didn't sit but collapsed into his seat. And thoroughly spent, he closed his eyes.

The human constitution is weak. He had proof: Mencken had said so. "All the errors and incompetencies of the Creator reach their climax in man. As a piece of mechanism he is the worst of all; put beside him, even a salmon or a staphylococcus is a sound and efficient machine." But Op Oloop still believed himself to be the heroic architect of his own destiny. And though he felt certain of his own order, at ease within the comforts provided by his system, he nonetheless

insisted on persevering, masochistically, in an attempt to overcome
. . . what? And what for? To suffer the shame of having crumbled?
To endure the ignominy of limping and hobbling through his own
ruins? A prickly uneasiness began to corrode his confidence. He saw that
he'd embraced, by means of all his weighty judgments upon life, an
intellectual vigor based wholly on failure. Failure was always there,
blatantly demonstrating his rarefied prejudices and the frailty of his
designs; demonstrating that he'd spend his life building arabesques
of eagerness rather than firm foundations; that his systems all represented an orgy of self-assessment rather than true ethological superiority. And just as he detested theatricality, he anguished now over
having a pochade box for a soul: one that would make everyone
laugh when the vicissitudes of the world at last revealed it as it truly
was . . . as seen beside what it should have been.

Lost in thought and discomfort, Op Oloop heard the spluttering
of the motor, and it suddenly began to interfere with his thoughts.
His ideas evaporated in a booming fog. And then the sound slowly
began to rankle, finally taking on a grating rattlety-bang tenor that
resembled outright enmity. He tried to stifle it by covering his ears—
but no, the clattering was coming from within! It persisted willfully.
And what's worse, it was jocular: a mocking, scornful flatulence.

The Statistician was suddenly overcome by an indignant outrage,
utterly irreconcilable with his upbringing. It had been no use inuring
his sensory organs to the asceticism of his phlegmatic temperament,
his temperament itself to a perpetual kinesthetic harmony. Anyone
who boasted, as he did, of utter neutrality, or rather, of a very neu-
tered neutrality achieved via gradual, intentional adaptation, by force
of will, by psychological absolutism, knew, at times such as these,
just how little their science truly mattered in matters of matter.

Glancing in the rearview mirror, the taxi driver picked up on his passenger's improbable gesticulations and, turning around, asked somewhat gruffly, "Just how long do you want me to drive around in circles?"

"Keep circling!"

The driver accelerated brusquely.

The interruption proved to have a calming effect: just as the driver addressed him, Op Oloop caught sight of Avenida de Mayo, and the thoroughfare embedded itself, jewel-like, into his mind. An image like that, for one whose attention has polyfurcated, signified a *ritorno al'antico*, a regaining of marbles. It was remarkable. He exhaled anxiously and repeatedly at the luck of having in this way recovered his self-possession.

But the mind has its avenues, its streets, its alleyways. Well-heeled neighborhoods lined with chic boutiques. And dirty, dismal quarters too. Dark, sleazy districts. Same as the city! Not far from the fetching Floridas, oozing elegance and extravagance, lie rank Recovas, where vice runs free and bestial instincts ferment all around. Near magnificent centers of art, finance, and culture squat shantytowns of wasted effort, the abulia of the unemployed, slumbering in slums: the hoi polloi who pick their fleas in misery.

Op Oloop soon left the smooth pavement of his consiousness behind. The images that had slipped briefly through his senses, bathing them in the clean reality of old, now snarled him up once more. He couldn't see clearly. There was just a great, tangled silence. And in that great, tangled silence, a droning came and went, cutting behind his eyes and forcing him to close them, slicing through his ears and forcing him to open them, as if to hear a great, redeeming ring from within the surrounding mayhem.

The droning was incessant. At best, as the cab careered around each corner, it would flutter away momentarily, but then it would return to hunt him down, like a trained falcon swooping down onto his brain.

12:50 P.M. His imprecations, twitches, and winks must have been quite off-putting, because at twelve-fifty precisely, the driver could no longer contain himself and screeched to a halt.

"Sir! Just how long do you want me to drive round in circles? We're up to six-eighty, sir!"

"Fine. Here you are."

Op Oloop extricated himself awkwardly from the cab, and while the driver busied himself changing the ten-peso note, he saw another car at the same corner, and cried, "Taxi!"

Heading for it, his hefty form teetered pendulum-like, rather resembling a rock at the edge of a cliff, about to tumble. He'd hardly sat down in his new cab before a voice inconvenienced him:

"Your change, sir."

"You can shove my change up your ass!"

It was a knee-jerk response, delivered by some sprightly sprite squatting in his subconscious. Though both drivers immediately froze, Op Oloop wasn't the least bit ruffled. His riposte had been so diametrically opposed to his own usual—albeit idiosyncratic—character that, while he may have spoken it, he hadn't actually heard himself. Which explains why, when the new driver asked fearfully, "Where to, sir?" Op Oloop's voice once more took on the half-pained, half-festive inflection of that morning:

"Drive round the plaza."

Ill will, hatred, and choler had no place in his soul. But sentiments of a low-class extraction still prowled within him, as they do in us all. The superego segregates or strangles them, but they're always there: lurking, waiting to explode unexpectedly the moment our resolve releases its grip, or delirium beckons.

The ceremonial solemnity of self-control was stamped on Op Oloop! A man who's spent his life inspecting himself, constricting himself, ministering to himself, attains—almost accidentally—inexcusable levels of urbanity. Propriety. Pulchritude. Virtue. Words, gestures, attitudes are the result of years and years of training, and so, such a man becomes almost mindless, given that—since respect for others begins with respect for oneself—he has erred by respecting himself altogether too much.

It's distressing when intellect can't detect its own defects. When this happens, others' deductions, no matter how late they may come, serve to confirm the sluggishness of one's internal censure and, consequently, the breakdown of one's sensibilities. Both drivers realized immediately. Thus, the one who was driving now, with a quick flick of the wrist, made his meter skip three consecutive hundreds. They'd circled the plaza thrice, at most, and already the meter read four pesos and ten centavos.

The Statistician hadn't noticed. Everything, in fact, was slipping by him unnoticed. He couldn't focus. His eyes had tuned into the droning, thereby affecting his ability to hear—which ability hovered awkwardly in the midst of all the urban traffic noise around him. Neuropathy had attached the characteristics of various other senses to Op Oloop's sight. He sat, perplexed, the sensorial wires leading to his brain having been switched around, as though he could listen with his sight or touch with his smell.

Did that ever-present droning mark the boundaries of his mental fog? Or else, was it the sound wave of a thought striving to escape its hazy prison? How tricky it was to attempt to define the seamless quality of that auditory mist! He found himself in that irrepressible state of rapture in which Rimbaud wrote his famous sonnet of the vowels. A fleeting rapture. Op Oloop's gaunt face suddenly came to life in a parade of grimaces: a screen onto which the freakish grotesqueries of some monstrous mask collection were being projected. And these monstrous faces bit him, mockingly. His soul felt dented, distorted, wrinkled. His mouth was distorted by fear. Op Oloop's suffering was indescribable.

Two more laps round.

The speed of the car cooled him down. And as the marks and wrinkles were smoothed off his face, he took on the look of a stupefied angel, astonishment illuminating him with a radiant, satisfied smile.

Suddenly, apropos of nothing, Op Oloop gave himself a little ovation, applauding joyfully several times. And he shouted, "Turn onto Callao. Quick. Quick!"

No doubt, the droning had been drowned out, transmogrified now into something more substantial in his mind . . . an idea? a wish? a feeling? After so many circles round and round Plaza del Congreso, perhaps his sudden impulse was the result of a process akin to the mysterious circles flown by carrier pigeons in order to orient themselves. Or else the inexplicable circling of dogs before they curl up for a nap. Instinct can become trapped inside such broken circumferences. It has to turn around and around inside itself until it finds the fissure, and then at last it rushes out to perform its duty. Circles are absolutely vital.

A reckless greengrocer helped Op Oloop stop his spiraling. The man's unexpected appearance in front of a truck parked at the side of the road caused some consternation for the Statistician's cab. Bruises. An overturned fruit cart.

An authority stepped in.

"And you, sir? See anything?"

"Nothing at all. I was thinking of Franziska. Of Franziska Hoerée."

The naïve glow on his face clearly made a bad impression on the Police Inspector, who couldn't help but mutter, "Unbelievable! A raving idiot. Gibberish."

In truth, Op Oloop was entirely absent. In a delicious trance. A mélange of fantasy and ecstasy. And he remained thus.

"You'll have to come down to the precinct tomorrow."

"Absolutely not! I was thinking of Franziska. Of Franziska Hoerée."

"I wasn't speaking to you, sir!"

The driver drove off, and the intrigued Inspector spent more time contemplating the passenger's curious behavior than he had the accident itself. On a whim, he decided to follow the cab.

The Inspector had mastered, over the course of his police career, the admirable science of speculation: speculating, that is, on probability, and often generating useful premonitions about insignificant details. Gut feelings, hunches, sixth senses, and the like, had always served him better than rational analysis. And so, fantasizing about a new stripe on his uniform, he lost himself in reflections as to when this particular nascent crime would be brought to term—because a crime is always a kind of spiritual pregnancy, and a good detective always has to be on the lookout to determine when the person or persons carrying it might go into labor. Many of the detectives in the department were expert abortionists. Why not emulate them? The Inspector knew that some criminals suffer so terribly from the pressure of their pregnancies that their heads practically burst—their eyes swell up, their good luck sweats out of their pores and disappears—before they finally give bloody birth to their own little crimes . . .

This time, however, his instinct had failed him.

Op Oloop stepped out of the taxi in front of a large house in the Inspector's jurisdiction, a mansion reputed to belong to a man of perfect propriety: the Finnish Consul. Somewhat disheartened, the Inspector turned around. Minutes later, passing by the grocer's, the squashed plums and trampled tomatoes taunted him, innocently demarcating the scene of the crime.

Quintín Hoerée and Piet Van Saal—one short and plump, his head bald and shiny as a helmet; the other pointy-faced, steel-chested, and built like a javelin thrower—stood up on seeing Op Oloop enter the parlor. The Statistician wasn't feeling deferential, but was unable to avoid making an awkward bow, since his friends were nearly eclipsed by his arboreal stature. The shame, the shame! He was overcome by a dense and solid shame . . .

"Forgive me! Forgive me! This is the first time I've ever been late for an engagement. You know that I'm methodical, even in spite of myself! Method is practically an organic function for me. I have never, never, never been in violation of the system that's guided my life. And yet, today . . . !"

"Bah! No need to fret. My brother-in-law and daughter have yet to return from their golf game."

"Nevertheless. It's inexcusable. Ernest Lavisse said that a method man who's catalogued pain, hunger, and sadness without feeling the crack of passion's whip must never fall victim to schisms in the rhythm of his life . . . And yet, today I . . ."

"Enough of this nonsense! Do sit down. Would you like a gin and tonic?"

"It isn't nonsense! A man who's aware of his own defects and does nothing to remonstrate with himself for them is nothing but a re-sounding failure! The very next day, when his tolerance becomes ingrained, systematized, it'll already be too late: he'll have been infected by inferiority, by his own immorality! I have no desire to step down off my throne. And yet, today . . . !"

Piet Van Saal's sharp, piqued tone interrupted him: "Look, Op Oloop. That's quite enough. We're all well aware that method is organic for you, something that rises up inside you with astonishing force and compels you at certain times—like this one, for instance—to make these asinine, inexplicable displays. Drink your drink and be done with it. Why all this sniveling about punctuality if the others haven't arrived yet? Do you see Franziska or the Consul here? Well, then!"

"I beg your pardon. It's been a day of unforeseen calamities. All my methodology has gone straight to hell. It's quite pathetic—perfectly, undeniably pathetic. Here, in my flesh, in my feelings, in my soul, I perceive a me that's gone out of focus, become deformed and imprecise. The austere, solid, resolute man that was *moi* has melted away. *Je suis un homme flou.* And I can't seem to bring the experience to a close. My personality is built on reflection, but I can no longer see myself. I've been captured. My moral and physical matter has become insubstantial. All that remains is the skeleton of my resolve and the scaffolding of old reveries. I'm in a pathetic trance—perfectly, undeniably pathetic."

Silence from one.

Silence from the other.

The unusual irritability with which Op Oloop had prattled on caused his two friends to exchange worried glances. Disconcerted, they approached him. Neither had understood a thing he'd said; both, however, attempted to calm him. Their attempts proved anodyne and ineffectual. The three remained thus for quite some time. Piet Van Saal attributed Op Oloop's behavior to a momentary breakdown brought on by overwork. Quintín Hoerée, more wisely, sought some sentimental explanation relating to Op Oloop's engagement to his, Quintín's, daughter.

They still were at this stage of their diagnosis and pacification when the Finnish Consul and his niece burst in, laughing uproariously and calling greetings.

They were stupefied by what they saw.

Undaunted, Op Oloop was still entirely absent. His eyes stared blankly, his soul stood empty.

No one dared break the vegetal, palpable silence.

The romantic expression worn by Op Oloop, so enigmatic and noble, quickly elicited pity from all, and tears from Franziska.

All at once, then, the tree came to life.

Some sort of internal breeze caused his eyelids to flutter like leaves. His pupils shone. And a smile broke out on the timber of his face.

The bystanders' anxiety, suddenly released in four isochronic sighs, turned to warmth, which filled the room.

And Op Oloop's eyes were drawn like magnets to Franziska's.

The man of the house led his brother-in-law and Piet Van Saal to the drawing room. Quintín Hoerée nearly exploded:

"This is very upsetting! You can't possibly fathom the scene we've just witnessed. A state of absolute delirium, and over what? The most bizarre rationale imaginable, a nonexistent lack of punctuality! It was appalling, pitiful. In the seven years I've known Op Oloop I've never seen him in such a state. And for this to happen on a day like today!"

"Luckily, your daughter didn't see the worst of it. As far as I'm concerned, it has to be a nervous disorder. My friend is a strong, healthy oak. I'm quite certain he hasn't picked up some disease, and that he isn't suffering any internal lesions. It's a nervous disorder, that's all, a nervous disorder. I think we ought to postpone the yachting trip to another day."

"Quite the contrary," said the Consul. "There's nothing like a little distraction. Franziska's presence seems to calm him."

Just then, booming laughter made all three turn their heads simultaneously. They ran back.

The Statistician was swaying like a poplar in a windstorm. Euphoria had stamped blood-red circles on the taught, matte-white muscles of his face. He was flushed. And he talked and talked, phrases flying from his mouth, minced and chopped, complete nonsense:

"Farcical, yes, farcical! . . . I counted one hundred twenty-eight adjectives . . . in a single paragraph . . . can you imagine? IN A SINGLE PARAGRAPH! . . . in an Almafuerte speech . . . When I can't find even one to describe you! . . . Farcical, yes, farcical! . . . It was in La Plata . . . in 1910 . . . at a student gathering . . . Isn't it disgraceful? . . . Hoarding all our adjectives! . . . Farcical, yes, farcical!"

Confronted with the groom's sardonic laugh, Franziska's tiny smile turned apprehensive. Her doll's face—"baby face," as Op Oloop called her, in English—suddenly clouded over. Her heart-shaped lips blanched, and she babbled like a doll, or a baby, "Da-da! Da-da!"

Op Oloop's cackling filled the front room. It made trinkets rattle and lampshades dance. It leapt from the grand piano to the cushions. Bounced off the checkered floor. Crept up the luxurious bindings of the books on the shelf. He watched his laughter, synesthetically, as though it was a little red comic-strip devil—nimbly naughty as it ricocheted around the room, oscillating between different tones, all being emitted at the highest possible register.

While the stunned father and uncle saw to Franziska, Piet Van Saal took a more forthright approach: he assumed a commanding posture, as was proper to dealing with hysterics:

"Op Oloop!" he shouted with all his might, "Op Oloop! That's enough!"

This reprimand struck the Statistician like a bolt of lightening to the head. And as if he'd been violently shoved, he proceeded to collapse into the squishy cushion of an armchair. The Statistician felt as if he'd fallen ass-first into a mud pit. He made a face and mimed cleaning himself off. Presently, and in great contrast to his friend's surly hostility, he went—in the space of a second—from a small smile to further guffawing.

Quintín Hoerée and the Consul, upon returning, cried out almost simultaneously:

"We must call a doctor at once."

"We must call a doctor at once."

Op Oloop bounced back to his feet, as though propelled by a spring.

"A doctor? For me? Why? Because I'm laughing? Ha, ha, ha! Now hear this: I laugh out of an inner obligation! . . . to vent the ill humors of my growing solitude, which thrives on the imbecility of my fellow men! . . . Ha, ha, ha! I don't need any doctor! No one can chase away the demon on duty in my mouth! . . . Ha, ha, ha! The demon confiscating my thoughts! . . . Ha, ha, ha! The demon jumping on my tongue . . . in my ear . . . in my larynx."

Those last words were spoken *in decrescendo*. Simultaneously, Op Oloop's trunk folded in at the middle, and he fell back once again into the armchair he'd sprung up from.

The phone rang immediately.

Exhaustion now welled up from within him and wedged its way

between his lips, like the tide of a rough sea surging up onto the beach. Everyone had a fleeting feeling of commiseration.

And with Op Oloop still soiled by his verbal dust storm, they led him to the Consul's bedroom, where he fell into the Consul's bed like a giant poplar into the sandy bank of a tiny brook.

There followed one of those deliberate, uncomfortable silences in which ideas begin to percolate through one's mind, gurgling around violently like gas in the gut. Each of the witnesses pondered Op Oloop's new, disturbing disconnection from his own usual, distinctive demeanor. And standing before the protagonist's rigid body, each interpreted the drama in his own way.

Quintín Hoerée said to himself:

"This is painful. But better today than tomorrow. Ever since Franziska fell in love with you, I've lived in a perpetual state of anxiety. What can you expect of a statistician! A man who counts, recounts, compares, controls, and catalogues for a living is no kind of man: he's a machine. I like numbers, why deny it, especially the ones in my bank statement. But those are *my* numbers, not others'. I've always wanted a young man for Franziska: slender, active, someone who'd take over my plywood distribution business—best wood on the market!—so it's always pained me that she gave her love to an older man, a portly man, a sluggish man, a man averse to risk, adventure, and audacity—all the best things life and commerce have to offer!—a man steeped in order, discipline, and the hierarchy of method. Truth be told, that he's had this little fit at their engagement party doesn't bother me one bit. Of course I feel bad for Franziska— poor thing!—but this is a sign from above! After all, she's still young. And though I know that daughters always dream of whatever their fathers *don't* want for them, perhaps time will set her heart back on track and she'll find a son-in-law I approve of, both for her and for my plywood import and distribution company."

Piet Van Saal said to himself:

"My poor friend! I can't help but think of the two things you said, that day when we were rowing down the Tigris. Do you remember? 'Solitude is the pleasure of one's own perspective,' you said, and 'Solitude is the academy of strong men.' . . . Now, however, you've tried to broaden the outlook of your soul by bowing to another, and instead all you've managed to do is muddle your own! Poor Op Oloop! Love is light and darkness both. Blinding light when the spirit is empty, virginal—but when it's knowledgeable and disciplined, my friend, it's all darkness, darkness all around. I could never get that across to you, since I felt I had no right to encroach on the mysterious magnificence of your soul . . . But you took a wrong turn! I thought you were educated in solitude—the school of experience at which we've all studied—and yet, look! Why, you're an absolute beginner . . . Poor friend! An absolute beginner who loses his pencil before an exam . . . An absolute beginner who knows what's on the test because he's had his nose in his book all night and studied himself silly, but never thought that passion could come along and trip him up . . . Op Oloop, don't you see where all of your strength, your mechanization, your method has gotten you? Op Oloop! Op Oloop! My poor, poor Op Oloop!"

The Finnish Consul said to himself:

"Well, well. Have patience. That's life! I just wish I could take that little siesta I was planning for our yachting trip. I can hardly keep my eyes open. What a nuisance! And of course he has to have his little fit today—and in my house! That's what really gets me. Next time, Op Oloop, find somewhere else. This is not what a Consul's house is for! It's all Franziska's fault. I've said it all along. But she wouldn't listen! A girl from sixty-five degrees north of the equator recklessly falling in love like a common Neapolitan! Ridiculous! Absolutely preposterous! It's all very, very odd. This morning she was a bundle of nerves, as though she sensed something. I insisted she play golf, to clear her mind. But it was no use! Her drives were strong, but not because she was concentrating on the game. Her approach was graceful. Worry seemed to excite and calm her both. She beat me by three strokes. But I'm convinced she wasn't playing against *me*! On the last green, after a marvelous shot, she could take no more, poor Franziska, and burst into tears. Crying when you're winning, now *that's* a bad sign! Well, well. Patience. That's life! But when is that doctor going to arrive? What a nuisance! You're an unforgivable idiot, Op Oloop. What a fabulous way to inconvenience people, really. Oh! I can hardly keep my eyes open!"

If Op Oloop, from the depths of his paralysis, could have scrutinized these adjacent characters in turn, he would certainly have gotten quite a fright. But his will had sunk, bogged down in a dense abulia.

Franziska's return seemed to clear things up.

Her simple presence guillotined both her father and her uncle's malicious musings. And it washed clean Van Saal's pious features, bathing him in grace.

She came as if in a trance, her face sunken with quiet anguish. Mute. In one hand, a jar of *sal volatile*, in the other, a glass of cognac. Her actions obeyed some unknown decorum. A touch of Ophelia, married with a bit of Charlotte's good sense. A bit of Ligeia, transfused into Eleanora's serenity. The instant her hand rested on her fiancé's forehead, he relaxed it. The creases faded away, waves of flesh blown flat by her tender breeze. Then, the instant the *sal volatile* pierced his pituitary, the grimace of humiliation and resignation that had weighed Op Oloop down vanished. The instant his lips sipped the cordial, the Statistician's burly chest contracted in relief.

"Just a moment, one moment, my love," she said. "I'm going to open the windows. The air in here is heavy with rumination."

Everyone heard her words, stunned. All at once, beckoned by their own surprise, they filed out, singly, only to gather again in the dining room.

Struggling to hold onto the images from his dream, Op Oloop sat up little by little, frowning. The very sweetness of Franziska's solicitousness bolstered him. He stood up straight and tall, all five feet eleven inches erect beside the Consul's bed, and the tiny fragility of his fiancée's frame was like an Egyptian statuette representing the pharaoh's wife in miniature, a single pleat in the enormous garment of her mate.

Op Oloop and Franziska's faces each searched for the other, their looks suspended halfway between them. Hers, since it was upward-facing, resembled ecstasy; his, since it was downward-facing, resembled compassion . . . But in reality, neither was either, and both were both, because that's what love is. It spans both downward-facing ecstasy and upward-facing compassion!

Solitary and solemn, Franziska and Op Oloop saw how sublime this moment was. And through the superlative strength of their spiritual symmetry, they set about certifying the fundamental purity of their souls with a single, absolutely irresponsible kiss.

Instincts adore contrast, and are most delighted when they can unite extremes. Thus is balance built. Op Oloop, on freeing himself from the embrace, blushed innocently, while Franziska took pleasure in the pride of feeling so loved. In perfect balance, then, Op Oloop's deep tuning-fork voice transcribed the images of his dream:

"Franziska. Love's vows, when signed by the soul, are inexorable commitments. There is no such thing as erotic insolvency, unless triggered by a show of false, paste-jewelry affection. Believe in mine as I believe in yours, so I can face our nuptial date with an anxiety born only of our mutual desires. *(Pause.)* With smiles as their only soundtrack, the eyes are a silent guide, setting many fixed-term desires in stone. Words are superfluous in spiritual commerce. The greatest characters in the history of love were always laconic. Werther's tribulations and Marie Bashkirtseff's anguish went unspoken. Those who have achieved the true sumptuousness of superior sentiment know how worthless rhetoric is! *(Deep sigh.)* Courtship can be a tournament of kindness or a diary of obsessions . . . my case exactly. Through successive feints and skillful evasions, one can avoid the wounds so often inflicted by the divine dart of love—or, rather, accepting it with peacocked chest, one can delight in the delectable torment of its myriad distressing discomforts, the pain festering on, rusted into place by your beloved's peculiar perversities. *(Despondency.)* One must always distrust those who stylize love. Professional seducers who value their vanity, who find womanizing a worthy recreation, who frequent those nightly festivals of frivolity in order to flirt. They boast—poor devils!—about their exploits, and thus curb the sources of their desire, so that it can never crystallize. Just as Stendhal feared!—and rightly so. Since love is the force of life itself, any constriction acts to frustrate it, and aesthetics are only fashionable extravagance. *(Exhausted lassitude.)* Passion is the generosity of selfishness. When love is so frenzied as to reach the highest heights of attraction, at its culmination, its climax, an elegant sentiment begins to dominate one's self-interest, begins to tame the hyenas of ego and sow seeds of sympathy, disdaining all else, as well as oneself. '*La société m'importune, la solitude m'accable*' . . . Dejectedly, I merely mimic Benjamin Constant's *Adolphe* . . . *(A few tears.)* It's useless depending on the easy alchemy of good advice to return to one's state of amiable effervescence. It's useless trying to appease this *exacerbatio cerebri* with anything aside from the sedative sanctity of the beloved one. The therapeutics of love are eternal. Love is a poison with only one antidote: love. *(Stifling sobs.)* Franziska: Let our tortured souls be healed in silence! Let joy erupt in an epithalamion of tears! Tears that are nothing more than decanted compassion!" *(His head drops onto his shoulders, inert, an overripe peach drooping off the tree of pain.)*

They might have carried on like this for all eternity. Such beatitude short-circuits the life of the senses and stops the flow of time. But the doorbell, strident, directed the lovers' attention to the foyer and the footsteps of Franziska's father, as well as the Consul and Van Saal, who'd all gone out to receive the doctor.

"I can't believe what's happening, Op Oloop!" Franziska said. "They don't understand you! They don't realize that it's love that's causing this crisis of yours! And they want to take away the trauma by taking me away from you!"

"Oh no, *cherie*! They'll never be able to abelardize us! Our union is incoercible. It can't be touched by vulgarity. If any difficulties arise, our mutual trust will overcome them. I'm nothing like Abelard. No one can abelardize me! And they'll certainly never manage to aberlardize us!"

He began repeating himself along these lines with progressive fury when the doctor and the others approached. This hitherto unexampled verb piqued their collective curiosity:

"Abelardize?"

"Abelardize?"

"Abelardize?"

The doctor, a recent graduate whose title, name, and office were identical to those of his father, was asking himself the same question. And, not knowing the word's meaning, he declared quietly to the men, "It's a neologism. That's a bad sign. Many types of extreme psychological alienation show a predisposition for neologisms."

The doctor approached Op Oloop.

His change had been so sudden. That ardent, deliberate declaration of love to Franziska had been followed by a convulsive phase. He hadn't been known to suffer from any sort of disorder, physical or degenerative, before now. The young physician could see no obvious anomalies in the Statistician, with the exception of his stature. The problem, then, was of an insidious, invisible nature. Suddenly, Op Oloop, panting, lay down on a nearby sofa. His facial muscles froze in a freakish frown and he looked as if he'd lapsed into unconsciousness.

When you're making a living off of another person's reputation, your own prestige can be put in extreme jeopardy by difficult cases like this. The young medic had come in place of his father, exploiting his identical title, name, and telephone number, and was now suffering the consequences of this audacity, and of his father's lack of foresight in launching the boy into the world under the protection of his own fame. But the doctor had to say something. The anxious bystanders were urging him on with their eyes.

Inventing an excuse, he stepped back a few steps and spoke:

"His pulse is normal. He has no fever. He's in a state of nervous shock. There's no doubt about it. The patient must have recently experienced some kind of very powerful emotion. The mind's deepest passions and miseries are equally capable of inducing these morbid manifestations. Perhaps some new abstract concept disturbed his thinking. It's all transitory. Unless it turns into a histological lesion, of course. That would be an entirely different story. But the strange thing is . . ."

"*You're* the strange thing," cried Op Oloop authoritatively, sitting up. "Even from the depths of my supposed stupor I can see how much you enjoy having these men heed your ravings. But I can tell you that my only abnormality is my perfect normality. The cerebrospinal cells generating my ideas and sensations are fine, thank you. I have no need of your services. Now leave."

Distress filled the air with choler, annoyance, mortification.

The physician, now quite ill-tempered, stepped away, grumbling to the Consul and to the bride's father, "He's a lunatic. A rational lunatic. This poses grave danger. If you ever run into a similar case, please don't bother calling me. I'm not a specialist in such matters."

"Fine, doctor. But, what do you recommend we do?"

"Do whatever you like. Take him to a loony bin . . . Give him cyanide . . . Good-bye."

His impudence made their embarrassment all the more palpable. Op Oloop's friends were oozing humiliation tinged with rage.

Under Franziska's kind gaze, the Statistician calmed his convulsive, ironic laughter. Piet Van Saal pondered the best way to proceed, intent on seeing his friend recapture his old, cautious state of mind.

"Come, come, Op Oloop, be honest. That simulated attack is in terrible taste. It's very unlike you to resort to such schemes. You know how well-loved you are in this house. I can't understand how—on the eve of your betrothal—you'd go out of your way to alarm us. Franziska, don't you agree that this is in rather poor taste?"

"Poor taste? But, how? Whatever *mon petit cheri* thinks, feels, or does is the epitome of perfection."

"Marvelous. This is all we need."

"All true, all true," interrupted Op Oloop. "Don't be shocked. You don't understand a thing. You've never been in love."

"Please! Don't be ridiculous. You're exasperating. I've known hundreds of men who've been in love and none have behaved this way!"

"That fact, as it happens, simply elevates our love," said Franziska. "Indeed, if it weren't the case that our love is unique, I myself would have to admonish Op Oloop. But, you see, I tolerate his dementia and his sanity, accept his vehemence and his dejection. A man such as yourself, smug and complacent in your normality, can't even approach the heights to which our souls have ascended. Love is the only arena worthy of our lives. Those who aren't in it are blind. Those who have left it, myopic. They can't see at all, or else barely make out the illuminated world we inhabit. It's all in vain—there's no reason for you, for my father, for my uncle to attempt to guide us. Your counsel only obstructs our path. You can never alter the course of our thoughts, because any intrusion from without becomes lost in our labyrinth."

Nearly ecstatic, Op Oloop took her right hand in his. He kissed it. And then, suspending his enchantment, touched by his and his beloved's *trouvaille*, he seconded Franziska's attenuated voice:

"Yes. A labyrinth. A labyrinth built of her faith and my faith, of her passion and my passion, of her anguish and my anguish. A labyrinth, Piet, with only one way out, a momentous and secret passage: our understanding."

"Who could have imagined! You, so erudite, so strict, so exact . . ."

"Forget your compassion. Don't annoy me. Meticulousness can be flaunted only until one's instinct rebels. I was methodical in spite of myself, tempted by the tawdry, rational benefits of such a life. My entire existence had been channeled so as to flow freely into servitude. I'd obstructed convenience, constricting myself so as to make the best use of every single hour. Regimen, order, culture . . . trinkets, garbage, baubles! True culture is a parrot's psittacosis . . . Ha, ha, ha! . . ."

"Hee, hee, hee . . ."

Van Saal froze, riveted.

A tiny trickle of laughter had escaped from between Franziska's lips, joining Op Oloop's hilarity, which by now was pooling up again around them. With each egging the other on, the noise soon took on quite absurd proportions. By the time the bride's family returned, Op Oloop's guffaws had formed an estuary, with Franziska's tee-heeing as its crystal clear tributary:

"Ha, ha, ha, ha, ha . . . !"

"Hee, hee, hee, hee, hee . . . !"

Such was the psychological commotion that the three comrades could hardly navigate the door leading to the foyer.

"Quick! We have to get this madman out of here! Tell the chauffeur to bring the car around. Call for the governess and the maid. Have them come for my daughter. We'll take Op Oloop away. This has gone too far. Entirely too far! He'll drive us all round the bend at this rate!"

Love is a very particular psychosis, one which soon impregnates the soul itself and can wreck the brains of two people at once. When it affects only one, it's not love but desire, disorder. This explains how, via spiritual and phenomenological identification, the beloved reasons and feels the reasoning and the feelings of her lover, and how, impervious to the arrogant normality surrounding her, she can take on the visions and obsessions of her visionary, obsessive groom.

Thus, Franziska was being colonized by just this sort of love. As it crossed her borders, she herself prowled the frontier between darkness and light, now counteracting Op Oloop's lucid imbalance with her own, makeshift, version of same.

Perception, in such circumstances, becomes purified, perfected. Abstractions fade away, forcing one's voice and comportment to obey the rules of the *beau monde*. Bride and groom were now quiet, dignified, refined to the very essence of their positions, attentive to all order-giving, doorbell-ringing, and hithering and thithering that could be heard out in the foyer.

"My love. They're plotting against you. It's inexcusable!"

"I know. I can sense it. These people don't love me. This is a living hell! You can't stay here. An angel in hell. It's unthinkable! I've resolved to run away with you. Come. We'll go."

Resolve was written all over his pallid face. He was panting. And, positioning her in front of him with a certain sculptural grace—a waif-like shield for his erect bulk—he made his way steadfastly towards the door.

The Consul and Franziska's father became conscious of this uncharacteristic maneuver. Their plan to get rid of Op Oloop had come undone before their eyes.

"How inconvenient!"

"This is all we need! I feel like someone's put a curse on me . . ."

"Now, now. Please calm down," Van Saal chirped. "This is a problem of the psyche and so must be handled prudently. Desperation won't help us. Franziska is under the same spell as Op Oloop. The risk of contagion is so great that his incoherencies are coming out of her mouth too! Please, please, I urge you—use caution!"

Certain Mediterranean peoples look longingly for a way out to the sea. They dream of the rhythmic expanse of the ocean and starry fairyland nights. In the same way, certain people feel landlocked by the dense layers of their souls—spiritual Mediterraneans—always anxious to find a way to love, because love, for them, is the great blissful ocean. And that passage out to sea, that *trait d'union*, always comes via the flesh.

Franziska had had a foretaste of this delight. With each kiss, each brush of her hands with his, her blood coursed as if magnetized to her lips and fingers, while her hidden compass, warm, throbbing eagerly, pointed to the real hidden treasure. Franziska was true to her passion. And she spoke to her father thus:

"Father, I'm leaving with Op Oloop. Such is the inexorable call of destiny!"

She said nothing else. But the implicit intention and strength of her words ran their course, through and beyond Quintín Hoerée's ears and into his conscience and that of the men standing beside him.

"Leaving? Leaving? My child, do you know what you're doing?"

"Yes. Perfectly. And no one can stop us," declared her fiancé.

And, taking her by the arm, tiny and submissive like a cane hooked over his own, he made for the door.

Everyone attempted to intercept them.

"Just a moment!"

"What does he think he's doing? Does he think he can really get away with this?"

"My dear friend! What's gotten into you?"

"Is Franziska not twenty-two years, three days, and five hours old? Is she not mistress of her own free will? Are we not engaged? Is betrothal not the equivalent of a trial run at marriage, just as divorce is more or less legal adultery? Is . . . ?"

There came the thunderous crack of a cane.

Simultaneously, as though this crack had sung out while traveling along the route of its trajectory, a great shriek sounded.

Op Oloop and Franziska fell, almost in unison, as if struck by lightning. He, brought down by the blow to a point just below his left ear; she, brought down by the cowardice of the crime thus committed.

The Finnish Consul, cane in hand, teeth on edge, appeared to be masticating his own indignation. He stood alone, muttering in mortification, under his breath:

"In my house . . . I'll show him . . . Bastard!"

Aside from Van Saal, no one paid him the least bit of attention. Having advised caution and prudence, Van Saal felt ridiculous as a result of this violence, felt as though he was drowning in disgrace. Silent, somber, his attitude a resolute rejoinder to the indignance brewing within him, he tended to the victims without a word. He lifted Franziska's body and laid her on a divan. He hoisted up his friend—bent into a square at waist and knees—and straightened him out, extending him over the carpet and placing a pillow beneath his head. After carefully cleaning his wound and straightening Op Oloop's clothing, he approached the Consul cautiously, his forehead wrinkled into a ball of rage.

"You pig! This was unworthy of a real man!"

And he slapped the Consul across the face.

The scandal went no further.

The Consul, paling noticeably, attempted to justify his action, but was unable. Fearful then, he slipped silently into his study.

Turning the other cheek. Bah! It just wasn't Christian! Responding to an offense with resignation was an abominable sort of masochism, frankly. He disagreed with the precept entirely. And that's how the Consul managed to avoid a second slap. When an offense can't be countered with a devastating triumph, the correct course of action is the one he'd taken: run away. But he'd learned his lesson. So well that Van Saal thought of Proudhon—he of the theory that property is theft—on the occasion when his noble opponent dealt him a solid smack with the words: "*Je vous le donne en toute propriété . . .*"

On returning to administer first aid to the two injured parties, Van Saal collided with the chauffeur, who was darting out to find the doctor. From the doorway, he caught a glimpse of the fiancée's face as she was carried to her room by servants. Such pathos, such bathos! He understood. Her divine countenance was bloated, droopy, pathetic, sorrow now stereotyped into her withered, magnolia flesh.

Op Oloop was still stretched out, shipwrecked, alone. Van Saal took his hands, shook his arms. The response was minimal. From time to time a far-off twinkle of life lit the Statistician's face; perhaps he was happy in his dreams. Yes, a far-off twinkle of the soul: the lighthouse illuminating this shipwreck! Quiet sighs. And that was all.

Silence was lost in still more silence. Piet Van Saal didn't know what to do or say.

Opportunely, the doctor was just arriving.

Handsome, fiftyish, he was the homonymous father of the homonymous doctor who had earlier paid them a call. A perfect specimen of cachet and capital, he'd come primarily to satisfy his great vocation, to vindicate the glory of his family name after the disgrace that had been precipitated by his progeny.

Seeing him arrive, the Finnish Consul went to bid him welcome.

"Hello, Doctor! How happy I am to see you! Another physician already paid us a visit, but his diagnosis was of no help whatsoever . . ."

"Yes. My son: Daniel Orús (Junior)."

"Your son! I didn't know that you had a son, Doctor."

"Yes. He told me everything. I'm here more on his account than for the patient. So, it seems we're dealing with a malingerer, yes? Someone pretending to be insane? Concealing who knows what unmentionable aims?"

"Well, something like that. No point in denying it."

Given how desperate things had become, a little dissimulation seemed perfectly in order.

The doctor glanced panoramically at the Statistician. More interested in an account of Op Oloop's actions than the *corpus delicti*, the older man became embroiled with the owner of the house in a lengthy and detailed overview of the recent events, peppered with over-general questions, uninspired replies, and *a priori* conclusions. Only then did he turn, patiently, to his patient. He knelt down in front of him. He prodded him. He listened to his chest. He opened his eyes. He took his pulse and checked his reflexes. But Op Oloop hardly registered any change at all. His face was now slightly more suggestive of something or other—his mouth was stretched into a shocked expression, and his pupils were as cloudy as a lamb's after its throat's been cut. When Doctor Orús stood, his expression confirmed the foregone conclusion of his diagnosis.

"I can assure you that the patient has fainted. Blacked out. No doubt he's of a tonic-sympathetic temperament. An injection will bring him round. Emotional type. Excitable. Unstable. Nothing to worry about. This too shall pass. He's predisposed to suffer. A likely candidate to develop depressive insanity. His stupor is standard in cases of *melancholia attonita*. I have no doubt whatsoever, from what I've observed and what you've told me, that his fainting spell is the result of a psycho-neuro-pathological attack . . ."

"A what?" cried Piet Van Saal, piqued by the physician's blasé tone. "Look! Why don't you take a look right here, behind his ear!"

The doctor was flabbergasted.

The entire theoretical foundation of his drivel now lay at his feet in a heap of ignominious rubble. He felt the opprobrium of his deceit. And staring intently at the Finnish Consul he seized his hat from its hook, ready to take his leave.

The maid, just then, came bounding down the stairs.

"Doctor, Doctor, please come quickly! Miss Franziska is raving . . ."

The doctor, now, was haughty and impassive.

The three conscious individuals present beseeched him with their eyes to go and see to the young lady. But still he stood, unruffled, furtively concocting a compensatory diatribe. The discomfiture generated by his aloof attitude was evidenced by three increasingly pitiful looks of entreaty. Oblivious to the call of duty, he remained heedless and unperturbed. The dramatic tension reached its climax. The three looks of entreaty, their twinkles turning steely, tried and tried to compel the doctor upstairs. In vain. He was anchored in his rancor.

"I want no more part of these farces. Take her to a loony bin . . . give her cyanide . . . Good-bye."

Flowers, the best part of plants, are what reveal their familial lineage. Moral attitudes, the best part of man, are what reveal his. Doctor Daniel Orús, father of the homonymous doctor, had just demonstrated, by means of his behavior, his common ancestry with his son.

Is it possible to plunge upward? Regardless: the three friends plunged upstairs. Fear inverts feelings. Unconsciously, all three rushed up the stairs as though they were rushing down.

Op Oloop remained stretched out, alone, shipwrecked.

Stormy seas rid themselves of foreign objects by tossing them onto any nearby beach: cadavers, debris, the wreckage of a ship destroyed in a squall. Instinct does the same: it tosses away everything that might interfere with its rhythms, rippling deep beneath the material world. So, for instance, sexual instinct tends to prevail over the censure, conventionality, and morality that attempt to restrain it. The self-preservation instinct, like egotism, tends to trump the desire to faint or collapse or otherwise put oneself in the path of some new trauma, those cowardly and counterproductive urges that so debilitate the life force with their transitory nervous contingencies and sudden incapacitations . . .

Had Op Oloop been in control of all of his faculties at that moment, he would've proven the veracity of the above assertion. But alas. His brain was a *camera obscura*, and the staff had taken the day off. No ideas, no images. It took some time for the supreme order of instinct to awaken him.

On rising, he found that all the shiny cabinets, tidy file folders, and other mental organizers that usually occupied his skull were now sitting out in the foyer. How did they get out there? His head felt hollow. It wasn't echoing in its usual fashion but seemed to have swollen to the size of the room in which he found himself. He was throbbing.

Mechanically, he put on his hat and found his cane. He headed for the door. Crossing the threshold, he experienced a strange phenomenon. He didn't fit through. It was a struggle to readjust the valve controlling the volume of his head. Having successfully reached the footpath, unrestrained joy lit up Op Oloop's face—though it was still pale and contrite.

Vacant, entirely vacant, with no destination of any kind, he began to saunter. Impervious to the noise pollution, to the pestilence of traffic, his automatic, uniform steps took him to the outskirts of nowhere. To a place where his colossal air bladder of a head could burst. Because by bursting, only by bursting, would he find the way back to his reality.

So he walked, and walked, and walked.

Franziska, meanwhile, after repeated requests, had indeed come to her senses. But only two of them: sight and hearing. Incoherent words took sporadic flight from the nest of her mouth like a flock of babbling loons. The nostrils of her thin, delicate nose flared and stiffened, as though some moist and overpowering jungle stench was paralyzing and then offending her in turn. Her spasmodically contracting fingers clutched and became entangled in her hair and the lace of her blouse.

The good sense of her governess—the only serene figure present—prevailed among the general pandemonium. The men, incapacitated by their anxiety and the desire to be useful, simply made nuisances of themselves. They were upset that the doctor had refused to attend the sickroom. The chauffeur rushed out in search of a replacement. And the governess said, peremptorily, in Finnish, "Please, everyone, out!"

No one paid the slightest attention. They had not quite understood her motive, and continued to lurk and prowl around the girl's bed.

"Everyone, please, give us some privacy," the governess repeated, more persuasively.

Franziska's father sensed something. And he exited, taking Van Saal and the Consul along with him, the two having more or less reconciled by now, thanks to their common anguish.

The moment they were gone, the governess locked the door. Turning back to the bed, without the slightest qualm, she raised Franziska's skirt. She had not been mistaken. The *odor di femina*—the genital bouquet, as it were—arose from the rose of the girl's menstrual flow.

For a Finn such as herself, equipped with snow-white hair, clothes, and intentions, this revelation was no more transcendental than a nosebleed. The governess did everything that was prophylactically required. For Nordic folk, these episodes carry no coefficient aside from the purely physiological. A governess from Cannes, in her stead, would have stroked her suspicions Sapphically across the girl's vulva, and, on seeing her clitoris swell—obeying who knows what mandate of the corpuscles of voluptuousness—she would have put two and two together, thinking back to that afternoon's interrupted performance, and seeing this blood as its morbid consequence. But no. The governess was Hyperborean. From a country full of robust young *mesdemoiselles* sporting thick pullovers and skis, living in log cabins beneath gray skies, unaware of all the comedies of love—yes, a representative of that psychologically upright race, so free of prejudices, and yet concealing a rich, sensual humus beneath the layer of snow that is their clinical secularism and acceptance of divorce. So she declined to complicate matters by hazarding any guesses as to the causes for Franziska's distress. The girl's repeated cries of "Ay!" and her contortions beneath the governess's hands had no effect—the woman carried out her duties with a natural austerity. Once she'd finished changing the girl's clothes, she made the bed, tidied the room, and then opened the door.

Quintín Hoerée was just coming back upstairs, anxious. He'd come personally to confide the following secret to the governess, in hushed tones: "Op Oloop has disappeared. I hope nothing happens to him! Not a word of this to my daughter. Don't let her leave her room."

Just at that moment, she was leaving her room.

"Miss," said the governess, "it would be better if you didn't leave your room. Miss, please do go back to your room. Miss . . ."

Franziska didn't bat an eyelid. A plan was taking shape within her, hardening her features. Her profile was a silent, white line. She floated past them, down the staircase, her nightdress billowing out about her, ghostlike. Each step she took reverberated in her father's heart.

"Sweetheart, why don't you go back upstairs? Listen to me, Franziska. Come with me, you need to rest."

She carried on, oblivious.

She'd reached the bottom of the stairs. She turned towards the *fumoir*. Despite the sense of expectant anxiety overwhelming her, her exhausted face showed no change whatever. Not a sign, not a sob, not a word. Franziska was now so thoroughly entrenched in their intimacy that the physical presence or absence of Op Oloop no longer mattered. Her impassivity began to disconcert her family. Indeed, *chez elle*, it was plain to see she was reverting to some furtive, vestigial personality. She had become introspective, as if a lockout had been decreed on all sentiments enabling her to relate to others.

Continuing on in haughty, silent arrogance, she opened the bar. Without vacillating for a moment before the arsenal of bottles, she snatched the apricot brandy and raised it to her lips. She drank greedily, avidly, but with no pleasure, until her father confiscated the bottle.

There followed a nervous, angry silence.

Her father tried to persuade her to speak to them, lavishing loving words on the girl. She rejected them, sickened. The governess, noting that Franziska's strange grunting sounds were getting louder, stepped away. Soon her face—Franziska's beautiful porcelain doll's face—was twisted up into something truly distasteful.

"*Tout se soumit aux lois de l'ivresse.*" Quintín Hoerée knew just how true Jules Romain's axiom was. His affections, his hopes, his honor, all trembled in humiliation before his daughter's toppling dignity.

For years, the field of psychology has been aware of a certain connection between anomalous states of mind and irregular menstruation. Sexual development—after puberty has been reached—only aggravates the situation. And the victim falls into hysteria or melancholy, leading in most cases to the emergence of delirious mystical beliefs or persecution complexes, regularly accompanied by two increasingly pronounced propensities: pyromania and dipsomania. (Franziska had reached the age when sex seems to seek out flames to add to its own fervent fires, and then alcohol to appease its terrible thirst).

Fathers frequently fret over these kinds of psychosexual theorem, when it comes to their own daughters. They observe their girls' various preoccupations, analyze their contradictory impulses, scrutinize their myriad crises. But that's as far as it goes. A general cowardice keeps them from making use of the information they glean via these observations. Diagnosing, coming to conclusions . . . that's the easy part. It's being heroic, stepping up and providing a cure—and without being a hypocrite—that's so difficult during this phase of civilization. The present conception of morality, which allows for every imaginable constraint of instinct—plunging it into the anguish of indescribable opprobrium, dressing it in cilices—has instituted an ignoble regimen of maceration, sinking flesh into penitence instead of sublimating it in the splendor and freedom of gratification. (Franziska felt victimized. Terrified and flabbergasted, in fact. From the lucid depths of her inebriation, she raged against familial orthodoxy and the preconceptions parrying her impulses.)

Fathers know that the cure for what ails their daughters often lies behind the fly of the man they love (or anyone with enough charisma). But they'll never "engage," as it were, to give their girl away, or let her give herself away. They would rather see them succumb, languid, wan, to the grief of virginal delirium, than see the glow of atavistic delight smolder on their cheeks and bosom. (Franziska, *anima plorans*, had shrunk, shriveled, weeping tearlessly.)

When the law, when religion, no longer seek to execrate desire, perhaps we'll return to times like those in the ancient Olympian era, when gods and men both took great delight in the glories of the flesh. Fathers, then, might burst through the dikes built by their scruples, and let flow the torrent of real life—and daughters might flaunt the virile desires they carry around in their obsessed little heads, like matrons and damsels of yore, who wore amulets and cameos pinned to their hearts as symbols of their *bon santé* . . .

Suddenly, Franziska fought back. She slid, catlike, towards the bar and strove to snatch another bottle from the polished chrome surface. To no avail. The hands that had been caressing her impeded the deed. Her eyes, which had been open wide in demented ecstasy, closed slowly when she realized she'd failed—finally fading into a sarcastic wink. She was sopping wet and turned slowly to look at both father and governess, sullying them both with her thick and smothering condemnation.

"Please! Don't do this, my child! Come with me."

This show of emotion made her flesh crawl. She made a sour, tooth-grinding expression. And with unrestrained rage, she screamed from what seemed the pit of her soul:

"Executioner! EXECUTIONER! EXECUTIONER!"

She stumbled. She couldn't feel her head. Like Charlotte Corday, receiving her infamous slap. Her head lolled, preventing her from exiting the room.

Finally, their attempts to restrain her failed. Staggering, she managed to make her way to the staircase in the hall.

The doorbell's urgent ring and the subsequent irruption of an Inspector and a Police Captain caused them all to freeze in their tracks.

"Which way to the wounded? Which way to the wounded?"

It was the voice of the same Inspector who, a few hours earlier, had intervened in the traffic accident involving the cab carrying Op Oloop. The same Inspector who, hearing the Statistician's ranting and intrigued as to his personality, had followed him to this very house.

Everyone stood stock-still. No one said a word.

"Is this or is this not the Finnish Consul's home?"

The members of the household nodded.

"Well then . . . speak up! Doctor Daniel Orús just telephoned headquarters to tell us that a crime was committed here. So: which way to the wounded?"

Piet Val Saal, who'd been planning to go out in search of Op Oloop, took the floor:

"Ah, Captain, sir . . ."

"Inspector, thank you," he interrupted, smiling, convinced he was about to be led to the man in question.

"Ah, Inspector, sir. No crime has been committed here. A friend of the Consul's slipped on the parquet and cut himself behind the left ear when his head hit the bottom step, that's all."

"That's a lie!" Franziska shrieked, electrifying the scene.

Already in a huff over having been contradicted, and now with the added incentive of this new revelation, the Inspector confronted Op Oloop's friend:

"Look here, sir, save your excuses for the indictment. Doctor Orús said the man had taken quite a beating. So, again: Which way to the wounded?"

Now the scene had become one of acute embarrassment. No one dared say a word. Van Saal worried Franziska's outburst had put him in a tight spot; Quintín Hoerée was still trying to restrain his daughter; while the Consul, confounded, contemplated how this *contretemps* could affect his career.

"Who owns the house? Let's get to the bottom of this," the Inspector asked authoritatively.

The Consul stepped forward, trembling, made an obsequious face, and explained, "I am the Finnish Consul. My brother-in-law and I were throwing an engagement party. Would you care to come through to the dining room? You'll see we were about to sit down to our lunch. Op Oloop, the fiancé of this young lady, arrived late, ill. He began to say and do queer things—crazy things, as it were."

"Crazy things? Allow me to interrupt. A tall man? Dressed in brown? Wearing a hat?"

"Quite so. Have you already made his acquaintance?"

"The automobile that brought him here was involved in an accident on Avenida Callao. I intervened. When I asked him if he'd seen how the accident happened, he said something along the lines of, 'Not at all. I was thinking about Francesca . . .' Can't recall the girl's last name."

"Hoerée."

"Yes. Well, anyway. He just kept repeating himself, like an idiot . . ."

"*You're* the idiot!" Franziska roared frantically, with a tragic windmilling of arms that made her silk nightdress flutter.

"Please. Pay her no mind. She too has fallen ill."

". . . so I followed him, on a hunch, and this is where he came. When I saw the consular coat of arms I didn't take it any further."

"Pity you didn't arrest him there and then! Well, you've already heard the rest of the story. All I can add is that Op Oloop has left the premises."

"Liar! LIAR! LIAR! They killed him. THEY KILLED HIM! THEY KILLED . . . !"

The girl failed to finish that last sentence. Her father had covered her mouth, and now hoisted her up violently and carried her upstairs to her bedroom.

Then came one of those excruciating moments during which one sweats, shuffles one's feet, wants to set things straight but can't, because anxiety is stifling reason, and confusion is making you skeptical even of yourself . . .

After fighting back his anxiety, the man of the house continued:

"Mr. Inspector, allow me to telephone a good friend: the Foreign Affairs office's Chief of Protocol. I feel his presence here will simplify matters and restore my reputation. My niece's mental turmoil seems to have put everything in a rather negative light."

"Go right ahead."

"Thank you. Come with me. I want you to hear everything. I am, in all honesty, a decent man who represents his country honorably—not an imposter and murderer."

Piet Van Saal allowed himself a tiny smile . . .

The Police Captain, meanwhile, had surreptitiously slipped down the hall. He scrutinized the furniture, the rugs, the corners of the room. He spied a few drops of blood by the center table. Spurred on by this substantiation, with velveteen fingers and velveteen toes, he slid silently over to the staircase, careful not to disturb the evidence. The bottom step showed no sign of anything untoward. Suspicion sprang up into a smug, self-satisfied smile, leading him to shake his head, slowly and significantly, from side to side. When he returned from whence he'd come, his eyes having become familiarized with everything in the hall, he noticed a strange absence: where was Van Saal? Pupils dilated in surprise, the Captain crept over to the office. He saw the Inspector holding the telephone. And froze, worrying that Van Saal might have left the premises entirely.

And so it was. While the Captain had been in hot pursuit of evidence, tracking the crime, and the Inspector had been otherwise occupied, the Statistician's friend had just taken his hat and left. Left to go look for *him*, naively, driven by his sentimental nature, just as the Captain in search of bloodstains had been driven by his professional instincts. But, how to reconcile the subjective imperatives each man had chosen to obey? The Captain was fuming, furious with himself and with everyone and with everything. Authority often turns a primitive temperament such as his into a well of jealousy, accompanied by a jaunty air of superiority that brooks neither contradiction nor derision—even if such contradiction or derision might stem from nobler and more profound deductions than those the authority in question would be capable of.

Van Saal hailed a taxi as soon as he reached the street. He gave Op Oloop's address. And then sunk into profound meditation.

He recalled a beautiful moral aphorism learned in English class at the Uleaborg Academy. "A friend is he who comes when all the world is going!" Yes, to arrive when others leave! To enter when they all exit! To offer your hand when selfishness retracts its own! To console while others cower!

"That!—that is true glory!" he cried, without hearing himself. The words sprang from him effortlessly, flowers growing from the sap of tenderness.

His state of mind verged on inebriation—kindness intoxicates like wine. The emotions that the events of the day had brought out in him had altered the meaning of much of the world without, however, upsetting the balance of his serenity. Contemplating his earlier comportment, he deemed it perfectly proper and appropriate, in retrospect. He boasted to himself about it, even with regard to his slapping the Consul. Yes, when his hand had delivered its sonorous smack, his conscience had told him he was doing the just thing, given the cowardice he was castigating.

Friendship is an affective theorem that must always be resolved vis-à-vis the absurd. If, that is, it is resolved at all. Most frequently, the unknown rules our minds. Of all the precious *eironea* handed down to us by Greek culture, the definition of friendship as "reciprocal goodwill"—as proposed by the philosopher from Stagira— wasn't, for Van Saal, one of the most valuable . . . caught up as it was in admiring its own beauty.

How to be a good friend is, and always has been, the core of the quandary. Love, at times, follows the path of truth. But friendship, almost unfailingly, follows a more tortuous path. Men, unable to achieve the sublime, prefer instead to play iniquitous, malevolent, envious games.

Throughout the centuries, people have bastardized congenial camaraderie. If friendship was what literature told us, humanity would
be better off. Grace and harmony between the masses. A perpetual
apotheosis of delicate subtleties from our intellects and bombas-
tic acts of munificent goodwill. Yet in reality, friendship is nothing
more or less than a *mare magnum* of contradiction!

Van Saal's mind clouded over, then, with unhappy memories. He
was besieged by thoughts of Franziska's father's secret hostility and
her uncle's marked fear of Op Oloop. Fear of a man so pure, so loyal,
so wise! And given that bride and groom both would be, in a sense,
the future father-in-law's children, how could Op Oloop ever truly
join Franziska's family, forced to crawl in through the trap door of
paternal contempt? And, too, given that spouses must be seen as
members of wide, affective communities, how could Op Oloop ever
symphonize with the stridencies of a cynical character like the Finnish Consul!

Those idealists who consider virtue to be an indispensable fea-
ture of life are often entirely overwhelmed by repugnance when they
happen to become familiar with the intimate details of some sordid
passion on the part of an acquaintance, or else the simple, ordinary
disloyalties dealt out over the course of any friendship. Van Saal,
generally a comforting exception to this rule, still couldn't escape a
sense of uneasiness on this day. And as he rode along, he jabbered
on in his diatribe against the men who'd so disappointed him. Because one must be candid at all times—even at the risk of despair,
even at the risk of leaving permanent macula on one's heretofore
unblemished acquaintances.

On the avenue, dark and tree-lined, shop windows began to
blink on.

If the subtle, metapsychic mechanisms required for successful tel-
esthesia had been in operation, the Consul's mental apparatus would

surely have trembled with rage at the waves now being emitted by Van Saal's brain. Alas—nothing doing. It seems most people are still basically impervious to the reception of others' intimate thoughts. Though, yes, there are occasional murmurs. And while these premonitions don't take concrete shape as words, even the most obtuse of oafs can occasionally sense them skulking about . . . in their ears and in the sudden contractions of their hearts.

Thus, turning on the light in the study, the man of the house felt an unexpected burning in his right tympanum.

"Someone is thinking ill of me," he murmured, smiling knowingly to himself.

The Inspector had just spoken to the Commissioner at headquarters, after having first conversed with the Chief of Protocol. His countenance now reflected a certain ambiguity: triumph, on the one hand, at having had his hunch confirmed; disappointment at having had his superiors insist he hold off on his investigation. There was something fishy about all this, he was sure of it. Trained in systematic doubt, he was used to grabbing the bull by the horns, used to picking up on and following the strings leading back behind the scenes. Conspiracy seemed all the more likely after his Captain calmly pointed out several bloodstains on the floor, and then that Van Saal had surreptitiously taken his leave, slipping past the subaltern's watchful eye.

"All right, then, sir," he said with restrained sarcasm, "apparently there's no cause for a police presence here."

The Consul ought to have kept quiet and opened the door and allowed him to leave. But instead, idiotically, he lapsed into a fit of loyalty to his Nordic nature. In a newly regained state of calm contentment, he forgot the elemental apothegm, which says that flattering the vanquished amounts to impudence. The Consul didn't quite grasp that the Inspector was suffering, having felt the faultlessness of his detectivesque reputation impugned. And, stupidly, he invited him to stay to tea.

"Come, come. Everything's ready. We have some fabulous Finnish fish pies, which I'm sure you'll love."

The official, eyes bloodshot, could bear no more. Strained tension—even when generated by graciousness—can reach a boiling-over point, at which gallantry seems outright insult.

"Enough with this idiocy," the Inspector blurted out. "I didn't come here to take tea with you but to investigate a crime. You can be as consular as you like, but you're not going to tangle me up in your lies. There is blood here, sir. A man was hurt here, sir. A poor madman, as I myself had occasion to verify this afternoon. You think you're going to buy me off with a few Finnish fish pies? A brutal, violent, vulgar crime has been committed. Your own niece admitted it. An esteemed doctor, Doctor Daniel Orús, saw the corpse. What did you want with the Chief of Protocol? You think he's Jesus Christ? You think he can make your Lazarus rise and walk again? Take tea! Take tea! You've got some nerve if you think you can pull one over on me!"

With that he walked out, swollen from the strain of his own anger, jutting out his bottom lip in disgust, to show his spite.

The opprobrium he'd experienced had made him giddy. Like a chocolate-bar vending machine, he'd had his thoughts well ordered, lined up, after tracking the evidence, in order to dispense the facts one by one. But, in the end, the whole heap of them tumbled out together, all turned around and jumbled up, with no logic to them whatsoever.

Once out on the road, riding on his motorcycle, swishing in and out of the bustle of traffic, he began to mutter furiously: "Fish pies! What an imbecile! Ha! Can't fool me. I'll catch that walking corpse yet. My hunches always pay off. I'll have the last laugh."

Whereas the Consul gave the Inspector's reaction no further

thought. He'd depleted his nervous energy and so simply held his bald head.

He stared off into space. Not three minutes had passed when, *subito*, the return of his personality—like a smack on the head—impelled him into the dining room. The table was set for five o'clock tea. Untouched. It was seven o'clock . . .

7:00 P.M. Six cups and saucers rested atop bright, happy linen place settings. Four candelabra with azure candles. Succulent fruit on two Saxon china plates. A cubical vase with long-stemmed gladioli, embroidered with purple and yellow Parmesan primroses. And little pies here and there. Fabulous little Finnish fish pies . . .

He gobbled them up one after the other until he'd had his fill. A copious libation of *amontillado* sherry placated them in his stomach. He snatched an enormous peach and the relish with which he bit into it stained his lips with its first juices, which then dribbled down into the wrinkled bulge of his big belly.

This animalistic act seemed to take him out of himself, and the Consul was overcome by a sense of well-being. A well-off well-being. He didn't think of anything or anyone. Franziska and Op Oloop, Quintín and Van Saal—clouds, and not even distant clouds—didn't register on his mental screen. No love, no business. No homeland, no family, no plywood. And he slid heavily into a steel armchair with plush, almond-colored cushions.

Up, upstairs, at home, lay Franziska in accompanied solitude.

Out, outside, in the city, wandered Op Oloop in crepuscular solitude.

Upstairs, the solicitude of father and governess, fighting to recover a spirit lost in sentiment.

Outside, the obstinate search of friend and Inspector, fighting to recover a spirit lost in life.

Up, upstairs and out of her mind, drowning in bad omens—the love of Franziska.

Out, outside, hovering above and over his mind, among the mental clouds—the love of Op Oloop.

Up and out . . .

The Statistician walked on . . . His enormous blister of air was intact, a supple layer covering his astral body. Dromomania and the delirium caused by aimless wandering give one unusual powers of exclusion and defense. It's second nature to such wanderers to evade danger, to avoid risk. Like waking-sleepwalkers, they're driven by instincts like a diviner's. Such was Op Oloop's state. Still taking uniform steps. Still retaining his automatic rhythm. Until his impulses exceeded the limits of his flesh. Fatigue set in.

He'd reached the entrance to the Botanical Gardens. His bulk—a trundling tree—found a way through the foliage, another plant penetrating twilight's autumnal penumbra. He didn't sit; he collapsed onto a bench, branch-like arms and legs akimbo. He was surrounded by the architecture of a Roman garden: slopes overgrown with privet, a grassy walkway, pond, two spectral cypresses, and the marbled nudity of Aphrodite.

Synchronically, father and governess left Franziska on her bed. She was neither asleep nor awake. (Stupor, mental atrophy, somnolence.) She was immobile, face down, her extremities—a cross of flesh!—open to the four cardinal points of love. She was neither asleep nor awake. (Repugnance, exhaustion, fever.) She was suspended, like Op Oloop in the park, in the shady silence of her room.

Death isn't always an inexorable fate. Parts of living beings die all the time, and yet the organism itself continues living despite the manifold deaths hidden within. Life itself—which for Goethe was multiple in character, and for Kant, rational—is not necessarily extinguished by the demise of one or even thousands of its integral elements. So, for people who are chronically infirm, the voyage of life is nothing more than a funeral *cortège* mathematically culminating in the necropolis, when matter finally becomes entirely overwhelmed, and perishes.

From a physiological standpoint, the organism is a federation of chemo-physical elements united in a solidarity of nerves and humors. If either of these goes bankrupt, as it were, the emergent imbalance affects life's credit rating—though it doesn't entirely ruin the personality, which can subsist. Or, better, can subexist.

When liberated from the attributes of differentiation, it recedes into an eternal simplicity. A protozoan is immortal in its proper habitat, but the higher animal life forms conspire in their complexity against infinite survival.

Franziska and Op Oloop both lay dislodged from the world. But this dislodging, which had ruptured their respective nervous solidarities, had served only to plunge what remained of them into those regions inhabited only by flesh . . . regions in which the flesh itself is inflamed, defending itself against all external coercion: swollen, alien to the yoke of reason, and speaking its own peculiar language, which is of course an instinctive tongue.

The fog that had been billowing in the corners of the bedroom and the park evaporated. A tension-filled night, now. A clear night, setting the stage for further scenes of egocentrism.

The word is man's eviternal anomaly. Clairvoyants see it as a mental extrusion that bulges out in front of one's mouth. Composed of concepts and modulations, of ideas and exhalations, of sensations and scintillations, this "bulge" can as easily attract as repel. Some chatterboxes, for instance, are constantly spewing up sludge from their verbal sewers—teratological specimens. And then, for those afflicted with the opposite pathology: what a privilege to be privy to the virgin intuition of the voiceless! Their aphasia leads nonetheless to maximal, exact states of understanding. Gender is irrelevant to the condition. Their speechlessness is a screen onto which our instinctive repulsion or attraction to words is refracted and projected. Baudelaire knew: ". . . *mon coeur que tout irrite, excepté le candeur de l'antique animal.*" Those to whom language has been denied are exceptionally sensible, and understand each other so well that there is never the least opportunity for doubt. That's why laughter is foreign to them: after all, laugher is itself aberration, a mechanism invented by men solely to overcome the atavism of their own intelligence!

For Franziska and for Op Oloop, it's now a perfect night. A night of amethyst and obsidian. A night of utter purity and otherworldliness. A night of diaphanous obscurity, with voices thundering through the lightning. A night of intimacy drawing near all that is far, gathering it into a single heart.

Franziska and Op Oloop sense each other's presence.

The lightness of the breeze impedes the rustling of leaves. But the lovers hear the sounds made by their souls. They hear them in the distance, like those Vedic hymns whose sounds can be heard clear across the jungle. They listen to and soak each other up. They listen to and bathe in each other's waves. They feel each other: a bubble of life inside a bubble of life. And they merge. They merge telestically in the grace of a Pythagorean rapture.

Following their lead, the sky now shows the same stunned paralysis it exhibits during seismic tremors. And the lovers talk and talk, a hermetic symphony mutely modulating the silence between them.

"   "
. . .
"   "
. . .

"Fran-zi . . . Fran-zis-ka . . ."

"Yes . . . I'm here . . ."

"Is that you, Franzi? Yes! It's you! I recognize the twinkling of your hair band and the cinnabar flame of your lips."

"Yes, mon cheri, it's me. But why is the air here so coarse, the land so craggy, in these unexpected surroundings—scratching your words, making them rasp?"

"Oh!"

"Please! Don't show surprise. It makes everything here so murky. Surprise calls up a plague of misty vapors . . ."

"Yet the sky is so limpid. A metempsychosic sky. Like a bell at rest, the heavens seem to guarantee our future rejoicing and jubilation and laughter, and the flights of doves . . ."

"You must be delirious! I see monsters far and wide! The firmament is furrowed! A lewd stench poisons the air! I loathe the land here, covered in flakes and flecks . . . Why did you bring me to this fantastical place, full of submarine flora, crawling with microbial fauna?"

"What! Can't you feel the streaming jets of milk, honey, wine?"

"No."

"No? And grace casting its spell into the ether?"

"No."

"In that case, mi amor, your spiritual orb must surely have been soiled by something or other. How did you sneak past the numina guarding the entrance to the otherworld? Never mind. I'll exorcize you."

"But why? My soul has always been an unquestionable pool of purity."

"Yes. But when base matter volatilizes, it sometimes leaves behind a residue of its memory. Purge yourself in a baptism of fire."

"I need your help . . . You're the only crucible for me."

"*Very well. Come here. Let our conjunction be perfect. Let our frenzies coincide and our effusions juxtapose . . . Yes, like that. Any improvement?*"

"*Yes. I see a viscous green dissolving . . .*"

"*The veins of hatred!*"

"*. . . opal caps liquefying . . .*"

"*Trivial aspirations!*"

"*. . . and an ochre swamp is vanishing . . .*"

"*Your desires!*"

"*How strange! Now I hear your voice so clearly! It's as though I'm now in a crimson cove.*"

"*That's my heart, enveloping you.*"

"*Yes! And yet . . . I can't comprehend this spectacular adventure. What witchcraft lies behind all this?*"

"*None at all. Haven't you ever talked in your sleep? We are, tonight, but two somniloquists conversing and communicating, that's all. During this union of ours, past life and future life will blend into one. You'll see . . . Here, in this place, you retreat by advancing, because there's no such thing as space in oneiric time.*"

"*Your voice is like a balm, a musical emanation!*"

"*In this place, apart from life, where we now dwell, all souls carry an ineffable accent of prayer. Yours caresses me with the sweetness of its sorrow.*"

"*How singular! Can such a tender breath truly exist? I was on an ecstatic plateau, my breasts thrust forward, eyes bloodshot. The air was austere. Prickly like a hyena's howl. And there were certainly hyenas . . .*"

"*I know, Franziska. Extirpate your memory. Oh, what I endured to find you! I heard your scream, broken and bruised, crossing the streets in all the awful clamor of these wastelands, of these denticu-*"

lated houses. But now a light and lovely breeze caresses us, so gently. Far away from flesh, the groaning flesh, a vast, spacious bed—the pure bed of true love—unites us. The pleasure! Can't you feel how we two vibrate in the deep beatitude of its resonances? Doesn't the fluvial feeling flowing from my heart to your soul sublimate you? The fluvial feeling refreshing the shores of the soul, fertilizing the wombs of death!"

"Ohhhh!"

"You mustn't sigh. There's no need for nostalgia to verify our inviolable solitude. Here, freedom determines our happiness. Kindred spirits share a special language all their own. And joy does not transcend, but merges with the ecumenical pleasure of free spirits . . ."

"Your consolation compensates my every sacrifice! Suffering is the best way to sow, and then, what a beautiful crop I harvest! I would gladly keep on suffering . . ."

"That's impossible. You can't. There's no suffering here. There's only being, you see? Just being. The present is the only place where we can escape pain. Being! Love is played out perfectly here . . . A luminous pool in which no one ever drowns. There, however, in the world, love brings pain."

"Let's not sink back into the mist. Come, let's stroll."

"But why, if we're ubiquitous?"

"Look! A sudden portent!"

"That's always the way. Look how it changes. What is ephemeral guarantees the perenniality of its image. We're lenses capturing the course of life. Everything flows towards us, under us, into us."

"I adore the straight-lined landscape here, the translucent reeds, linear water, skyless sky. Shall we have a dip in the water? But first divest yourself of your physicality. Be a nude psyche, like me."

"Oh, Franzi! How silly of me to forget! There, it's done. Can you still see me?"

"No, not anymore. The last adorable little vestiges of your carnal deceit have been extinguished."

"Thank you. I know I'm a diaphanous shadow. I'm aware of my occasional occlusion in light. But sometimes my own sylphs follow me and dress me in the vestures of reason, the nervous tunic of the terrestrial Op Oloop. But I still have my secrets. And I can vanish to such an extent that when I keep silent, even I can't see myself. Physiognomy represents the boundary of the flesh of the spirit, you know. But now we can perceive our true faces—the ones that emanate wisdom, perfume, and music."

"I intuited all that when I first met you. I felt that your entire being was penetrating—like a melody—an ear I was unaware I possessed."

"Yes. When one isn't in love, one's face is a dam where the audacity and interference of others break and fall back. When you're in love, the ardent flow of tenderness and the coursing stream of words from your beloved burst the dike."

"Why are my father and uncle unaware of that?"

"Because they've dammed up their pride. Matter dominates them and desiccates their souls. Forgive them. Instead, evoke the spirit of your ancestors. They're within you. The souls of our ancestors, mildewed or fresh, are eternal. And when they're resuscitated in us, it's easy to ponder both the lofty heights and base depths of their passions. Don't worry, the gnawing worms won't follow them back from their side to ours. Concentrate. As soon as you evoke them, they'll arrive within you. Miracles flourish here."

"Will wonders never cease! Look how many spirits surround me! Here's my grandmother's grandmother, blessing me. Here's my grandmother's mother, kissing me. Here's my grandmother, laughing. And here's my mother, silent. It's a miracle!"

"Take advantage of this magic. The bond of blood can't be broken.

Speak to them a while. Consult with them. Here, secrets are infallible oracles, and premonitions carry the weight of the deeds they foretell."

"Consult with them . . . about what?"

"About what concerns us. They know. Every thought, sentiment, decision, rises up to the immortal world. Since we've inherited the cosmic element of their souls, and since spiritual affiliation links the episodes they lived through to the ones we're living now, our ancestors instill us and epitomize us. Having worried over the same doubts, cried the same tears, they possess the a priori experience of all our failures and our joys. What's more, in the other world, everything is clear to them—all are clairvoyant. Permeating the strata of dreams, they're able to reach the authentic waters, where the conscience bathes, far more quickly than we . . ."

". . ."

"Well?"

"Hallelujah! Hallelujah! I was right! They encircled me. I heard a polyphony of praise. And my mother's advice: 'Hew to what is constant, not what is ardent—dignified inflexibility, not transitory audacity.' And they all urged me back to you, urged me to graft myself to your soul until our enigma is finally spent."

"Tell me, was your mother happy during her short life?"

"No. She told me so herself. She took the wrong path to reach the sublime. She was widowed in her love long before being reborn in death. And she still is. Hers was an isolated love. And since such desolation is considered the worst tragedy in the otherworld, she now endures the endless, living death of a dead love . . ."

"That's why one mustn't fail. True love enslaves both parties reciprocally."

"Our love, for example . . ."

"Yes. Let's both agree that love be our yoke."

"So be it. The grand cru *love favored by our afflictions.*"

"So be it. *A love sanctified by many tears and much suffering.*"

"*And let's ensure that our physical forms withstand all coming vicissitudes.*"

"*Your strength comforts me, Franziska. I know now that engagement is the beauty of an unread book; the wedding, the sensation of opening its pages; matrimony, the spouses' errata to the edition . . .*"

"*Don't worry. I know what I have to do. My affection has now been leavened with the yeast of torment. The loaf is golden and succulent. Interests that unite on earth are lost in heaven. My mother just told me as much. When I become corporeal again, I'll take to wearing masks. I'll be exquisite yet perverse like a prostitute-nun. I'll cordon off my sensorial side with lily garlands and barbed wire.*"

"*A prostitute-nun! That's an outrage! Why disturb our serenity with thoughts of human interference? Serenity is a fine crystal vase that vibrates and makes a sumptuous sound when filled with the ecstasy of two souls in love. But, oh, if it breaks! All the complicit glory evaporates. No matter how imperceptible or tiny the fissure, the harmony becomes dissonant. And though formal beauty appears to be intact, the vibration and the sound will never be the same again.*"

"*. . . !*"

"*. . .*"

"*Oh! What's happened? Why have the diamanté stars stopped shining on us, twinkling their astral tresses so?*"

"*It's us. We have scorned pure thought.*"

"*And those sickly colors? Mauve, amaranth, and gray? And this febrile pageant in the chamois-colored twilight?*"

"*It's us. We have tainted the beatitude.*"

"*And this dazzling copper-colored languor, now dissolving? And this air that cobalts the night and imprisons us as though by concrete in the rigid skeleton of its spell?*"

"It's us. We shouldn't have detoured, shouldn't have forayed yearningly into the exclusive regions of the flesh. It's not uncommon. Love is immersion, not excess. Those who stride thirstily, ruthlessly, through the desert of love become sensualized the moment they reach its oasis."

"I . . ."

"Yes. You and I both. In the desert of love, sex is the oasis. Deep well, beautiful flower, slippery snake. A deep well where the infrapersonality succumbs to the unconscious. A beautiful flower that blossoms out of the chaos and destroys all elegance. A slippery snake that slithers through the instinctual swamp and peeps its face over the muddy surface."

"Let's escape, let's run away from here. Let's seek out some scenery of greater moral probity . . ."

"Impossible. We walk but cannot advance. We must recover the key to our lost serenity. If a single link is broken, as you've seen, shameful repercussions rock the entire chain . . ."

"Meaning, we'll be smothered in this . . ."

"Reality."

". . . everlasting, all-encompassing delusion?"

"It's obvious: we've sinned. It's been confirmed by this ineluctable assault."

"If only I could shut down my senses!"

"Au contraire, your perceptions will only increase. We're ardent mirrors. We'll see everything except each other. A mirror's sorrow resides in this blind lucidity, in the inability to gaze into its beloved. Don't prick me, mi vida!"

"It isn't me. It's this loathsome foliage, emitting scorching poison and a fetid, morgue-like odor . . ."

"Are your arms like lianas or venomous vipers?"

"I don't know. Don't whine. Let me rest here a moment. I can see a metal armchair."

"Quick! Step back! Can't you see the mucilaginous marrow, the lar-vae writhing on the chrome? Can't you see that the leaves fanning you are the ears of leprous elephants? Step away!"

"All right. But don't bite me."

"I'm not. It's the ravenous crocodiles hiding in the shadows. Observe. They and other chimera are stuck here, where modernity mixes with the world's most primitive horrors. Be careful! Everything is deceitful. Keep away from the squishy fruit on those trees. They're macabre grafts, the invention of drunken demons. Don't yield to a single temptation. It's not water but caustic lavalike soda spurting from those springs. Phosphoric, phantasmagoric life forms filter through the cracks in the walls and the fissures in the onyx floor, expanding and then entwining themselves in the sweltering air. We must shield ourselves in the inno-cent faith that first brought us to this otherworld, recover the light that will guide us out of the labyrinth—or else we'll perish!"

"Such mammoth misfortune! What I wouldn't give to uproot this undergrowth! What I wouldn't give to be back on the path of periwin-kle and forget-me-nots, the trail that will take us back to the telepathic viaduct bridging normality and the supernormal!"

"Giving things is meaningless. Giving yourself is what matters. Our selfishness cut short that idyll of sacrifice and sadness. We wished for the immediacy of desire. We're to blame. We dispossessed the heroic sincerity of pure love, which is selfless."

"Hold on! I hear laughter . . . Several people laughing . . ."

"Laughter?"

"Yes. Over there . . . Look, look!"

"Ah. Of course. I know them. Malignancy tickles certain shame-less souls. They're laughing for no good reason, naturally. They're laughing at Henri Landru, that ardent lover fanning the ashes of his sweethearts, stoking the fire of his kiln. They're laughing at Henry the Eighth, assessing his conjugal clearcutting: Catherine of Aragon, Anne

Boleyn, Catherine Howard, Anne de Cléves . . . *They're laughing at everyone who experienced an instinctive love and sought sexual truth in death—in the death fuck. Idiots!"*

"Who are they?"

"Failures. Ratés. *Casanova and Madame Bovary, Lucrezia Borgia and Werther, Francis of Assisi and Nana, Christina of Sweden and Rasputin, Rudolph Valentino and Teresa de Jesús . . ."*

"And that sardonic hyena ogling the cinnamon statue?"

"That's no statue. *It's the only faithful spouse of Koresh II. The other fourteen wives loll in the same disrespectful derision as Rama V's three thousand wives, their breasts dried up and shriveled by vampires, their genitalia withered and worn away by incubi with emery phalli. The hyena is Leporello. Don't you know Leporello? He's one of my colleagues. Don Juan's Statistician. He catalogued his seductions and computed his conquests. Sing. Would you care to hear the aria Mozart composed for him? It will inform you, as it did Doña Elvira, of how many lovers Don Juan had spurned:*

640 Italians

100 Frenchwomen

91 Turks

231 Germans

1003 Spaniards . . ."

"No, no. Enough of your statistics. *Please, let's get out of this suffocating and self-important atmosphere. These alternating gusts of penury and Sapphism, of perversion and derision vex me . . ."*

"Leaving is arriving. *We're gloves turned inside out. Everything is inverted for us. Torture and punishment are ineluctable. I know. It was just as inescapable on the other foggy occasions when I furtively traversed these same paranormal premises on my own."*

"There, I see a clearing. Let's go."

"Don't be fooled. *It's a counterfeit clearing. The hostile hovel where*

Descartes dwells, after having been iced up in Elizabeth of Bohemia's love. He's a crafty, cagey traffic warden who can't be counted on. His directions all lead to dead ends and blind alleys. I know the narrow pass we need. We have to take the path marked with priapic milestones. This must be the one. If the immodesty of it mortifies you, I pray you, mold your mood, modify your manners. Here, you see, a blushing woman is a lost woman, because such a flush proves that you understand sex and its pleasures. There will be an infinite number of magnetic forces attempting to control you, possess you. Be apathetic. If you can manage this, our travels will be brief."

"I think I'm going to faint. Since I'm still pure, innocent of the shame of sex, this great big, strapping, nightmarish reality seems to me like an enormous phallic crystallization of every female anxiety rolled into one . . ."

"It's much more than that . . . But we mustn't speak. Be strong. This battalion of erect phalli serves to counteract witchcraft and sorcery. Salute these jaunty captains, whose prophylactic effectiveness against the evil eye and other curses is proverbial. Prepare yourself: there's the abode of Osiris, overflowing with italophallic paintings and amulets. The atmosphere is orgasmic. Can you smell the sickening stench of spikenards?"

"Yes."

"Those are the seminal rivers born deep within—they fertilize the barren wastelands of the world."

"I can't stomach it. I'll asphyxiate!"

"Come on, Franziska! You see, here's a recreational bend in the road. See the cult of Shiva. The dancers contort lustily. Their ritual embodies sacred obscenity. It's symbolic!"

"I can breathe again! But what muddy waters! What terrifying skies! I was suffocating in sorrow, a sorrow bordering vesania . . ."

"The sky hasn't changed, though. We have. Our depravity, our thoughts, our auras stain it. We must find shelter in the innocent faith that matches and unites pure souls, free from ulterior motives. The sky is always an upturned cup, and we're trapped underneath. The only way out is to transmogrify ourselves into beams of light."

"Beams of light! What use are beams of light in this sick, mysterious place?"

"Light will shine its way through the labyrinth. We'll emerge from ourselves. And we'll reach the golden sands where the life-giving forces of virtue and balance are found."

"Then hurry! Has anyone ever told you that you're an overly loquacious dragoman? Stop wasting time."

"Wasting time . . . Don't you see that time expands and contracts, adjusting to our every whim? Love is the seed that inseminates eternity. The only thing that matters is taking care of that which is everlasting: our love. We must love!"

"We must love! Of course. I know that. But—why is that old man in his crown of shoots and roses smiling at me so?"

"He always smiles. That's Anacreon. He's the one who said, 'We must love.' But, observe. Behind him stand Sappho and Socrates disputing the point, dissuading damsels and ephebes both. Listen to their squabbling. 'Yes, we must love, but in our own way . . .'"

"Scioccante!"

"Let's turn here. Feel how the air is fresher? What are you worried about now? Oh! No need to hesitate. Those are merely the athletes who accompany the Olympiad. Naked, their bodies glistening with fresh stadium sweat and Egyptian ointments. Sex is sublimated in their epics and shines forth in their triumphs. Feel how the air is fresher? That's our spirit, the pure breeze of our spirit."

"Hallelujah! But . . . what's that?"

"*Don't be upset. Condescend. Accept the offering that Euripides and Aristophanes—finally friends!—are making to you.*"

"*More phalli!*"

"*Those are the phallic pastries they used to distribute during the Thesmophoria. Repress your revulsion. You see, the panorama expands, exalting in a breadth of blue as vast as our very souls. But . . . what's this I see? Oh, misfortune! Misfortune! They execrate us. They make obscene gestures, thrusting their thumbs between their index and middle fingers. Your condemnation has caused them offense. We've aroused their disdain. The fig is an evil omen—it bodes ill. I fear an ambush.*"

"*Pity. I was just beginning to feel a cool fountain filled with . . . Oh!*"

"*Oh!*"

"*Again this frond of flesh with teratological flowers and foul aromas! Again the assault of reality, rife with aberration. Where are you going, mi vida? Don't you dare cross that corridor carpeted with creatures' buttocks. It's lusciously lucent, but it conceals terrifying traps. I know—I poked around. Now it's my turn to guide you through these infernos. Behind them lie vaginal grottoes where every disease imaginable festers in fetid stickiness. Come. Close your eyes and summon all your will. We're going to cross some difficult terrain, paved with Hyperborean damsels' breasts and nubile mestiza girls' thighs: a slippery, sensual locale. Hold on to me.*"

"*I'm slipping, Franzi . . .*"

"*You mustn't weaken, Op Oloop. Your demeanor must demonstrate even more contempt than before . . .*"

"*But my sense of touch has been numbed, and my hearing . . .*"

"*Remember: touch is the language of the flesh. It surges in pleasure, contorts and weeps. Blood is its spirit—a smug spirit, seldom strong or*" salubrious, especially when suffering the stigmas of sex. Sweetheart, you must learn to loathe blood."

"Oh, cherie! Your reasoning drains the sorrow from my soul. I am comforted. But I can't . . . I'm slipping . . ."

"Don't fall victim to your own desire!"

"What bliss, to drown in vice!"

"I know vices are appealing. But come on! I can't believe you'd accede to the temptations offered by these sirens, succubae, and centauresses, disgracing my honor, which is also your honor—my chastity belt. Wake up! On your feet! That's it. That's right. Three cheers for your affectations! Your dandy-bored-with-the-world posture! Bravo! Now turn away, close your shutters. We're going to pass through foul, filthy markets, where pimps and ruffians—with vertical vulvae for mouths—lewdly peddle their wares in a thousand tongues. Whores' cohorts—breasts on their shoulders and buttocks for backpacks—ply their wares like disemboweled carmagnoles. Thank God there's only one more crowd left to pass through . . ."

"Thank God. Disgust infuriates me, and fury makes me terribly tense. But now my heart flutters sweetly once more . . ."

"I'm confused by this turbulence in your heart—a melodious bird, singing in the prison of your ribs. With us disembodied, what veiled designs can be controlling it, urging it to flee?"

"They're not veiled. They're diaphanous. The heart is a camera obscura and what it reveals are instincts. It's obvious! I've lived my whole life in regimented continuity and implacable restraint. This fresh air . . . these stimuli . . . Liberty leads to libidinousness."

"Your sincerity moves me. It was a difficult test, but you passed, and you've convinced me."

"And you. You too overcame our odyssey with marvelous modesty. The grief and opprobrium, ire and tolerance we've experienced on our travels persuade me that your hitherto unknown feelings and my own are in synchronicity. The staff paper of love contains both unfinished symphonies and complete ones: the former conspire against the souls of creatures who still dream their deceptive dreams, who are still attached to the pleasures of life. The latter are composed by souls advancing towards mortality. Such are we. Without leaving this world, summoned by pure ideality, we've lived in eternal exile and faced the mass of esoteric horrors that undermine the temple of love. And we conquered them. And when reedy childlike voices and gruff subconscious whispers and soft hypnotic registers sing in unison, we bask in a near-posthumous euphoria, inexpressible in the terrestrial world, submerged in each other—you and I."

"What delight!"

"Franzi, all that's left is to bask in the light we radiate. To rest in the glowing panoramas opening like flowers in the morning breeze. And to drink in the peace that these hills—auspicious giants for we two stunned specks—offer in their cupped hands, their valleys."

"What delight! I feel an ancient sort of fulfillment in this peace, I feel blissfully submissive, I feel a new renaissance approaching!"

"Exactly: me. That's our glory! When love is perfectly ripe it's both young and old at once. And when it begins to climax, the foretaste brings joy. And the profundity of time and the relief of overcoming destiny are one."

"Let us kiss."

"Yes. Let us kiss. And may our kiss last until past and future are extinct, and may it tie the fluid knot that makes the present immemorial . . ."

Had anyone—skilled in the arts of ubiquity—snuck up on Franziska and Op Oloop at that precise moment, he'd have seen their faces brighten, the result of the deep current of insufferable cuteness then charging through them. In spite of the circumstances in which they found themselves—one laying on her bed, the other collapsed on a bench in the Botanical Gardens—the same mysterious force had simultaneously penetrated their corporeal tissue, invigorating them, coloring their lips and flushing their cheeks.

In the same way that a blood transfusion revives exhausted organisms, injecting stores of new hope, new energy, souls too are rejuvenated when their fallow fields are flooded with the white waters of love . . .

Love, like blood, contains biologically permanent characteristics. Everybody has a predetermined love type, which is suitable for subdividing into further analogous and dissimilar types based on certain unalterable psychological postulates. A love transfusion is essentially the same as a blood transfusion. Just as humans are divided into four hematic groups, they're also grouped into four erotic types; let's call them *A*, *B*, *C*, and *D*. An *A*-type lover is always an *A*, a *C* is always a *C*, and so forth. What's interesting is that the question of love transfusions has yet to be tackled. Both socially and eugenically it would be quite useful. When sympathies are on their way towards turning into love, lovers could consult a specialized psychiatrist—an *amoristrist*—who would then rule on the fitness of their selection, based on their respective libidinal tendencies. There are some disparate souls quite skilled at the game of concealing their own disparities, just as there are temperaments that agglutinate, and those that dissolve others' feelings entirely. A perfect amorous combination results from the kind of scrutiny that—the vast majority of the time—lovers don't even consider undertaking. If a blood transfusion is never undertaken when the blood type of donor and recipient aren't compatible, why then are spiritual injections not regulated in the same way? The *A* group, the universal recipients, for example, could be called the "egotistical group." People in this category can successfully receive love from anyone in the world. But they can only transfuse it into those in their same group. Hetaeras, for example, are a case in point: they can love only thugs and gangsters. In complete opposition to this group are the *D*s, the "altruists," or universal donors, whose love can be given to anyone in the world but who can only receive it from other *D*s in turn. Jesus and Don Quixote, for instance. They possessed enough warmth to fill all of humanity, but they were spiritually celibate, due to Mary Magdalene's pettiness and Dulcinea's coarse pastorality. Groups *B* and *C*, who can receive love from groups *B*, *C*, and *D*, are made up of standard lovers, *tellement ordinaire*, and they possess entirely routine passions and pedestrian habits. Sometimes, when they receive altruistic love, they become transformed—pompously—in the eyes of the world. Such would be the case, for instance, of George Sand basking in Chopin's genial effluvia . . .

Franziska and Op Oloop were compatible lovers and kindred spirits, both *D*-type. Both were generous, but their generosity was retractable. She, orphaned by her mother, curbed her love so as to allow only what was absolutely necessary to filter out into the world, once she realized affection's role in life. She had no reason to be lavish with the gushing, unruly flow inherited from her deceased *mamá*. While he, fashioned in the farthest forge of loneliness, had carefully and compassionately dissected all universal ills, as mandated by humanism and method, knowledge and number. He contained a wealth of tenderness, yet knew how not to wear it on his sleeve.

Within the heart's great opulence, there's always a transversal egotism that advises you to be stingy when extolling your affections, the better to appreciate the crucial moment when you can at last squander them luxuriously . . .

They had both arrived at that lucid moment.

Friendship—which is trust—had become love—which is confidence. Mutual desires—upheld by illusions that were all still intact—became foretastes of pleasure. Their rapport had reinstated their bonds with the sensorial world. All that was missing was the psychic fusion that dissolves one's scruples and others' preconceptions. And when each of their feelings entered the other, fusion was ignited—heating their beakers, setting the liquids in them to boil, and, finally, decanting their spiritual essences.

When unconsciousness is brought on by shock and trauma, it later results in a dazed state of wakefulness, which itself finally leads into a hypnotic state. This mysterious phenomenon played out in both Franziska and Op Oloop. If the body is attacked or ill-treated, it clamors for refuge or succor. Man's awareness grows faint, but his most intimate senses never faint away. These mechanisms are invulnerable. In such circumstances, cerebral fluid still emits and receives orders and suggestions imparted by one's consciousness. And two consciousnesses that are in sync can therefore communicate. Leaving behind external stimuli, souls turn to those utterly interior expanses whose paranormality enjoys the privilege of never leaving so much as a trace upon the world outside.

The modern sciences tend more and more to delve into the invisible, as Sir Oliver Lodge maintained. Man's inherent faculties are becoming increasingly fine-tuned. They still show the scars of theological, political, and rational filth, of course. We've besmirched all that is simple and pure in animals. Soon, perhaps, we'll recover our clairvoyant transmissive and receptive powers, currently suspended, and attain the vital attributes prolonged after death that separate thought from matter. All otherworldly phenomenologicality will lose its unsettling character. What's now seen as "supernatural" will become "entirely natural." Intelligence hammers at the blocks of our atavism. Intuition, which perforates the toughest leathers of enigma, is already hinting at the truth. Symbols and allegories are being founded, established. Mediums, rummaging around in transcendentality, offer us clear signs in ectoplasmic inkblots. Richet delves; William Crookes experiments. These are no longer simple premonitions: these are certainties. There are strong indications that a discovery is near. An inverse Christopher Columbus, setting sail from our physical continent, will conquer the primacy of its innermost spirit: he'll be the greatest conquistador in history. The ships are approaching. Light, electricity, magnetism, gravity—entities that only yesterday were imponderables in the vastness of the universe—have now yielded to intellectualization. The four axes of philosophy are about to be revealed in the tiny space of the spirit. A strange fluttering indicates that the joy of triumph is near. On this side of that great orb-filled void, and on the other side of that flesh-covered void, a heart beats . . . a heart beats! Is it ours, or the heart of the world? The science of the invisible will tell . . . Perhaps two hearts beat as one in the pulse of the cosmos.

9:00 P.M. The night fog bewildered. It was nine o'clock. A gentle breeze, fluttering like a frilly frock, caressed the trees. Sharper gusts stripped them of autumnal leaves.

Op Oloop was a shadow.

A night watchman, on his rounds, came upon him. He noted his regular breathing, his distinguished appearance, and his astoundingly crumpled and uncomfortable-looking position. Accustomed as he was to kicking out drunks, ejecting idlers, and ambushing those intent on suicide, he now found himself quite perplexed. He knew not what was expected of him, which procedure to follow. He coughed. He coughed again. Nothing! Having failed in this attempt to wake the man, he took Samaritanical compassion. He replaced the man's hat on his head. He closed his legs. He gently lifted an arm that had been hanging askew. And, tapping him lightly on his curved back, he asked, "Anything wrong, sir?"

No reply.

He spoke louder, tapped harder.

"Anything wrong, sir?"

The Statistician made an enormous and obvious effort to rouse himself. But then collapsed back into the same position, inert.

The night watchman must have discerned something extraordinary here, for he refrained from pestering the man again and instead took a few steps back.

Op Oloop was lost in a dream world. His mental faculties were rejecting all external stimuli. Something like a magnetic force seemed to be drawing him inward. Intimacy was still a placid pool full of marvelous matter—but on diving back into it, he felt a ferocious sense of rejection, as if the pool had suddenly petrified.

Telestically speaking, when his dream state shattered, this reverberated in Franziska. She'd sensed the commotion caused by the night watchman's presence. (Her internal images were startled.) That cough of his had created an implacable gale. (Bliss turned to dismay.) His tapping produced horrific thunder. (Enchantment disappeared entirely.) Then Franziska was seized by an indescribable anxiety. And at the very instant that Op Oloop finally stood, she wailed and cried out at the hypnotic disruption.

The governess, charged with overseeing her depression, ran in immediately. She saw Franziska's eyes were still closed and assumed it was nothing. But she soon changed her mind: the girl was writh-

ing in exasperation and, desiring an uninterrupted dialogue, called
out numerous times to her idyllic interlocutor:

"Don't go! Don't go! DON'T GO!"

The Consul shook his bald head back and forth.

"I think, Quintín, that it would be best if we took her to a sanato-
rium. Right away . . ."

It's very difficult to differentiate between truth and imagination,
particularly for obsessives. The surreal atmosphere that their dreams
inhabit is, for them, still the only unstifling air to be found. While
their inner world conforms to their desires—the specters they see
symbolically embodying a made-to-order reality—as soon as they
awaken, the external atmosphere seems intent on choking them,
and harsh reality only incites their rebellion.

Franziska refused to let her senses function properly. She couldn't
relinquish the images she was holding on to, nor force herself to
accept the abrupt confines of a state of wakefulness. She rolled over
unconditionally. And sprawled out, face down on the bed.

Op Oloop, who was now attempting to walk, stumbled like a
drunken shadow.

The night watchman ran to his aid. He held him up. And he asked,
once more, "Anything wrong, sir?"

Before responding, he fixed the man with an icy glare: an attempt
to communicate inquisitive indignation.

"Yes, something's wrong. What's wrong is that I am now back in my
body . . . Thanks to you . . . Again in a suit of flesh . . . Thanks to you . . .
I had been swimming, naked, just a ball of light in a greater ocean of
light, and then you came along to disturb me . . . Who are you?"

The night watchman let go of his arm. Instantly, he thought he
was dealing with a lunatic. And instilled with the significance of his
position—grave, with all the valiance afforded by his ten-foot dis-

tance from the madman—he commenced his little homily:

"I am the night watchman here. I don't bother anybody. I'm just doing my job. Here in the Botanical Gardens, sleeping, lovemaking, and committing suicide are not permitted. I must now ask you to leave."

Op Oloop didn't fully comprehend his words, but the imperative was clear enough. So he headed down a narrow brick path. His steps were lighter, but still clumsy. Aphrodite's buttocks were spread before him on the privet-covered slope in the moonlight. Above her, like a menagerie of monks in pointy cowls, the pine trees peeked down on her delightful derrière.

Op Oloop took the wrong path.

"You're going the wrong way, sir! Turn right!" the night watchman shouted after him.

Op Oloop didn't hear him, or pretended not to hear. He was now striding along, taking great big steps, losing himself further and further in the darkness of the path. His shadow was barely visible among the gigantic shadows of the trees.

"I have a feeling this lunatic's going to be a real headache," the night watchman murmured. And he started off in pursuit, intent on kicking him out of the Gardens.

Confusing the different senses and obsessing over erotic images are both typical of systematized delirium. Storybook love or fanatical Platonism might well be what spurred on the knight errant or the sweet troubadour. Likewise any of their modern-day equivalents. In such a state, mania and fever overcome reality. A woman's tiniest gestures are magnified out of all proportion. Innocent displays of common courtesy convince the sufferer of a sublime love. The entire relationship is hallucinatory, and yet, for that very reason, it's wholly invincible, thanks to the reigning supremacy of autosuggestion.

Op Oloop may not have been suffering this particular type of paranoia, but some hint of it was in the air that night. Though apparently still in his right mind, he behaved discordantly, a victim of the imperfection of his senses. There's no doubt that fantasy had taken him over. Another awareness of reality—perhaps more diaphanous—had sprung up inside him. And his personality split, jumping back and forth, alternately, between its normal state and the circumstantial state whose influence he'd most recently been under.

It was then that Franziska appeared beside him. Said materialization made him exceptionally nervous. He pressed her to himself. He spun her from left to right. He held her before him like a shield. The foliage was taking on frightening shapes and sounds in his mind. Branches were debauched arms. Leaves were a monstrous whirl.

The night watchman snuck up on him while Op Oloop was executing these maneuvers. He was baffled. He crept on, more stealthily.

Para-amnesia, which is a distortion of the memory, was stalking the Statistician. His view of reality was "covered" by unfathomable recollections, and the illusion created by these memories adulterated his reason. Lacking the clarity to distinguish between the two, he was more affected by his feelings of fantasy than by any genuine awareness of the real world.

Just when the night watchman was about to grab hold of him, Op Oloop took off toward an illuminated flowerbed. The electric light dazzled him. His absurd contortions beneath the shaded canopy of foliage suddenly froze into a hard, inquisitional look. He was looking for Franziska. Hardly moving, he searched the air, his surroundings, his thoughts. The hallucination had been so lifelike that he began to suspect Franziska had been spirited away via some trap door.

On spotting the night watchman, he began interrogating him:

"Where is Franziska? Hand over Franziska!"

And then he abruptly made amends.

"Oh, no, no! . . . Forgive me. I was delirious . . . Man fools himself often, you know . . . Our spirits are to blame . . . When the flesh sleeps, the spirit likes to go out and wreak a bit of havoc . . . If the spirit returns home in time, no one thinks to blame it for all the chaos it's caused . . . But on certain occasions, it can't get back in. Yes, yes! That's it! . . . You see, my spirit's still out . . . Forgive me."

"I do, sir. But please, come with me. I'll take you to Plaza Italia. Then you can catch a taxi or a tram and go rest, preferably in the comfort of your own domicile."

"My do-mi-cile? What a thought! I'm hosting a banquet tonight!"

"Well then you'd better be off . . ."

Op Oloop fell into step with the night watchman. He was reacting energetically now, whether on his own incentive or the converse— something quite unusual in melancholic types. Perhaps it had to do with his vigorous constitution. Built up by sports since childhood, his strength forbade him to become one of those pitiful, wandering caryatids—the introverts. In the bright foliage of a crossroads, the night watchman glanced back at him out of the corner of his eye. He looked happy enough, his face was smooth and worry-free, he bore the idiotic grin of a schoolboy who's just passed his exams. And so the watchman tempered his pace, decelerating to his usual lope and loosening his tongue:

"Not a very nice night, eh? Bit windy . . ."

"It's a magnificent night. Clearly you've never felt the glacial Arctic north winds . . ."

"No, that's true. Me, I'm from San Juan—we have the hot Zonda winds there. This little river breeze drives me crazy. If it weren't for my old lady and the little ones, I'd say to hell with this damn job!"

"You have a job?"

"Well, what do you think I'm doing here with you?"

"Oh! Yes, yes of course."

Op Oloop erupted suddenly in a nasal cackle.

Health is simply a matter of inner hygiene. Illness results from a dirty soul. Pain is the grime caked on it. This little walk and laugh did Op Oloop well. A large portion of his self was being treated, cleansed.

"These days, Sundays especially, it's all work, work, work. So many poor bastards lose at the racetrack and then sneak in here. They're afraid to go home broke. The second you turn your back they're stealing flowers. They want to fool their wives, lead them up the garden path, so to speak. Then there are the drunks, poets, couples . . . Christ! You name it!"

"Well, well! Many chary souls indeed!"

"You're telling me! And there's nothing you can do about it. Just got to keep alert, do your rounds all night, enforce the rules . . ."

"What rules?"

"The ones that prohibit sleeping on the benches, making love in the grass, and committing suicide in the Botanical Gardens."

Their little chat had taken a turn. Op Oloop was suddenly besieged by gnawing doubts. Seized by anxiety, he re-examined his own motives on entering the Gardens, and came to an abject conclusion. He assigned himself all sorts of implausible faults, whose transcendence now overwhelmed him. His expression altered, his voice deepened to tuning-fork pitch, and he sputtered:

"Come now! Tell me, in all honesty, did you think that I . . ."

"No, no, not to worry. You're a decent guy, I can tell. Feel free to come back whenever you like."

They'd reached the gates.

Suddenly, the Statistician experienced a sort of tingling in his consciousness. His thoughts became imprecise, fluctuant. He couldn't decide how to interpret the night watchman's invitation. For a few seconds, he blushed, recalling the incidents that had just transpired—for a few seconds, he made an effort to placate the myriad neurons seething inside his cranium. Deep down, Op Oloop was naïve, overwhelmingly naïve. He was within a hair's breadth of falling into another delirious fit. Self-accusation and guilt plowed through his mind exalting every trivial incident to the heights of monstrosity. But then he was inspired. He slid his hand down into his pocket. He extracted twenty pesos. And, expressing his profound humility and mortification, he handed them to the night watchman.

"Please, friend, accept this token of my appreciation. I won't be troubling you this way ever again."

The San Juan watchman went cross-eyed. He was so shocked that he forgot to express his thanks, and when he finally remembered, he was too dumbfounded to get it out. Op Oloop, crossing the street, was already opening the back door of a taxi. And the car, heeding the demands of traffic, slipped into the chaos of screeching, squealing, and honking.

The taxi driver circled round the Statue of Garibaldi and headed towards the Monument to the Spaniards.

The night watchman remained stupefied. The speed with which the entire transaction had taken place filled him with suspicion. He cocked his head in concentration.

"He didn't seem to care about the money at all! Wonder if it's counterfeit?"

He leaned against a lamppost. He held the bills up to the light. He saw the watermark. And deeming them to be legitimate, he likewise legitimized his casual ingratitude.

Meanwhile, Op Oloop was taking great delight in simply allowing himself to be transported.

More and more air came into the car as it sped along. And more and more air came into the passenger too, who sat, yogi-like, his chest near to bursting. Invigorated, he seemed to have come to his senses, emotionally. He'd been so absent the entire day that he was flattered by this reconciliation with his faculties. He leaned his head out. Set with stars, as watches are set with rubies, the celestial skies drew appreciative sighs from him. Yes, he remembered now: exactitude was the mainspring of his life! On sighing, a resinous perfume filled his lungs. The rows of trees lining the avenue had aroused his instant sympathy. He reflected briefly on their immobile discipline and the benevolent tribute they paid humanity, their only reward being the municipal axe and schoolboys' urine. And then, on inspecting them, he felt the tenderness of a defeated general regarding his ramshackle regiment. Nearing the end of the avenue, he noted how the excessive lighting overheated the trees, desiccating the branches and tingeing them with nacre and celluloid tones. He was overcome. He mused that soon they'd begin to grow their buds, to cast summer shadows, to attract warblers who would fly off again come winter; they had no ulterior motive. This generosity, this quality of giving oneself just because, because of innate goodness, this obeying a higher order, warmed the cockles of his heart. In his estimation, it was the supreme thing. And he himself, personally, could also boast of being a tree, one that bore fruit and flowers without ever asking for gratitude or being carried away by his own imagination.

"To give, to give! Yes, I'll emulate them down to my core—learn to give and give until I can give all of myself and vanish! To give one's spirit to life and one's matter to death, that these may be the very perfume and humus of humanity! To give, and to give oneself!"

"Talking to me, sir?"

"Yes. Turn right. Take me to the Plaza Hotel."

The aptness of Op Oloop's lie prompted him to assume a friendly, sorrowful smile—although indispensable, lying distressed him. But he was calmed again almost at once, the absence of guilt establishing the legitimacy of this last resort—and that he'd resorted to this resort filled him with satisfaction. It signaled a return to his faculties, Argentinified by irony and spontaneity.

He was almost happy. Almost, that is, because the troubles of the day had still laid waste to his punctuality. He was late for everything. An ominous feeling clouded over him. It seemed fate was now allowing him to worry about his punctuality again, and he nursed this quality accordingly, as carefully as if it were a graft being affixed to one of the trees he'd so admired; because punctuality is a way of grafting oneself seamlessly onto the trunk of time.

Luckily his discomfiture was short-lived. The smooth pavement of Avenida Alvear restored his characteristic aplomb, which had been so woefully lacking on this particular Sunday. He was once again the strong, grave, pure man, as complicated by excessive simplicity as he'd always been. He once again located the formula that synthesized all the elements of his lifestyle: equal parts skill and diligence, numen and capital. And, shrewd as he was, he thus fell back on the mental stratagem of using the imminence of the banquet he was hosting to obscure all of his latent preoccupations.

His custom of offering dinners to small nuclei of dearly beloved friends was one rooted in secrecy. His motives always sparked off great curiosity and intrigue. Especially since he himself never accepted invitations or attended parties. His long, slow, copious dinners—tailored to his aphorism, "The art of the gourmand resides in tasting everything and eating nothing"—were always perfect: Op Oloop's friends esteemed his tactful way of veiling his own triumphs, and thus, by attending, they were already applauding a well-earned victory.

As per the invitations that he had personally inscribed that morning, he imagined his guests, already seated at the table, which, being round, happily prioritized each of them only according to his coincidental connection to whatever the cause might be for that particular gathering. With the exception of Ivar Kittilä, who was attending one of Op Oloop's dinners for the first time that night, he intuited that the guests would all forgive his tardiness, as true friends do, without a word, carrying on as if nothing had happened, strolling carefree on the carpet of times past.

The motive for the evening's soiree was perfectly comical. He was prepared to divulge it, so long as the tragedy it presupposed didn't produce any pain. For Op Oloop these banquets were quite palliative. They made him forget not his successes, but the laborious torture of achieving them. That's why, the moment he arrived, he strove to eliminate any cerebral distance between himself and his friends, imbuing his conversation with a good-natured, carefree tone. From time to time, he surpassed everyone with astonishing naiveté or audacity, precisely with the purpose of expunging any sense of his superiority.

Just at that moment, he had a sudden presentiment. And that presentiment added to the irony—now insuperable—of the fact that he, the host, would be the single latecomer. Uneasiness and pride generate vibrations that aggravate one's temperament. Feeling victimized yet again, Op Oloop clouded over. He was irritated by the unreliability of his internal climate. He felt his emotions must be light, wispy cirrus clouds. And yet the rays of understanding didn't burn them off. Subsequently he saw an urgent need to soothe his inner self via his usual, programmatic amnesia—and to spruce up his external self, so as to conform to his habitual toilet.

He was unable to achieve his objective.

The car had just arrived in Plaza San Martín.

When it pulled to a stop, he stepped out so solemnly that his grayish pallor traumatized even himself.

He strode immediately to the lavatory. Fortunately, he was alone. Staring into the mirror he perceived each of the day's masks superimposed over one another, forming an expression of authentic anguish. He turned on the cold tap and moistened a towel. He scrubbed his face vigorously, splashing himself liberally with eau de toilette to dispel the other faces still showing through. And, once he was ready—like a man finally pulling down the shutters and closing up shop on a doomed business—he closed up his exasperation, lowering the palm of his right hand over his face, forehead to chin, while applying firm pressure.

The effect verged on the miraculous.

The mirror now reflected an entirely different image. Once again, elegance was the measure of Op Oloop's striking appearance. The kind of vibrant veneer usually evidenced only on the epidermis of those experiencing intense embarrassment or excitement was visible on his visage.

Straightening his tie, he grumbled to himself, "What a sight I must have been today! It was as though I were another. Frightening, to have succumbed, restrained, surrendered, been suffocated by an iron will just for this: to be a human automaton, who shouts, jumps, and raves at the first little failure. If only they understood me . . . But I fear they got me all wrong, Franziska's family doesn't truly know me. Ignorance is always dogmatic and aprioristic! If only they knew that my psychosis is for my own personal use, so unique that it's yet to be catalogued . . . If only . . ."

A snap decision cut short his soliloquy.

He exited.

Striding surefootedly toward the bar, he decided to swap his current self for the self on quotidian display.

10:04 P.M. The guests were all there. But he didn't see them. His eyes froze in shock at the sight of the spherical clock, which read 10:04, and the calendar just below it, indicating that today was the twenty-second day of the fourth month. All his apprehension at arriving so late dissipated with this coincidence. Trivialities penetrate to a man's most inaccessible regions in the most unforeseen of ways! He himself had often observed how, in people overcome with fear, inconsequential twists of fate often dispelled their anxieties. He knew one poor soul plagued by the monstrous guilt of incest who kept his obsession at bay by wearing narrow-ankled boots. And one colleague (from his days at the Ministry of Agriculture) who'd suffered two defamatory rulings escaped his painful memories by regularly flaunting new ties. But Op Oloop didn't think about him at this moment. He was lost in ruminations and who knows what calculations involving 22.4, 224, 4.22, 422, 42.2, and so forth.

Robín Sureda—olive-skinned, curly haired, and built like a stevedore—brought him back to reality.

"Hello, Op Oloop! Very strange, your being so late!"

"Yes, it is. I can't explain it myself."

Op Oloop spoke perfunctorily. But the sound of his own voice seemed to spur him on, serving as an enticement to keep speculating aloud:

"But it makes no difference, really. After all, the clock reads forty-two hours and two minutes—I mean, twenty-two hours and four minutes. Did you notice? Look. You see, today is the twenty-second day of the fourth month, and I arrived at twenty-two oh-four. A wonderful omen! Invert the figures and you'll see why. Forty-two is twenty-one doubled, and twenty-one is my favorite number, based on nineteen being the Greeks' lucky number, then adding two, which in Pythagoras's esoteric scale was . . ."

He was interrupted.

At just that moment, Ivar Kittilä, the sound engineer for a local film studio, and Erik Joensun, an ex-Submarine Captain, approached.

He made a tremendous effort to greet them. His mind, still reeling with his calculations screeched to a halt.

"You two are acquainted, aren't you? Robín Sureda . . ."

"Yes."

"Of course, the 'Eternal Student' . . ."

"The E-ter-nal Stu-dent?" the party in question stammered.

"Yes, just one of my little jokes. Ivar had heard your name mentioned before. And since I've always alluded to the painstaking parsimony with which you undertake your studies . . . failing your subjects deliberately . . ."

"You're always fucking with me! It's true, though. I do fail deliberately."

"Of course you do!"

"Obviously!"

"No doubt, no doubt . . . But, let's move along. Come, the others are over there."

Alone, affected, drinking a glass of Byrrh, standing beside a mysterious bottle and a completely intact tray of hors d'oeuvres, was Gastón Marietti. No fifty-two-year-old could be more dignified!

Carefully ensconced behind a banister adorned with ferns and aspidistras so as to remain unseen, Cipriano Slatter—his face as perfect as an anthropometric chart—and Luis Augusto Peñaranda—pale and sweaty, his obesity still in its incipient stage—were each on their fourth Manhattan.

Op Oloop was radiant on thus discovering his guests' punctuality. He gathered up the group. With the exception of Ivar Kittilä, they all knew one another. They met up fairly frequently and had dined together on several occasions, at Op Oloop's invitation.

"Ivar, Monsieur Slatter is the Head of Sanitation I was telling you about."

"Ah! Excellent. So that means you must be the mackerel?"

"Mackerel? As in *maquereau*? Ha, ha. Would that I were! Luis Augusto Peñaranda, Commissioner of Air Traffic Control for the Republic, at your service."

The frolicking laugh that arose from this quid pro quo suddenly ceased. Gastón Marietti approached, his *tenue* quite impeccable, a blonde cigarette held by manicured fingernails—just so.

"I, sir, am the 'mackerel' to whom you refer."

The austerity of his response left the sound engineer daunted.

"Er . . . I assure you I meant nothing by it."

"Nor do I. I'm simply an exploiter of women, the way capitalists are exploiters of men—nothing more, nothing less."

"Hm . . . Well, you must admit there is some difference."

"The way I see it, the only difference is that I don't beat up the elderly."

"No, just adolescents."

"Bah! They're happy to do it! I can assure you, it's a nice job for a little lady . . ."

Op Oloop intervened.

"Well. So, there we have it. Let's go in to the dining room. I find it's best to have everything at just the right moment: an aperitif when one is at the table, ready to *aperire* the appetite! I've ordered us one that will flatter the palate: excipient: tonic water; backbone: French vermouth; kick: Old Parr whisky; warmth: *crème de cassis*; perfume: Angostura bitters; poise: drops of absinthe; poetry: rose petals."

Erik Joensun strode over to snatch the first glass. He raised the crystal to his nose and inhaled deeply.

"Magnificent. Stupendous!"

And he drank. The rose petals stuck in his throat, which he cleared repeatedly in disgust. And, on finally spitting them out, also spat out this invective:

"Blech! I've always hated poetry!"

"And yet, it's the nectar of life."

"It is, is it?" he boomed, as Peñaranda wrenched the glass from his hands.

And handing him the petals he'd extracted with his fingers, he downed it in one gulp, finding the contents all the more delicious for the laughter and jeering that accompanied them.

The men's nonsense continued tumultuously, with no reproof of any sort, and the only thing that strained their jovial jocularity was the envy seeping through their squinting eyes. Op Oloop, from his corner, so measured, so balanced, let the friendly repartee waft over him like smoke from a joss stick.

Their banter now became obscured in a debate over the superiority of the classic cocktails—a position sustained by Gastón Marietti—versus the gustative preponderance of the modern—sustained by Cipriano Slatter.

". . . When you're acquainted with the melody of a Haymarket or a Bronx, and are able to discern the mirth of cherry brandy or the cunning of maraschino from within an orchestra of Canadian Club . . . when your palate can perceive the devious flow of a gin fizz or the lonely force of a whisky sour, then, Gastón, you will see the beauty of the new art of imbibing."

"I'm not of your opinion," Ivar Kittilä interrupted. "Accustomed as I was to the Volstead Act, I don't have the physical tolerance for such *feux d'artifice*. Because they are, of course, *feux d'artifice* . . ."

"Do you mean to say that you actually abided by Prohibition? Poor man!"

"Let me tell you. I used to haunt every speakeasy there ever was in New York and Los Angeles. But I did respect puritan morals with regard to one point: if it tastes bad going down, it must be good for you."

"I appreciate your joining the debate, but I must reject your thesis. Taken to its logical conclusion one would have to devour detritus in order to satisfy the stomach. Or, put simply, to eat shit before making it. No, my dear sir. The key to stomatophilic beverages resides in the tonicity of their bitterness. Thus we have Fernet Branca, cola, quinine, Underberg . . ."

"Nonsense! Tonics!"

"Who drinks such things these days?"

"Exactly the same men who invent cocktails . . . No bartender worth his weight actually consumes the concoctions he crafts. You're still in the primary school of mixology. You drink names, things you hear about, rather than liquors, as you should."

Meanwhile, the waiter was handing out a new round of glasses. Gastón Marietti accepted one. Robín Sureda, then, ready to make the most of the inconsistency he'd just observed, as well as to defend the Head of Sanitation, made a point of remarking, "Jesus Christ, you're a fine one to talk! Practice what you preach, why don't you?"

The Maquereau gave an arrogant smile.

"I don't preach. And I don't set examples. I'm too honest for that. I accept these cocktails for two reasons: to toast Op Oloop's health, and to honor a bona fide beverage of his own concoction. Because, really, cocktails are almost always a mélange of deceptions. Keep your eye on any good—that is, sneaky—bartender and you'll see: his arsenal is always a battery of anonymous, unidentifiable bottles and jars. Wicker-wrapped demijohns! It's a universally established principle that only the sublime, the near unattainable, is not adulterated. You see, when I order *something*, they always open a bottle of that very *something* right before my eyes. The astute connoisseur ascertains what is genuine."

Op Oloop accepted the toast with veiled uneasiness. It went straight to his head. He'd eaten nothing all day. From the time he'd had his Turkish bath until now, everything, absolutely everything, had conspired against his synesthesia and ataraxia, that is, against the chemo-emotional equilibrium of his temperament and the psycho-physical equilibrium of his organism. The alcohol, now, was beginning to elevate his effluvia and inundate him with an indefinable anxiety . . .

His good friend Erik Joensun was incredibly opportune with another of his habitually brutal explosions: miming mastication, his irate voice raged, "Well? Are we eating or not?"

"Yes. Let's eat."

Then came the disorder that always precedes the order of guests sitting down in their appointed places.

"Why is this seat empty?" the Student demanded.

"This is Piet Van Saal's place. I was sure I'd be able to invite my friend in person since I see him so often. However . . ."

The excuse rang false before it had even escaped his lips. He fell silent. His falsehood was lost in the prevailing euphoria, but he felt himself flush unexpectedly at the wretchedness of the lie. Instantaneously, the ultra-emotional events of the day paraded past the hitherto neutral screen of his two open eyes. He saw how surreal and infrapsychic it had all been. He wouldn't have bat an eye, but on remembering Piet, that old unsettling anxiety made his heart beat erratically. It occurred to him that as soon as his friend heard of the dinner, as soon as he realized he'd been excluded, he would have cause to doubt Op Oloop's affections. And that subtle, embryonic idea suddenly grew, expanded, and unfolded itself like a mantle, cloaking the revelry around him. Op Oloop could take it no more. Losing control, he banged the table violently, unjustifiably.

All looks converged upon him. The waiter did too.

"Did you want something, sir?"

That was his salvation.

"Yes. Call the maitre d'hôtel at once. How long are we going to be forced to sit here and wait?"

Following his fictional outrage, a hypocritical smattering of smirks and jibes. Beneath the surface of his skin, the truth: fear, and the volatility of his utter emptiness.

Keeping quiet would have given the game away. He could tell. He had to speak, to say something; in a word, to superimpose more masks. And he did, with a notably forced fluency:

"Listen to this! It's quite funny. I tell you, I'm evolving. All of my customary composure has crumbled. Used as I was to timing everything down to the minute for every occasion, I now find myself squandering entire hours on idiocies. When I read Plato's *Timaeus* and learned that time is the image of eternity in motion, I climbed on it like a tread-wheel. I read while I tread, I designed while I dined, I meditated while I fornicated. I wanted to graft myself onto eternity, an auspicious, rosy bough on the trunk of immortality. To be everlastingly in bloom. To be, after my flesh expired, a fruit of light, an everlasting perfume. But, as you can see, I'm headed for failure, full steam ahead. Time does what it pleases, and so do I! Because in order to beat time, one must beat oneself, and I've grown weary of my petty victories against my own person!"

"Well, lovely sentiments indeed, but that doesn't justify your lateness. Waiting for one's own host! Honestly!"

"Well, well, well. Here's the maitre d'hôtel."

And, indeed, handing him the menu, he made the following announcement:

"Monsieur Op Oloop, as per your suggestions I've prepared for you the following international menu:

Malossol Kaviar in eis

Rollmops

Foies gras

Schildkrotensuppe

Spargel

Fresh ox tongue, Creole-style

Empanada de pollo

Welsh rarebit

Goulash à la hongroise

Cassoulet comme à castelnaudary

Osso bucco

Tendron de veau braisé

. . . as you can see, an exquisite gastronomic repertoire."

"Yes, but very heavy indeed."

"A judgment with which I completely concur. However, serving only a morsel of each provides just twelve bites. As for desserts:

Assorted cakes

Kirschkuchen

Camembert

Pumpernickel

Pineapple . . ."

"Op Oloop," interrupted the cantankerous Student. "Tell him we want the menu in Spanish. I don't want any galoshes! He just said something about galoshes!"

"*Goulash à la hongroise*: that would be Hungarian goulash."

"Got it?"

"Well, all right. But all those foreign names piss me off."

"Fear not. I've accounted for everyone's taste. It's all been taken into consideration: caviar, herring, turtle soup, asparagus, chicken pie . . ."

"Jesus, all we need now is a bone for the dogs!"

"Precisely: osso bucco."

Contagious laughter broke out, and Robín Sureda would have joined in too, had the maitre d'hôtel himself not chuckled, and in so doing infuriated the Student:

"Look here, mister. Your job is to serve, not to have a giggle."

Shocked by the reprimand, the maitre d'hôtel backed away. He kept his eyes on Op Oloop and Marietti, as if to steady himself by using their straight lines of thought as an anchor.

The conversation had again turned back to more pleasant topics, and Ivar Kittilä was recounting to his neighbors the triflingly minute portions that he'd seen film stars eat; at the behest of Peñaranda, he widened his audience and spoke up:

"In Hollywood, everyone knows the caloric value of everything. Just as they all aspire unanimously to stardom, they're all equally fanatical about being *très mince* rather than overweight. Truly, there's a veritable obsession with fat. Dieting forces them all to undertake endless calculations and combinations. All portions are measured on a basis of one-hundred-calorie units. For example, one hundred calories equals: a tablespoon of honey, or two mandarin oranges, or four dates, or twenty asparagus tips, or a quarter-inch thick steak measuring five inches long and two and a half inches wide . . ."

"So you must've gone round with tape measures, eyedroppers, and scales. . ."

"It's not a joke. You know, I've noticed that Argentines in general tend to be quite sarcastic, yet they're entirely lacking in humor deep down. They make fun of everything in particular, and yet as a nation are all unanimously dull. It's truly incongruous!"

"Here's mud in your eye!"

"But getting back to the subject, there are innumerable recipes for breakfast, lunch, dinner—it's fascinating. Nothing can exceed the fourteen hundred calories that the organism requires for its daily functioning, and therefore any useless fat stores are burned off. Would you like to hear what Greta Garbo eats? Or Carole Lombard?"

"Nonsense! What I require—and urgently!—is what Op Oloop ordered for *us* to eat, even if it has three hundred thousand calories!" roared the Submarine Captain.

The caviar was served.

The Statistician was relishing his sturgeon eggs. He paused ecstatically. And before sinking his teeth into another morsel, he deigned to offer these words:

"Although you might laugh, Slatter, what Ivar says is quite accurate. I have the figures to support his observation. A full one-fifth of Yanks are obese. Obesity is an anomalous state, you know, one which leads to glandular failure and an irregular metabolism. Insurance companies suffer the effects of the disease more than anyone: the shorter the life spans of the insured, the greater the drain on their income. That's why they promote collective thinness, so that the companies themselves can always be fat. Accordingly they endorse sobriety, exercise. Here's an interesting tidbit for you: Metropolitan Life Insurance, based on a study of two hundred thousand clinical exams, advocates first . . ."

"Please, no statistics! You'd reel off the annual indices on the universal exchange of crab lice if we let you . . ."

"Bravo, bravo!"

"Instead, why don't you tell us: what's behind all this? Why are you spoiling us with twenty dishes tonight?"

Sureda and Peñaranda's ironic volley crushed Op Oloop's doctrinaire exposé. Defenseless in the face of their dying laughter, he was reduced to repeating simply, "It's an old gentleman's trick, 'Feed 'em to defeat 'em.' You'll all find out by the end of the night . . ."

A commanding cough called them to attention: the Maquereau's. He was indicating that he wished to take the floor.

"While I hold that the various theories concerning excessive weight and alimentary rationing are indeed quite seductive, they are also, dear sirs, quite complicated. In Marseille, Barcelona, Shanghai, Paris, and even here, whenever my *enbonpoint* exceeds itself, I take a disciplinary action that I find to be more efficient as well as more enjoyable. I simply frequent the most luxurious *ristoranti*, grills and so forth. I can assure anyone trying to slim down that there is no greater dietetic regimen than that resulting from the exorbitant prices they charge . . ."

The waiters were removing the silverware. For a moment, the table's uproarious geometry was incomplete.

The arrival of the rolled-up herrings produced a jocular commotion made up by the guests' sundry impressions. Ivar, Erik, and Op Oloop laid their pungent claims to the delicacy now awaiting consumption on the tablecloth. The others—with the exception of Slatter, who remained neutral—begged that the turtle soup be allowed to stand in by proxy.

"Let the Head of Sanitation decide."

"Let the Head of Sanitation decide."

"Well, my father was of Scottish origin," Slatter began, "so I have no bone to pick with herring, nor do I have an aversion to turtle. I'm afraid we're at an impasse."

"He must decide! I can't stand that pestilence! Myself, I've always extolled the wisdom of attempting to place one's nose right up to one's anus regardless of the impossibility of making the twain meet, even when bent in half. I fear this dish ruins that exercise by placing the pollution directly *in front of* one's nose. Now: decide!"

"Hurrah, Peñaranda! And I thought you had such wonderful manners!"

"Gentlemen: I see that opinions are as split as they were at that famous bullfight in which some cursed the mother of a useless *torero* and others impugned the father. Split down the middle! However, it's up to me to come to a decision, and decide I shall. Let them bring . . ."

"Herring!"

"Turtle!"

". . . wine. And let each man eat what he pleases."

The immediate applause served to second the plan categorically.

Op Oloop shouted: "Maitre, we need wine, wine! What unforgivable laxity!"

And he blushed like a schoolgirl, perhaps recalling Brillat-Savarin's well known postulate: *"Celui que reçoit ses amis et ne donne aucun soin personnel au repas qu'il leur a préparé, n'est pas digne d'avoir des amis."*

Happily, the maitre rushed in, brandishing two bottles.

"Sir, here we have a 1926 Wiltinger Dohr, and a 1925 Liebfraumilch Riesling."

"Stupendous. Bring as many bottles as required. And don't forget to bring a Chablis. Not everyone likes Mosel and Rhine wines."

"Though I dearly adore the golden liquid of Burgundy, pour me just a wee bit of the milk of the beloved! Rhine wines slide down the throat so smoothly," oozed Gastón voluptuously, already imagining the taste.

"And you, sir?"

"For me, Chablis."

The maitre returned at once. He uncorked the bottle ceremoniously and, on pouring the first stream into Slatter's glass, the fresh, ripe scent of a just-bathed bride set the diners' olfaction atwitter.

Then, approaching the host, he presented the following list:

1920 Chateau Beychevelle, St. Julien

1920 Mercurey, Beaume

Champagne G. H. Mumm, Cordon Rouge

Napoleon Cognac, Pellison Pere Grand Marnier

"Not bad, not bad at all, in fact. However it's not particularly well suited to the dishes being served. Wine should underscore food as accompaniment does song. The selection should set the tone and the mood and the pace: it should be harmonious, as light or as heavy as whatever is being devoured. A dish like osso bucco, for instance, could never go with a Mousseux. That reminds me, we'll need an Italian red. Bring out the most venerable Barolo you have in the cellar. At any rate, with such a motley menu as this—in which a collective complacency seems to have taken precedence—we'll have our bases covered with the smooth Bordeaux and warm Borgogne."

They hung on his words in rapt attention. The Student, still feeling vexed by the maitre, couldn't resist a vengeful intervention:

"You tell him, Op Oloop. Those maitres are all alike: self-important, petulant. But once you strip them of their pomposity, why, they're just a miserable bunch of idiots. I'm sure the lesson you've just taught him will have him shitting in his pants."

"No, sir. I fail to see why," the Maquereau quickly rebuffed, puffing out his chest grandly. "The wines selected are exquisite and relatively well tailored to the meal. Even the most refined gourmet could hardly object, because—if you forgive my saying so, my dear Op Oloop—the error resides in the heterogeneity of the *carte du jour*. We white slavers dine in lavish hotels—just part of the job—as well as pestilent penitentiaries—just part of the law . . . At any rate, that being the case, we're more concerned with wine than with food, since, being pure spirit, matter is subjected to its transcendental hierarchy. In those circumstances, a crystal flute of Heidsieck Monopole is as worthy as a glass of cheap Mendoza pigswill. You see, what we appreciate is not the taste but rather the intention of the wine, not the bouquet that perfumes the palate but the aroma released into our inner worlds."

"Shall we drink to that?"

"Let's drink to that."

"*Salud*! To our illustrious pimp!"

And they each raised a glass.

The toast, jovially thunderous, discomfited Gastón Marietti. He was a man who deplored all things stentorian. And since the very last word of their toast kept ringing in his ears, he proffered a wily, diffident expression and retorted without bothering to stand up:

"Bravo. I appreciate your concerns for my health and accept the title of 'illustrious pimp.' But allow me to pose a question: which is better and more dignified, my state of pimphood, exposed as I am to a thousand risks, or the complacent pimphood of certain public administration officials who procure their posts at the cost of their honor?"

This allusion sank the group into a pensive state that, seen from a distance, each man staring intently down at his plate, could have been mistaken for a gluttonous zeal.

Since the waitstaff had become bustling and attentive, the meal, fortuitously, was nonetheless able to progress with some degree of normality. Erik Joensun invariably emptied his plate and asked for second helpings of everything. His ruddy cheeks, loosely hanging jowls, and shrill idiosyncratic manner contrasted greatly with the haggard countenance and controlled dynamism of his neighbor, Ivar Kittilä.

"You keep grumbling, and yet you eat on, come what may. Reminds me of Lionel Barrymore . . ."

"Of course I'm grumbling! The asparagus is going bad."

"But that's your second helping . . ."

"I'm telling you, it's rotting . . ."

"Don't you think it's probably the cream that's gone bad? After all, culinary arts are all about the creative exploitation of leftovers . . ."

"Poppycock, Peñaranda. I've been dining in hotels since I left Finland, in March of 1919. People criticize hotel kitchens too often. It stems, perhaps, from the envy of those who are forced to suffer the domestic stewpot. Even worse for those with dyspepsia . . . Me, I've never had any trouble at all with my digestive tract. I wholeheartedly defend hotel kitchens against the habitual insults showered upon them. After all, the *gourmandises* who nourished me and the delicacies they've given me were all created in their laboratories. I'm one of Gasterea's peaceful minions, not some common glutton. Look at me. My body is not that of a Benedictine or a Trappist monk attempting to sidetrack his quotidian abstinence with a few measly vegetables and a quarter liter of wine or cider. My body makes demands and I satisfy them. Which is to say, hotels have been my mother and my school: mother, because they taught me the proper way to venerate health; school, because they initiated me into that wonderful science that elevates the stomach to the level of the brain: gastrosophy. And that is why, wherever I go, my gratitude can always be seen—in the form of a generous wine stain—on the hotel tablecloth."

"Drown them in Mosel, you who drowned so many in the underwater wars . . . But be careful, now: we're all radicals here," warned Sureda.

"Radicals? I know Op Oloop was in the Red Guard and took part in the taking of Helsingfors. But Ivar, Gastón, Slatter . . ."

"Yes. We are all radicals . . . in our asparagus-eating methodology . . ."

"Very cute. But the as-pa-ra-gus has gone bad."

The roar of laughter that flew up brought him crashing down like a clay pigeon. Teeth on edge, he attempted to mutter a muffled invective through his flaccid lips.

Cordial conviviality soon reigned once more and a toast was made to the Eternal Student, whose joke even the Captain himself now feted.

But Op Oloop was no longer the same man. His was staring off into the hazy distance. While the guests cooed over the succulence of each new dish, he choked back nostalgia as though swallowing bitter pills. He sighed with each new longing that developed. It was all Erik's fault. He'd called to mind the greatest episode of his now-remote youth. How, then, could he dodge the multitude of memories, both woeful and wonderful? At one point, that whole multitude—inundated by alcohol—attempted to escape via his mouth, but finding the way blocked, instead rushed up to form tears in his eyes.

He had to make a tremendous effort to pull himself together. He knew that, as Jean Rostand said, true moral courage resides in altering your own image in front of others, in order to save it for yourself. And so, curbing the secret sequence of his intimate tributes to the past, he forced himself simply to eat, in stony silence.

Like a charm, Rostand's name took his train of thought down other tracks. He reflected that it was quite natural for the son of a poet to have become a sage. It was not reversion but continuity. Why, he himself, as an adolescent, had delighted in writing pastoral tales after having read his favorite Finnish authors, Pietari Päivärinta and Juhani Aho, and had even dared to pen a play after having seen the works of J. H. Erkko. Now, as an adult, he thought literature seemed risible: naïve child's play compared to the ferocity of cosmic laws, a game of tiddlywinks in the face of the terror of human destiny. Science was the only way, science was the only way . . . And so he submerged himself in numbers, abstract capsules containing the essence of all knowledge and wisdom.

In pondering all this, he stopped concentrating on keeping quiet, and this mental laxity allowed enunciation to make a sudden break for it. Without realizing it, just when his guests were beginning to worry about his self-absorption, he lost control and blurted out, "These are difficult times, the times we live in: no romanticism, no bohemia! Times when we must all make propositions of our personal equations, elucidate and illuminate any unknowns we carry within us. When that happens, we'll all be better off. When that happens, we'll see the whole picture, make it a little bit clearer with each problem we solve, each error we rectify . . ."

"Magnificent. But what on earth are you going on about?"

Op Oloop, jolted, shook his head as if he'd only just awoken. His ears were burning. Proffering them a rueful smile, he stammered, "Nothing, nothing. Just talking nonsense . . ."

"Isn't it curious that at your age you still talk nonsense? I remember at the Uleaborg Academy you went gaga for the literature teacher's daughter and did exactly the same . . ."

"Well, 1=1. One is always one, mathematically and psychologically."

"Yes, but you! You're inundated, submerged, underwater, like an island. You're an island of meditations. And that's dangerous! When I was in the Biscay Bay . . ."

"You mean the Bay of Biscay . . ."

". . . I never thought about islands. Can you imagine the responsibility I had as Captain? No time to deliberate. No islands."

"The truth is, Op Oloop," the Maquereau chimed in, "your friends are right. I was watching you. How easily you plunged into the depths of your own private pond! Interior monologue is always better than Voltairian dialogue, I grant you that. The former signifies that one's personality is fully formed while the latter indicates that one is seeking some external validation. Cultured men, truly educated men, the monstrously urbane men of the future will suffer from intellectual aphasia brought on by their refusal to speak. You . . ."

"Oh, no!"

"Yes."

"No, no."

"Yes."

"Well, I must be honest with you. When Erik brought up the taking of Helsingfors, it brought to mind certain episodes in which I played a part. Even then, I was a man inclined to ruminate on the past, and I'm still not free of that little cul-de-sac. From the parapet of my mechanized life, I like to gaze down into the well of my adolescence. To stare into the water. To see the fish I held under the water, like so many bright ideas . . . To see the celestial discuses that I, romantic decathlete, once hurled into the ideal blue."

"You're unbearably trite," Peñaranda spat. "I'm often in the blue and have never come across any discus or any ideal. There's something the matter with you—you're in a shell. First you're withdrawn, now you're twee. Even if it's just to satisfy my incredulity, I insist that you explain yourself."

The Commissioner of Air Traffic Control was curt. Because he was so categorical, his sentences exploded under the intense mental concentration that formed them, almost shredding his words.

The host was perplexed. He decided to practice the axiom: Never explain, never complain. Pondering, he took a glass of wine. He caressed it with his eyes and his fingers. He breathed in the bouquet unhurriedly, taking several sips. And then he spoke.

"Fine. Since you insist, I shall expand upon my state of mind. But the truth remains: the key to real exasperation resides in this need to have everything explained . . . Yes, gentlemen, I've been lost in my own thoughts, engrossed in a world all my own. What's so twee about that? Nothing. Aside from the fleeting discourtesy of having briefly taken leave of you, it's scarcely even a faux pas. I detest mirrors because they bear witness to my existence. But how can one steer clear of the mirrors inside? The moment our attention is directed inward, our incorruptible narcissism leads us to a hall of metaphysical mirrors. Curious mirrors, to be sure, which don't reflect the present but the images of past selves, or the fantasy of future selves. The present is invisible. You simply sense it by its stench . . ."

"Look out! You might fall off a cliff . . ."

". . . the way Merovingians perceived the devil's presence by the stink of sulfur. I'm not insulting anyone, Robín. I'm simply stating my personal views for the record. Because what we all do hic et nunc is entirely inconsequential in terms of the historical reality of a banquet among friends—it matters only as the preterit of a wish I had nurtured for my immediate future. Time is only the present. We're all in motion. And we move in order to exhibit our past: photographs already developed—and our future: photos to be developed . . ."

"OK! All right! So it's all exhibition. Fine. I'm with you up to that point. But from another perspective I could just as easily hold to quite the contrary view: that man is immobile, always frozen in a pose, while the world passes him by. Like a mime at a fair who pretends to saunter along, never taking a step, while behind him a backdrop with painted scenery rolls past."

"Wrong, Ivar. I know from experience that both cinema and philosophy have their tricks, their artifices, and then their other, more terrible ruses. But don't allow yourself to be misled. That's a hedonistic perspective: one that gets fat by exploiting our illusions—illusions are the real chattel on the auction block these days—in the most appalling of illicit traffics."

"Hear, hear! Magnificent, Op Oloop! I agree entirely: film producers are humanity's worst sort of maquereaux."

"Precisely."

"What do you mean, 'precisely'?"

"Let's not argue. Hartmann said that the world is invincible and life, unbearable. We must challenge that blasphemy—we must buff and polish life until we're able to remove all its calluses. Let's not argue. I've traveled a great deal and suffered a great deal, too. Everywhere I went, I saw a world in search of pleasure . . . and the market on that pleasure monopolized by a select few. And everywhere I went, I rebelled."

"Rebelled? You?"

"Yes. Are you not aware, my friend, that composure is the most dignified, most effective form of rebellion? Peñaranda, you're a hothead. And as such, you ignore the fact that such heat is a verbal dust cloud that always vanishes after the first spray of bullets. I should have liked to see you beside me in the cantons of the Red Guard in January 1919. The cries of political passion were more fervent than the fighting itself. And yet, in our hearts there was a determined courage, a courage that made us set our jaws and soon forced us further and further into the fray—to fight oppression. Often I've pondered the empiricism of history, the algebraic determination of destiny. We're numbers, and events are calculations. The taking of Helsingfors and the subsequent collapse of privilege made us believe in the axiom of our justice. The Soldiers' and Workers' Council was an idiotic delusion. The Red Terror, a gruesome fallacy. Because negative numbers can change position and become positivized. Because events equate and cancel each other out, just as in arithmetic proportion, maximums and minimums are canceled out by averages. Extremism and mesocracy; extremity and mediocrity. Indeed: Germany, which according to the Treaty of Brest-Litovsk had ceded its interests in Finland, came to the aid of the White Guard. And the success of the Bolsheviks was drowned in the rivers of blood unleashed by von der Goltz and the intractable hangmen of the White Terror."

"Von der Goltz? The one who was here for the Centenary?"

"The very same. The most pigheaded generals are the ones who honor their homelands most fervently. They're sent to parade around in their laurel-covered nooses and display their dripping fangs. By May, the revolution had been crushed. I fled, carrying my youth on my back like a satchel full of bitterness. At the time I was just twenty-five years old . . . twenty-five years old . . ."

He repeated the last phrase, echoing himself as though his words had reverberated in the valley his eyes might have been peering into. And then he fell silent.

His hands—psychic hands—came to his aid, however. They resembled the hands of a mother, silently soothing the memory from his feverish forehead and smoothing the static of ideas from his hair.

The waiters, unruffled, carried on serving the multiple courses that remained of the meal.

The glasses were stained purple with Mercurey.

And a withered, brooding silence descended.

There was a desperate need for someone to break it. Cipriano Slatter assumed command of this mission. He was sensitive and sensitized. He leaned forward his anthropometrically perfect face and blurted, "I share your views, Op Oloop. When sacrifice is made in vain, it's tragic, terrible. What's the use of fighting? What's the point of risking everything? Absurd. In politics, enemies see generosity as an offense, while friends see offense as a virtue. Politics are a pestilence."

"Hear, hear! A pestilence!" concurred Peñaranda. "Politicians have always pestered us with their lily-white principles and tried our patience with their austerity. So what? Deep down, they're all the same. After securing their places in history, secluded in their ivory towers with all their perks, not doing a bit of real work, they proceed with their declamations . . ."

"Hold on there. Tell me, are you not public employees?" the Student interpolated.

"Yes."

"Yes."

"Well then?"

"Well then, what? Do you think salaries are manna? We owe no one any gratitude!"

"And even if we did, we're perfectly within our rights to fail to express it! I was late to learn that decency is a heavy cross to bear. My culture charged me with being a 'bird-man,' meant to rise to the skies in the eyes of the public—but decency held me down at the level of necessity. I was riddled with debts and forced to become a 'mouth-man,' sponging off public funds."

"So you don't fly, then?" the Maquereau asked sardonically.

"Correct, sir: I do not fly," the Commissioner of Air Traffic Control replied with absolute solemnity.

The Statistician watched his guests in bemusement.

The impassioned silence that followed this latest interruption cheered rather than worried him. Skepticism was a drug for him. Life's vicissitudes had taught him never to be caught without it. A most useful drug, it magically invigorated his heart, transforming opprobrium into piety and ignominy into tolerance.

Gastón Marietti perceptively picked up on this complacency.

"It's a shame we interrupted you, Op Oloop. Please, carry on with your story."

"I'd love to. On one condition. Allow me to toast to the man I once was, from the belvedere of the man I now am."

"Certainly. Unanimously."

"Yes. Fate made me a sentinel. I see the sad, serious boy who left the comforts of home of his own free will . . . I see the adventurous teen who wandered the length and breadth of Finland, from Ladoga to the Glacial Arctic, sharing in the misery of his fellow man who suffered through the frost, the sheets of ice, and the blanket of snow . . . I see the dreamy young Marxist who, intoxicated by poetry on glassy lakes and in birch and larch forests, fought for Love, Truth, and Justice . . . And I can't help but be overcome and aggrieved by the great landscape of humanity, so full of candor, so full of passion, so full of purity! And so I toast: my tears to the Op Oloop who once was, and my wine to the Op Oloop who will never again be . . ."

Their skills honed by the evening's near-constant libations, they raised their glasses fluently and drank.

The sibylline tone of Op Oloop's last words rang in the ears of several guests.

"To the Op Oloop that will never again be . . ."

Ivar and Erik exchanged glances, frowning.

The Student remarked to Slatter on their host's temperamental dithering: loquaciousness, absence, smugness, tears . . .

Gastón Marietti plunged right in to deep reflection:

"That will never again be! Is our poor, dear, unfortunate Op Oloop a *uomo finito*, perchance? I think not. His education, the extraordinary vitality of his culture, should forcibly impede this will of his to renounce his humanism, the superior art of becoming as much a man as he is able. His recent eloquence—industrious in its content, syrupy in its effusion—nevertheless displayed a definitive fatigue that seemed to prompt him to wallow in his past. What aberration is this? It is true that certain ambivalences coexist in the spirit, elements that tug one's personality in different directions simultaneously, attempting to lead it down different paths. I myself have experienced the phenomenon. For instance: it's paradoxical that I should thrive and prosper on the vileness of current morality, given that I'm a futurist."

A rain of flowers and laughter, fronted by Op Oloop, brought the Maquereau back to the banquet's hue and cry.

"Was it really you who criticized my abstractions and my interior monologues? You ought to see yourself when you dive in! You must not be accustomed to the practice. You gesticulate as though you were drowning."

Gastón blushed.

"Forgive me. It was on your account, actually. Your toast to 'the Op Oloop who will never again be' perturbed me."

"Nietzsche said that man is an accident in a world of accidents."

"Fine. But your implicit renunciation of the future, your intention to bedeck the soul in the outmoded suits of the past . . . And speaking of the past: my hatred of it is so absolute that I downright refuse to have children, out of knowing that their age would necessarily reveal my own."

"I, on the other hand, could not bear and cannot bear being childless. For the same reason: so that they can reveal my age. The illusion of youth is nothing more than an illusion, after all."

Having made this proclamation, Op Oloop's thinking suddenly hit an air pocket. He sighed. And without the slightest trace of shame, he hid his eyes with one hand.

This time, Peñaranda gave his neighbors a "technical" explanation of Op Oloop's curious agitation. While it was true that he himself had only flown *beside* the pilot and never *as* the pilot, he was well aware of the theory of aviation and the laws and international conventions legislating air traffic:

"When one's spirit takes to the skies—transcendentally, so to speak—climbing towards the altitudes of clear conscience, a kind of anguish often rarifies the air. That's when the subjective motors stall and illusion rushes in. The finest and bravest pilots can often glide back safely into their own carnal hangars. But others, colliding with nostalgia in midair, experience a sense of immobility: the wreckage of their souls drifts aimlessly through the skies, which is what happens to fallen angels in their descent . . ."

Erik thought he'd figured it all out and, in his ever brutal, opportunistic manner, took over from his compatriot.

"Go on, go on, Op Oloop. The entire table is hanging on your every word. You must have set this up, timed it perfectly. So go ahead and tell us what you're about to tell us. Say it."

Op Oloop nodded. He was far away indeed. His expression was austere, and he appeared to be experiencing an incommunicable desire to weep. The opacity of his spiritual aura and the dust of the carnal deserts he'd just crossed were visible on him. He spoke in a lugubrious tone.

"I know people who speak aloud in public to convince themselves of their own existence simply because they can be heard. I distrust that articulacy. I don't enjoy speaking. My voice is always an intruder in the theater where I perform, and where I listen—playwright and spectator simultaneously—to the secret drama of my life. So forgive me, and let's change the subject, please."

"No, Op Oloop. Say something. Your invitation to this banquet, which displayed the groveling gentility of a petty bureaucrat, was quite remarkable:

> *Honorable Ivar: I would be most grateful if you would lend my spirit your services by joining me at the cloth I shall lay tonight, at 9:30 P.M., at the Plaza Grill.*

You must admit, that's not the style of an ordinary man. You're hiding something. Tell me what it is—what's the murmur, the sound, the din that your spirit requires, and I'll provide it. I'll do my part. But don't give me that opaque, Clive Brooks face . . ."

Op Oloop was cornered. The Student and the Maquereau, each with matching invitations in hand, repeatedly reread the term: Honorable. And they too joined the mob confronting him.

"Gentlemen, your expectations wound me. So you want me to tell you about it? My life, after I fled Finland, was stable, constant, flat, and rectilinear. And it has remained so. You, Ivar, first met me at the Uleaborg Academy. I couldn't resist Minna's love or her father's— the literature teacher—literature lessons. And I traveled. I traveled all over Suomen-Maa, from Arkangel to the Gulf of Bothnia, everywhere between sixty to seventy degrees latitude. Lakes, rocks, marshes. Freezing cold, aching hunger, bad luck. Until I finally landed on my rear in the Aabo Timber Emporium Inspection Office. That's when I first came into contact with statistics. The genuine truth of numbers and the relative truth of mathematical probability pervaded everything: I was overcome. For years I knew the exact tonnage of the world consumption of paper pulp, plywood, tar. Those who have not been touched by this divine hand ignore the supreme hierarchy of statistics, the science that links pure mathematics with the study of the real world. The *esprit de géometrie* with *the esprit de finesse*. Using censuses, diagrams, and rows and columns of figures, the static history of humanity can be described and synthesized. Plywood was my point of departure. By studying the export statistics on plywood, ply-wood . . . Hoerée! . . . Franziska! FRANZISKA! FRAN-ZIS-KA!"

A truly redoubtable performance!

Sudden and stentorian, Op Oloop's new exaltation stupefied his guests. Some stood. Recovering immediately, however, he motioned for them to take their places once more.

"Forgive that little outburst. I can't fathom what Bacchic significance or impulse lay behind it."

He was lying.

And with a syrupy voice, a gentle, weary sweetness, he cried, again, "Hoerée! Franziska! FRANZISKA! FRAN-ZIS-KAAA! . . . Evohé! Io, ío, eleleleu! . . ."

General stupefaction escalated into consternation. No one understood a thing. Op Oloop emitted this bacchante screech of devotion and simultaneously tapped his lips in syncopation. Given the gravity of the situation, even Gastón Marietti stood up. Everyone noted how the host's exasperation at the start of his story had turned to deferential pride during its continuation. But this illogical slip? What lay behind it?

"Perhaps it was the Mercurey . . ."

"Or mixing different wines."

"No. He's scarcely drunk anything at all," Erik affirmed, whispering into Slatter's ear.

Then, as if nothing had happened, their host picked up the thread once more:

"By studying the export statistics of plywood, I was able to make endless assertions about the nature and idiosyncrasies of the country in question, much like the condom dealer who estimated the birthrate of his fatherland based on his sales . . ."

He gave a suspicious little laugh. The joke, however, did induce each guest to sit back down. And then the banqueters gobbled down their latest dish with relish.

The residue of Op Oloop's outburst plagued him, however. As did the scrutiny of those seated around him.

Garrulous, poorly disguising his fretful desire to set them at ease, he continued.

"After I moved to Helsingfors, the scientific autonomy and experimental discipline demanded by statistics won me over. And that's where my love of method stems from. All phenomena have mechanical explanations that demand certain prerequisites for their analysis: first, a critique of their origin; second, interpretation; third, sincerity; and fourth, exactitude. Just as all investigation requires rational judgment in order to deduce, first, a computation of the probable forces of historical materialism; second, an awareness of what was wrong with the old notion of an infinite future; and third, a functional equation that synchronizes the past within the principles of occult law. Pure philosophy, my friends! Helmholtz and Hertz introduced it to the world, whispering like gamblers, 'The numbers! The numbers! It's all in the numbers!' Later on, as an employee of the Demographic Institute, my analyses were used to interpret the capital's archives on love and death. By speculating philosophically on the figures, one can determine the crisis of modern morality that will be upon us in the near future judging by the rates of divorce, crimes of passion, and the production of bastard children. My thesis on the subject—that a societal organization suitable to the betterment of the individual biotype is prone to eugenic manifestation—was deemed praiseworthy by the London Statistical Society, and several conferences subsequently accepted papers based on my work.

Additionally, the Annuaire Statistique de la Societé des Nations, 1932–33, avows the technical superiority of the 'Op Oloop Method' for collating data on phenomena common to different countries. Because, gentlemen, method is all. Bacon himself said so. '*Claudus in via antecedit cursorem extra viam*,' which means, essentially, that a mediocre intelligence guided by good method will make more scientific progress than a keen mind working without a plan. In that sense, I've been methodical and will be methodical until the day I die. Death, as a phenomenon, is a proposition under the hormono-nervous aegis by recognized physio-chemical axioms. Fine. When I was exiled from my country, when the reactionary dictatorship of Senator Svinhufvud began, I settled in France. My family moved heaven and earth trying to persuade me to return. They even obtained a special pardon from the first Finnish President, Professor Kaarlo Juho Stahlberg, which would have restored me to my prior post. Ha, ha! Brilliant invention, the family—I seethed, like *Poil de Carotte*. I accept pardons from no one, and in particular not from anyone dangling the promise of a rosy future before me in the attempt to make me forget the red blood of twenty thousand comrades murdered during the White Terror. So I stayed on in France, a magnificent, unbearable country. I stayed on and suffered untold horrors, because a Nordic man always suffers from the intensity of the depths of love, order, and freedom in Latin climes."

"That makes no sense to me," Marietti interrupted.

"That's because I've explained it poorly. Love and freedom have specific coefficients that are poles apart in people who reside by the Baltic. Passion there has been drilled. Here, love is wild and untamed: liberty is brusque. Order, too, is wholly different. There, at home, it resides in the spontaneous rejection of individual will, in paying homage to collective well-being. You go there and everything is silky smooth and straightforward: self-sacrifice and honor. Here, people are prickly and try to procure their own well-being. So society's surface is rough and bumpy. I confess, at first I was something of a clod, stumbling and lurching about as though I were lame . . ."

"Speaking of lame . . . In that translation of '*Claudus in via . . .*'"

". . . *antecedit cursorem extra viam . . .*"

". . . you lamely overlooked the lame . . ."

"True. I gave a periphrastic translation. A more literal one would be, 'The lame man who follows the good road outstrips the runner who departs from it.'"

"I agree. I adore all three Claudes . . ."

"Tell me, are you a maquereau or a philosopher?" exhorted the Student, sparking uproarious laughter.

"Both. A maquereau when I stoop down to speak to you, and a philosopher when I ascend for a tête-à-tête with Op Oloop."

"Here's mud in your eye!"

"As I was saying, I adore France's three great clods: Claude Bernard, Claude Monet, and Claude Debussy. You, Op Oloop, as someone who measures men Pythagorically, must know what they represent. *Basta*. Forgive me for having interrupted you."

"Not at all. I, too, adore them. Though not as much as the other cripples, those belonging to the second sex, whose muscular defect—which is of course their sex itself—is also a veritable fount of strange voluptuousness . . . Montaigne, a connoisseur of both wine and women, is, so far as I know, the only one to have beat me to proclaiming the pleasures of this experience. But let's not 'limp' along any longer. Let's get back to the story. In Paris, I lived for four years in an attic in Montparnasse, accompanied by a Yank who spent the entire four years drunk, celebrating the armistice. He was insatiable. In 1922, his father, a Kentucky tobacco grower, came to fetch him, but, having honed his binging down to a flawless system that involved trekking from La Cigogne to La Coupole and from Vicking's to La Rotonde, he opposed the idea of returning to the United States. Soon the monthly checks from papa stopped arriving. In an attempt to reeducate him, the American's father had used his sway with some senator to secure him a job as a clerk at the American Battle Monument Commission. He had no choice but to concede. But he made a pact with me: we'd split his salary fifty-fifty, and I'd do his job while he continued to celebrate the armistice. Since there was no supervision, the scheme worked for a while. By the time the truth was discovered, the quality of my work had been acknowledged and was undeniable. Indeed, I was brevetted, put in charge of the archives at the American Graves Registration Service. The organization not only registered American soldiers killed in France, but is also in charge of the upkeep of war monuments and cemeteries, and there my arithmetic vocation found its expression in a serious period of research into method. I became a macabre strategist. An entire recumbent army—eighty thousand expeditionary soldiers— obeyed my every order. And I was the director of death, in the same places where Allied command had earlier ordered a massacre . . ."

He suddenly slumped into silence.

The guests, who'd been rather skeptical of Op Oloop's verbosity when he first resumed the telling of his tale, had by this time become beguiled by his bleak account. His discourse was no longer seen as a sophism required by circumstances to cover up the disgrace of his having burst into incoherent gibberish. Now they'd been listening closely, riveted, trying to stifle the sounds of their silverware. And with the exception of the Maquereau, everyone became upset at his latest upset when Op Oloop's voice trailed off and his gaze grew distant.

"A little Mercurey?" Gastón inquired, brandishing the bottle.

No reply.

When a man plunges headlong down into his own vertical scarp, the vertigo brought on by emotions and memories exceeds the impact of the fall itself. Words wane and waste away, or stream out nonsensically, insanely.

After a short time, Op Oloop began to prattle, "Wine: blood— blood: wine. No. NO! Sun: Mosel, Champagne . . ."

Were the obscurity and wisdom of this hieratic utterance legitimate?

No one knew, nor would they ever find out. Some enigmatic psychological processes are unknown even to the subject himself. Sometimes the spirit's manifestations are authentic postures, coinciding with emphatic states of depression or exaltation that could never be faked. Op Oloop's hieratic posture was real, *malgré lui*. But in its mystery lay its perspicacity—for mystery is, quite simply, a cunningly concealed entelechy, a potentiality become a reality.

At one point he almost seemed prepared to unburden himself. All eyes became all ears. Each man hung on the morbid magnetism of Op Oloop's words. And then he spoke quietly, breathily, with the strange inflections of an underwater bell:

"Wine: blood—blood: wine! I've seen farmers who, on raising a glass of local red, made the sign of the cross and wept, believing themselves to be drinking the blood of their children. I've seen landscapes riddled with mortar craters, where cadavers were twisted and contorted like vines. I've seen blond heads clustered like grapes, their juices watering the greedy ground before being bottled and sold as the fizz in champagne. I've seen deciduous vines rise up on limpid mornings like ghosts by the banks of the Mosel, out of burning orchards. And everywhere, wearing crowns of tendrils and barbed wire, the green flesh of youth fermenting with blight, ignominy, shadow. So wine makes me drunk on sorrow, and then oblivion. And knowing that human essence is transmuted therein, each new sip scorns my sorrow and embalms my oblivion."

Lengthy, taciturn pause.

He downed his glass in four sips.

The others did the same.

No liturgy had ever been more unctuous. They sat in sacred silence, in the "euphemy" that the prytaneis once demanded at the Pnyx.

And in the same hushed, breathy tones, and with the same bizarre, underwater bell inflections, Op Oloop continued:

"Wine: blood—blood: wine! . . . In the cemeteries of Aisne-Marne, Oise-Aisne, Meuse-Argonne, of Somme, Suresnes, Saint-Mihiel, and Flanders, I have bottled death's harvest in the ground. More than thirty thousand identified bodies lie in flowering fields: flesh that flowered in the torment of shrapnel and grapeshot. For nearly two years I was a macabre strategist. How meekly their docile remains submitted to my will! So sublime, the acquiescence I always attained from bones and rags! It was as if they did the work for me. The decomposed remains of a forearm, the shredded front of a carmagnole, the rust-colored blood on the butt of a gun, these all made transparent the mysteries of death—identifying the corpse, narrowing down the options to one. We lined death up in stock-still squadrons in order to defeat it, to conquer the alleged barbarity and notorious massacres of the war. Everlasting evil, perverse discipline, and armed injustice surrendered to the mystic fervor of my organization. Every record in the American Graves Registration Service was a victory over man's despicable amnesia. Every record documented a life lost in its pledge to abolish war. But what good is a pledge? The beast of the Apocalypse grazes anew among the fourteen thousand two hundred crosses at Romagne-Sous Montfaucon, amongst the six thousand twelve of the Ourq Cemetery, amongst the four thousand one hundred fifty-two of Thiacourt . . . Because the glory that grows in the shadows of those "heroes" is its fodder of choice. Encouraging a life of danger: that's sacrilege! Honoring the heroic passion of Bayard and not the prudence of Fabius Cunctatur: that's sacrilege! . . . In doing so, you ignore the majesty of war cemeteries. Row after row of crosses as far as the eye can see. The repeated geometry of suffering written across the blackboard of the night. Lily-covered putrefaction stretching all the way to the horizon . . . You ignore the pathetic quintessence of millions of beings lying beneath perpendicular beams of marble or cement. The lechery of Mars, traversing the centuries, satisfying his cesarean frenzy . . . The immeasurable mercy begged for by those open arms, only to have crows defecate on them derisively . . . Because that's what happens! I've seen Pershing and Foch inspect my recumbent troops, guiding the Gold Star Mothers along. What a revolting recollection! No tenderness, no respect: just pride. The ranking officers of the hecatomb. They seemed to demand that their own victims salute them posthumously. And when the tattered crosses defied their orders, they turned their grudges into praise for the beauty of burial mounds and the magnificence of war memorials . . . Nonsense! The fools who wage war always try to cover their tracks with that kind of talk. And what's more loathsome still is that mothers defend them, bought off with a few cheap medals and honors! For them to march alongside the generals like sheep, forgetting that what's left of their sons has decomposed into dust and putrefaction. For them to yearn—oh, their menopausal nationalism!—to be young again, so as to give birth to even more cannon fodder! Mothers are poor wretches. They never should have given birth to begin with. When the vaginas of the world institute a genesic lockdown, only then will humanity change the course of its deadly regime. That pure love should spawn hatred is so unjust! That the perverse seed of Nebuchadnezzar and Alexander can continue to be propagated in an age when even oatmeal requires the proper pedigree is so unjust! Throngs exultant in their patriotism. Pastures garlanded in green. Unworthy camouflage! Arms manufacturers—Maxim, Vickers, Armstrong—tend to their commercial interests. They were the first to hide any trace of their crimes from the terrain and from the pulp of their consciences. And the order came to plow, plow, plow . . . Nature perjures itself, wombs perjure themselves, brains perjure themselves. All the lies: peace, employment, harmony will all be prisoners of their licentious desire to annihilate. I heard it all. Me! It was in Chateau-Thierry, on the famous Hill 204, the outstanding ossuary of thirty thousand boys from the U.S. Armed Forces. There, from the pavilion commemorating the recent holocaust, they, the directors of the consortia—Bethlehem Steel Company and Creusot Iron—banged out some cock-and-bull story about loving one's country and the grandeur of sacrifice. Meanwhile, their managers were surreptitiously selling arms to the enemy and signing treaties that granted them exclusive rights of manufacture . . . Business first; everything else is secondary . . . And thus they carry on with their double-crossing: beautifying wastelands and decorating soldiers' chests . . . Camouflage! La Fontaine, whose soul once wandered that much-loved place, taught us the moral of that story. And my recumbent army, their mouths set ironically, held onto this moral for dear life while they were in the trenches . . . Trenches! *Tierra de nadie*! Haunted caves. No-man's-land. Horror, hunger, wounds. No-man's-land. A living hell. Lice, scurvy, asphyxia. I know the cavernous tragedy of sap and rubble. Of petrified fear and instant insanity. I addressed you—you answered me. You knew I was a servant of sadness. You knew I detested the senseless show of honor. You knew I wandered alone through the shadows of your grounds, searching, searching, always searching. And you answered me. 'Here they are! Raise them up! Deposit them in the memory of mankind! Weigh them on the world's scale!' . . . I raised them up. And now they've been laid to rest. But not how I would have liked. Not back in their mothers' vulvas, not in the world's face, but in a false grave, flanked by two tiny percale flags . . . It's not my fault. My mirror shattered in horror. Such lifeless images! Specters, not people! And yet, I have their records here. All neat and tidy, all in order. But how to resuscitate their decomposed nerves, their spent souls? It's not my fault. Look at me! I'm the same macabre strategist. The same servant of sadness. The same Statistician who found all the coefficients of human solidarity in the number of crosses on the hill, in the methodical order of death. Look at me, no-man's-land: I am Op Oloop!"

The first bottle of champagne was just being uncorked. Its pop provided a sonorous finale to the saga.

The host sat stiffly, with altered expression. Slight subcutaneous shudders shook the skin of his egg-shaped, lusterless face and fiery eyes: the scene he'd been reliving had not ceased for him.

A sudden and unforeseen swinging of his head alarmed all present. He seemed to be trying to scare off a flock of vampires biting into in his brain.

But swiftly he returned to his determined rigidity.

Subsequently he relaxed his face muscles. He beatified himself. And, raising his head, he lowered his eyes, as though he were inhaling light.

He sat there.

It's hard to strike a balance in the tension between differing temperaments. Op Oloop's story, while having captivated everyone's attention marvelously, also produced a singular emotional effect in each man. In particular, the Statistician's demagogic cries and lugubrious tones sparked off Erik's Red repulsion and Gastón's sheer skepticism. Given the morbid mood of the situation, what would have been most wise was to show some respect, some simple respect. But after assessing the circumstances, not everyone was subtle enough to summon such respect up. So, while the Maquereau was quite careful in his reserve, the old Submarine Captain let his caustic diatribe flow like an overturned jar of fetid, fatty fluids . . .

"I'd have liked to remain silent. But my distant homeland won't stand for it. I shall speak. Hard as I try, I can't find the foundation for your ingratitude. Finland gave you life and you rebuke her. Finland brought you out of darkness and you defame her. Why? The right response, after you fled, would have been to forgive and forget. She forgot first. And when she called you back, you just whined at her. That's not right. I don't discount the sincerity of your Bolshevism. I don't give a damn about that. I do applaud, however, the failure of you and all your comrades, in your rash attempt to Russify my country in 1919. What the hell were you playing at? The Reds' atrocities were the most despicable that the Finnish public ever endured! You know that. My family in Yrjölä and your wealthy aunt and uncle in Riihimaki are proof enough. So I can't allow you to yell about your so-called heroism. Absolutely not! I signed up immediately with von der Goltz and his army. And I thank my lucky stars that I never came up against you head to head. I was indignant, infuriated, in those days. I'd just offered my services to a nation that had been backed into a corner by the Allied scum . . ."

"Just a minute!" Gastón Marietti demanded, albeit without losing his composure. "When you allude to the Allied Forces in that manner, don't include France. I won't stand for it!"

"Oh, shut up with your nonsense! You of all people! If you'd been a valiant, saintly, good French soldier in the war, maybe I could stand for it. But you! You were a coward . . ."

". . . a defeatist and a traitor, yes. But leave France out of it!"

"Yes, a defeatist on Miguel Almereyda and Bolo Baja's side, taking refuge in Barcelona, and a traitor paid by the Spanish consortium that supplied intelligence and fuel to German submarines. Why, I myself received your communications!"

"Precisely."

"So what's this bullshit about France? If you love your country, don't offend her!"

"You're wrong. I've always loved my country in my own way. The thing is, my love is so painstakingly pure that it's sadistic. It doesn't side with France's chauvinism and bloated sense of self-worth. All of my cowardice, all my defeatism, my treachery—which on the surface seem negative—are, deep down, positive. They aim to cure France. To cure her of her civic defects and ethical traumas. In fact, these motives explain my behavior even now. In the same way French morality grumbles at the fact that white slavery is a national industry, I take fierce pleasure in it. When an epidemic really begins to spread, one finally takes measures. By publicizing a disease, perhaps one day it will be eradicated. Then you'll appreciate everything we've done, our labors, which are as vital to society as bismuth to radioscopy. And that's why I'll never allow France to be insulted in my presence. My mother may be a whore—that's her right, or her fate. But I'll never let anyone say so to my face. That is all."

Uncertainty.

The air grew heavy with ill will.

With the exception of Op Oloop, who was now nearly ecstatic, the guests all looked at each other as if attempting to determine something in particular. Were they meant to take this episode seriously, or not? The Maquereau's paradoxical remonstrance had disarmed Erik. Big as he was, his smooth cheeks burned in shame and rage. He struggled to keep his peace but was, again, unable. Finally, turning an even brighter shade of crimson, he spat out his response:

"You make no sense. Since when have traitors loved their countries? Since when have thugs been concerned with social status? They're the ones who sink it! They sully it! I don't understand you. Or you, Op Oloop, rebelling against the old Finnish ways, against the land that made you who you are. Have you no feelings? What did you think you were doing, trying to Sovietize us? Eradicating the old Scandinavian race? Tarnishing the blue cross of our flag? Silencing the 'Suomen Laulu,' Runeberg's heroic, melancholy hymn? I can't fathom such contradictions: being romantic yet cruel . . . educated yet idiotic. Why curse the sacrifice of war if you took part in the Reds' ignominies? Why weep over Yankees' whitewashed tombs if you left your own comrades unburied?"

Op Oloop, his face held high and his eyelids closed, kept on inhaling light—allowing the Maquereau's remonstration to continue to reverberate.

"Come on! Answer me!" the Captain reproached them furiously. "You, spouting off about the other side's crimes without philosophizing at all about the crimes your own side committed. You, seeing in every cross the sign of a man crying out to God and not in every man a cross covered in rags . . . You, who knows that to win at war one must take pleasure in killing, and yet ridiculing duty with your eloquence. And *you* . . ."

"Me? Leave me out of it! It seems you can't hold your wine."

That unsolicited remark felled the Captain from his oratory pedestal. As inconceivable as it was, it left him dumbfounded. (One often tends to have a bigger reaction to a simple truth than to an outright falsehood.) Grumbling, he inspected Marietti—who was straightening his tie—and added a large dose of loathing to the as-yet undisclosed ingredients of his spleen . . .

This time the uncertainty was short-lived. Slatter and Sureda, almost in unison, demanded they all change the subject. No one paid them any heed. On the contrary, Ivar Kittilä, pupils gleaming like two steel buttons, took the occasion as an opportunity to let fly with his own little homily.

"War is beautiful. It's the heroic symphony of cinema. Sounds both hushed and thunderous take on their greatest hierarchical expression in war. The abbreviated explosion of howitzers and the pithy whistling of bullets are taken up for the first time in its specta-tors' acoustic souls. War is magnificent: its effects, its surprises, its explosive *trouvailles*. A good sound engineer easily surpasses any purely scenic phantasmagoria. Thunder over lightning. The moan over the wound. A dying soldier's groan in the shadows of a muddy trench full of corpses has more impact than the pain described in a hundred pages of Henri Barbusse. Not to mention the faint, almost inaudible whimpering of a baby lying amid the smoldering rubble of a decimated village. Hearing your account, Op Oloop, even a blind soul would rebel. But war is beautiful in cinema. In fiction, everyone weeps. In reality, everyone suffers. What people need most is cathar-sis for their souls, because tears cleanse and purify. We in cinema do more than all your idealistic speeches and conferences put together. Sound requires no meditation, no cogitation—just feeling, heart. We're proud of that. Vision is not enough. Imagination is too rarely linked to audition. Fear, desperation, Dantesque horror—these are nothing without the clamor of imminent death, without a sardonic laugh erupting like a geyser, without the macabre hiss of intuition and the cosmic forces around you. But for sound technicians all that's just child's play. The tools of terror are risible, in themselves. And I know something about the ridiculous. I was a gagman for Harold Lloyd. Comedy always left the bitterest taste in my mouth. And then, as an almost complete novice, I took part in sound production for the adaptations of Roland Dorgelès's *Le croix du bois* and Remarque's *All Quiet on the Western Front*. Neither of these films were particularly outstanding, and yet they made the whole world shudder. And the world promised to reconsider its actions. I assure you, I will make a splendid little war, the most persuasive yet. I have collected nearly two hundred aural sources whose pathos is so overwhelming that, when I find the right producer, the film I put them in will be the definitive, unprecedented plea for world peace. I am considering Stalin or the Pope as producers. They're the only ones who could really do it right. I've already invested enormous amounts of my own money on patents and archives. Almost all of the recordings belong to me. In order to gather them I went out on military maneuvers, visited hospitals, sat in during real battles— Shanghai and Paraguay—always recording the sounds, the cries, the bombing and shelling . . ."

"You did, eh?" interrupted the Student. "Well, record this."

Thunderous flatulence reverberated throughout the room.

His unseemly audacity awoke a general indignation, but before it could be made more manifest, Robín bent his right arm into a v-shape and, cupping his elbow jocularly, added, "That one was on the house. Next time, it'll cost you!"

Hilarity exploded like a grenade.

To hide his true feelings, the sound engineer too joined in the revelry. His laughter was affected. His two steel-button pupils grew misty. He was infuriated to find his solemnity succumb to these snubs. His feelings inadvertently made themselves known:

"This is nothing new. In Hollywood there are hundreds of different kinds of farts, real and simulated, on record. I have exclusive rights to some rather amusing military flatulence emitted by field marshals and sergeants full of airs and graces. Yours, however, does not suit my purposes. It is coarse. From what I heard, I would venture that you suffer from aerophagy. I advise you to see if you might be suffering from any gaseous bloating of the stomach. Belladonna, liver salts, antispasmodics—there are numerous methods of treatment. If left unchecked, you might end up with heart trouble when you least expect it. The heart is the first thing to suffer the effects of such filth."

The giggling, already *in decrescendo*, ceased suddenly when the engineer finished this sentence. Everyone took the hint. But suddenly, boomingly, Peñaranda repeated the chorus: "That one was on the house. Next time, it'll cost you!"

And merrymaking prevailed once more.

Op Oloop was just beginning to open his eyes. Back from his own private voyage, he glanced contentedly from face to face. With the eager jubilation of a newcomer—as though he'd only just arrived at the party—he broke excitedly into the conversation, which had begun to grow hazy with the champagne.

"What happened? Tell me. When I left, you were all dismal, preoccupied. Wherefore this metamorphosis?"

"What do you mean, 'When I left'? Were you or were you not present?"

"Yes, really, Op Oloop!"

"I was present, but absent, like Adam before Eve handed him the apple. And now on returning, I discover the joy of their sin, which is the joy of finding oneself, although God may curse me for saying so."

"Fine. We were laughing at a little joke Robín played while Ivar was talking about a film project. These Creoles are unbelievable!

They can't stomach anything serious. The moment they find a crack, they let in the sun . . ."

"Thank you, Captain."

". . . and annoy everyone. It was the same with your distinguished traitor friend Gastón Marietti. I nearly punched him. You heard what he said! It was vile!"

"I didn't hear a thing."

"What? How can that be? It was you he was contesting! If you take it upon yourself to overwhelm us with your eloquence, it's only fair that you accept the correlative duty to pay attention to responses subsequently submitted."

"You are delusional. I do not overwhelm, I simply speak. And while I spoke, I put up the shutters. If I persuade, it is without eloquence. I detest all artifice. The vast majority of wicked men are emphatic and eloquent—Stendhal himself said as much."

"Do you mean to tell me that you paid no attention to my denunciation of your discourse and your extremist conduct?"

"None whatsoever."

"Why, you little . . ."

The maitre approached Op Oloop.

Erik choked back the insult he'd been on the verge of uttering. Judging by his expression, it was viler than a castor-oil purgative.

"You have a telephone call, sir. Someone wanting to know if you're here."

"Van Saal?"

"Yes, sir. What shall I tell him?"

Op Oloop deliberated. The idea of having to either affirm or negate his presence pained him. His friend's absence, on the one hand; a public lie on the other. He sought an ambiguous excuse.

"Tell him that I have just stepped out." A cloud came over his newest phase of jollity.

Shot through with premonitions and presentiments, he set sail for his private world once more. Departing the wide, deep cove of his friendship with Van Saal, he navigated his way to Franziska's port of perplexity. There she was, pretty as a statuette, her arms held aloft like an imam. Their dialogue was as brief and laconic as the encounter itself. And they fused, effusively, in the warm affective currents of their ecstasy.

When again he recovered, he found himself bidding farewell on arrival. He didn't care. Neither the superimposition of his sensations nor the surprise of those surrounding him concerned him in the slightest.

"Franziska! *Franziiiska! Franziiiiska!*"

He was feeling so tender, so pampered and full of endearments on his return, that it pained him to find Erik's eyes turned upon him, relentless and round with rage.

He shrugged humbly by way of excuse and attempted to dodge his friend. No luck. The Captain wanted to fire off a new volley.

"What's all this idiocy about Franziska! What am I, an uninvited guest who warrants no consideration at all? Why are you ignoring me? Can't you see it bothers me?"

Peñaranda, always circumspect, butted in: "Don't you think you've badgered him quite enough for one evening? We'd like to know the reason for this banquet, please. Every time there's been a banquet, Op Oloop has eventually told us what prompted it . . ."

"Hear, hear! Just what I wanted to know!" echoed Ivar Kittilä.

The Statistician, before they could collectively insist, resorted to a cunning ruse. The banquet's true motive made him feel self-conscious in front of some of them, and so snatching up any old story—random refuse from his intellectual storeroom—he expounded without much conviction, in an attempt to change the course of their insistence:

"One day, while eating steak Provençal, I considered the question of the existence of God. I said to myself, 'The world exists: we have it here before us. Now, if one needs a bricklayer simply to make a ball of mortar, cement, and water, then clearly vast materials and a 'super-subject' were required in order to create the world. But researching the origin of these materials and the genealogy of this hypothetical miracle worker, I was struck by an unfathomable mystery: since nothing can come from nothing, causality must predate intention. This drove me to distraction. So I gave up on my steak, as gristly and absolute as the notion of God, and I plunged into the appetizing reality of the *pommes frittes* that served as garnish. The garlic and parsley pointed to *un certain logique* in the same way that theology is the garlic and parsley of believers. And thus I realized that our senses grasp objective reality just as it is, while the brain plays tricks, transcendentalizing it. The intellect, dear friends, is the greatest liar there is. The entire world is nothing more than a mental preconception. It does not exist as a concrete reality, only an illusory one. Therefore, God is not a subject, but a parasitic entelechy located in the consciousness—just as a rubbery steak is located in the stomach. Therefore: it is only appearance. And since appearance is what it is *not*, but only simulates—like a conman—I came to the conclusion that the idea of God and rubbery steaks are both things that people willingly swallow, but which are toxic and, finally, stomach-churning."

This *boutade* did not gratify. It was not philosophy but pure eutrapelia. Nearly everyone was aware of the covert purpose it was intended to serve. And they sealed their lips, awaiting an explanation.

The explanation, alas, was not forthcoming.

Erik Joensun could not sit still. Of all those present, he was the only one with a real violent streak. He simply couldn't bear the silence. And he said so.

"When you next decide to speak, skip the half-witted bullshit you just fed us. Your blasphemy distresses me. Our Lord God is the love of all men."

"If God is male, he ain't my love. I'm no fairy!"

Duplicitous laughter curled their lips, staining their teeth with its essences.

The Captain protested, irate.

Robín interrupted.

"Calm down, man! It was a joke! There's no need to get your panties in a twist just because the man doesn't like to eat—how shall I put it?—'meatloaf' . . ."

"This has gone too far! It's insufferable! I'm burning like a lice-ridden twat, as you might say. If things carry on like this, I'm leaving!"

"Oh no!"

"You can't leave!"

Op Oloop was bubbling over with joy. When one's sympathy is pure and unblemished, being incommodious and annoying one's friends can be very agreeable indeed. Particularly when one succeeds in diverting the conversation from more sensitive subjects.

At that juncture, someone coughed presumptuously: Gastón Marietti. Once he'd attracted everyone's attention, he proffered the subsequent assessment:

"You always operate *ad modum astutum*. Sometimes you're naturally astute, other times you feign it. I, for one, still cannot discern when Op Oloop is absolutely Op Oloop. Limiting himself to just one self that expresses the very essence of his being must have fused some genetic defenses together, and also caused others to be acquired via cerebral systematization. Your brain mediates everything, Op Oloop. You possess a powerful yet fine-tuned transmitter that soaks you with waves from within and saturates others with its frequencies. And what an *oratore*, gentlemen! When you speak, the whole world is rapt, and when you stop, it's unwrapped. Because if silence is golden, only silence can value you, discover your true essence. And I can assure you that with this exordium I'm not just 'licking your boots,' as Robín would say . . ."

"You're really pissing me off!"

". . . but expressing an axiom that must be established in order to prove certain theorems. Over the course of this feast, I've noticed a thousand new nuances in our host's eccentricity. His inner climes betray great instability. We've all undergone or enjoyed the vicissitudes and splendors of his torments and his joys. Look at him now! He wears a smile as serene as the autumn sun. He gives off the fragrant air of ripe fruit. But he won't share the fruit! Why not, if he's the one who invited us to partake of it? Your recent subterfuge, Op Oloop my friend, is ingenious but unconvincing. I accept neither the gristly steak nor the existence of God. I concur with that thesis set forth by Coulomb, a famous thinker who dealt in abstractions as I deal in women. He maintained that aside from discovery, which is the greatest science there is—*rerum magistra sciencia*—all we do is dress up the same old impenetrable philosophical spirit in dazzlingly *nouveau* fashions. So, in sum, stop cheating us and explain what's behind this banquet. But skip the garlic and parsley, eh? Anything is possible, you know. Indeed, a French Hellenist has proven that the spirits drunk by the gods were actually *aioli*, the Provençal sauce made of oil, garlic, and eggs, rather like mayonnaise. That was fine on Olympus, as it is at my favorite restaurant. But for now, Op Oloop, omit all garniture and simply expound."

A resounding applause rounded off the Maquereau's speech.

"I'll drink to that!" several voices shouted in unison.

Op Oloop filled the Maquereau's glass and his own with champagne. And, caressing the flute like a breast, he brought it to his lips in what amounted to a kiss.

"Gastón: your kindness overwhelms me. You can twist my arm as much as you like, just don't break it in the process. I'm almost tempted to respond like the nonchalant son called to his father's deathbed. 'Why the hurry? He's still got a few hours. I thought he was breathing his last!' Because it's all well and good for you to charm the pants off people professionally, but not to strip me of my will and force me to let slip what I'd like to keep under wraps. I confess that feeling exposed disarms me. Once stripped of their verbal pretense, our intentions, ideas, and hidden feelings suffer the shame of not being what they seemed. Everything is embellished by the narcissism that accompanies one's personality, from the simplest subconscious act to the most arduous and deliberate one. Fine. I'll explain my motive for the feast. But I shall do it with garlic and parsley. And since you're the one who insisted, you must also suffer my breath. That way, as well as punishing you, I'll also continue my flirtation with one of the demigods of international cuisine. When I learned that garlic prolongs life, I ate it with resignation, but when I found out that it belongs to the lily family, I devoured it with romantic zeal."

"Indeed, it's true: garlic is liliaceous. Just as potatoes are solanaceous and peaches are rosaceous. So you actually smoke by eating mash—you perfume yourself . . ."

"All right, all right, Peñaranda! Don't get carried away now. Taking that route you could add that I dissolve diamonds in my coffee since sugar is made of carbon. It's entirely logical that, being Commissioner of Air Traffic Control, you respect and recognize all things terrestrial. But don't forget that parsley kills parrots, and that I'm going to speak with parsley and garlic . . ."

"Here's mud in your *ail!*"

"This is quite serious, Robín. Tonight, we are seven orchestrated variations on a cynical theme. Perhaps without realizing it, we're actually composing an *opera buffa*. Our ludicrousness is illustrious. It surpasses the echelons of academic inanity and ostentatious rhetoric. Personally, I laugh at Plato, Dante, Kierkegaard, and their symposia. No demerit to ourselves, of course. That's why I'm not taken in by the erroneous belief of that Parisian journalist who finds it cruel to compare firecrackers like Swift and Diderot to a damp squib like Bernard Shaw. Damp squib indeed! That's a regrettably routine error in judgment. Classical morons bask in the sort of praise that we'll never receive. Tell me, in what way is Alcibiades superior to me? Only, perhaps, in his love of 'meatloaf,' as Robín calls it . . ."

"Ooh la la, Op Oloop!"

". . . Tell me, in what way are Saint Paul's journeys superior to Erik's submarine voyages? In speech alone, for one's faith in eventual triumph is identical in the mystical piracy of hands joined in prayer and the military piracy of hands firing torpedoes. What were the literary exploits of Sophocles, Virgil, and Cicero but the extraction of words from extreme idleness? And yet the manly feats of Bird, Italo Balbo, and Alain Gerbault lie consigned to the wastelands of our memory. I protest! I protest against the mob filling libraries, seminaries, and universities, longing for old buskins and medieval sandals. I protest the erudite who appropriate the beauty of the past and disdain the sublimities of the present. And I revile them for valuing Asclepius's twaddle over German therapeutics, Saint Augustine's filth over Romain Rolland's uncontaminated morality."

The Statistician's paroxysmal voice brought the maitre and waiters running.

On seeing them he became infuriated.

"What are you doing here? Your job is to serve. More Cordon Rouge for me. Napoleon Cognac, Grand Marnier . . . Pour, lackeys, pour!"

And then he waffled on, enraged.

"Each man must administer his hatred cautiously. Mine is equitable. I distribute it evenly among those who are frozen in the past and those who perspire in the present. Because while the former are hemorrhoidal in their sensibility, the latter are constipated in the brain. And they complement each other by both betraying the law of life that demands the immediate defecation of all useless detritus, be it antiquated illusion or contemporary cowardice. I've always been a loyal man. You know that. So much so that I've never believed that knowledge is a race or injustice a necessary evil. My feelings are bristly and need no comb or pomade. The same goes for my instincts—educated yet untamed, nothing has ever disturbed their unruly naiveté! I coddle them, I accept them, I'm captivated by them. They are my greatest triumph. I'm a man whose character is quite structured. Cold, firm, *sui generis*. Not a scaffolder, like those who plan projects, accumulate aims, and finally manage to erect a few lunatic schemes. My *oeuvre*, my masterpiece, is internal. I admire it. It's no mere platform, sullied by failure, that will collapse one day under the weight of that filth to reveal the desolate, vacant lot of the soul once more. No. My soul is inhabited by memories—the only currency in circulation there—and with it, it buys up the future beyond my borders. Because in the *pampas* of my solitude, I've found the most beautiful and most enjoyable sort of isolation: that of living out man's complex aloneness."

He took a quick sip and carried on.

"My happiness is remunerative, it pays me in purity. All the riches tycoons accumulate are surplus. All the wealth poor wretches lack, I lavish upon them. By giving, I purge myself. But I eliminate only what is superfluous. I, then, am *un Hombre* with a capital *H,* not an orthodox *jongleur* doing flips on the crossbeam of that august letter. I've always said, 'Despise tributes . . . They're specious waves rolling onto your beach . . . Become smooth and polished like a rock in the swell . . . Let your vainglory froth in the surf around you . . . It makes no difference . . . It is always better . . . to be covered . . . with the . . . moss . . . of self . . . ab . . . sorp . . . tion . . . than to have . . . the undercurrent . . . of . . . your . . . vanity . . . lap . . . vulgar . . . shores . . .'"

Fade out.

Op Oloop's voice trailed off, grew faint, and then suddenly boomed, amplified, and he flooded his listeners with its torrent. Then, tapering off, it again grew faint until it had become a nearly imperceptible whisper.

Analogously, his eyes twinkled, then dimmed, and then opened wide in stupefaction.

What mysterious tides lay behind the ebb and flow of his speech and gaze?

No one dared to find out. They chose instead to wane with him in the lassitude of his languorous spasms. And the ruthlessness of the phenomenon remained relatively unremitting. Until . . .

Cipriano Slatter, insatiable, was on his fourth Napoleon. He was rather drunk. His anthropometrically perfect profile had fixed on his friend, in search of the crucial explanation. And suddenly he hit on it.

"Op Oloop is in love!"

"What?"

"Shut up!"

"Don't be ridiculous!"

"Op Oloop is in love, I repeat. Aren't I entitled to my own opinion? Take a look. Don't criticize. Op Oloop is in love!"

Gastón Marietti broke free of his own pomposity for a moment to glance back and forth between the Statistician and his interrupter. The lucid vision of the one and the sibylline stance of the other both upset him greatly. And he muttered under his breath, "It just might be true. Drunkards have an insight that reveals the intrinsic value of their actions, of their words, of everything. They're straightforwardly analytical and discerning, under the influence. In them, expression is reduced to its intentions, form to its essence, and words to their intrinsic truth. It just might be true . . ."

Op Oloop was just tuning in, back from the netherworld of his meta-psychic intimacy. And he was sighing. Sighing so loudly that his own exhalations seemed to startle him.

The Maquereau's face lit up. He no longer had any doubt. But he'd have to catch Op Oloop at a weak moment to wheedle a confession out of him. So he attacked mercilessly.

"No beating around the bush, Op Oloop. You're in love. Don't hold back, own up to it once and for all. That's the reason for the banquet. You're in love."

The host was speechless. Flabbergasted. The surprise attack chilled his soul and changed his so-changeable expression.

He glanced round. Each man's gaze was one of interrogation, a taciturn diorama of anticipation. He reviewed. He pulled himself together. He overcame his misery. And without further ado he responded, slowly nodding his head up and down.

Peñaranda stood and called for a toast.

"I'm the only married man here. Consequently, I can attest to the fact that love seasons life. Let us drink to Op Oloop . . . and to his new spice."

"Long live seasonings!"

"Hear, hear!"

Applause and congratulations.

After the concomitant rejoicing, Op Oloop paused decisively, emotionally. The others waited attentively, in silence.

"I hate to disappoint you. It's true, I'm in love, but profoundly sad. The more I think about it, the more nonsense I talk. It's deplorable! I always thought it was ridiculous and 'inhuman' that love—just one instinct among many—was the only thing that could fulfill mankind. I can't accept the idea. Yet it must be so. I know from experience that nothing beats that affective adventure—there is no more extravagant enterprise, certainly not in the intellectual sphere, for example. But I'm distraught. Full of misgivings. And still today, my own derision rebukes me. Even within the enchanted circle, I hear my own skepticism mocking me. It's deplorable! I sense my ruin is near. The miracle of love has plotted the definitive sabotage of my spirit. I note intolerable obstacles, steel traps that make my psychological gears slip and destroy the harmonious mechanics of my system. It's deplorable!"

His right hand concealed his obsession; his left, lying slack upon the tablecloth, cried out for solace.

Peñaranda granted it, with erudition:

"Relax, my friend, relax. Love is a plane crash of the soul. Like you, I flew my heart cautiously, skillfully. Like you, I had the brevets granted by experience, life, and literature. I flew perfectly, avoiding all the traps set by wild effusion. But how can one account for others' imprudence? One afternoon, suspecting nothing, an impetuous soul collided with my feelings. It was a serious accident. I sounded all the alarms, making my solitude known. And I altered my course, but not in time. It was fatal. We fell. Only the wings of an angel saved me. A divine tree broke her fall. Should I have put in a claim? Bah! The trial was slow, full of wiles and embraces. When the heart has a breakdown there are no spare parts. I demanded another heart entirely, and love brought it to me. Since then, Op Oloop, all of the damage has been compensated: I live in a passion that glides merrily towards death with another soul by my side, never reaching for the brakes . . ."

Erik and Ivar—first riveted and then whispering—dovetailed into the subject at hand. The old Submarine Captain charged first.

"Instincts wage open war, while reason goes in for trench warfare. If you had mulled this over, you wouldn't be so upset. It's your fault for being so convinced that the brain controls everything. It's unfathomable that a man your age should be caught up in this sort of nonsense. What good is all your alleged wisdom if it can't save you from the malady of love? Because love is like a rat in a tin can: it's fun to catch, it makes your heart race. But then it squeals and thrashes, agitating your innards and causing nothing but desperation. Finally, unable to escape, it dies in the can and rots your spirit forever . . ."

"Exactly. And your spirit becomes a living hell. Santa Teresa said so herself: *Inferi sunt ubi foetet et non amantur*, which means, 'hell is where it reeks and there is no love.'"

Stunned silence.

"You needn't be so shocked. I did graduate from the Lycee de Marseilles."

"That's not what I find shocking. It's that a maquereau like you believes in love."

"Of course I do. I exploit it for a living."

The hurtful sarcasm of the others was equaled by the kindness Op Oloop had expressed.

Then Ivar began his diatribe: "Love is a society sport, subject to the rules of fashion and the laws of distinction . . ."

"Never!" Peñaranda refuted. "Love is warm tenderness, it's an immeasurable poetry that begins with kisses and ends in tears. It conquers all; it trammels anything in its path. Gentle, it tickles like a memory. Passionate, it makes us as drunk as all the Greek symposia combined. Man is its endorsement. I believe in its gallantry. Sometimes, a *coup de foudre* starts hearts beating unstoppably. Sometimes, spirits go deaf with a wild drum roll of anguish and desire. Love . . ."

"Love! Bah! It's immoral! . . . *hic!*"

"Please, Slatter!"

"I'm a victim . . . *hic.* Love is the great go-between . . . *hic.* It's both clean and dirty, like a bidet . . . *hic.* You trust its whiteness . . . *hic.* And then it turns out to be full of spirochetes . . . *hic! hic!*"

"Slatter, please!"

"Don't interrupt him. He's not saying anything improper. Love is nothing but an *affiche* for our genetic instincts. And an ignoble *affiche* at that!"

"Watch your mouth, Ivar."

"I, too, speak from experience. In Hollywood I fell for a wonderful girl. Her father—President of the Los Angeles Eugenics Society, no less—assured me she was a virgin. He was trying out an experiment on me. What a con! Feminine beauty is nothing but pus and viruses glued together with make-up . . . I had to undergo intensive treatment. In fact, I still do. Love was the end of me. I traveled around, trying to forget her. Yachts, *paquebots*, sweethearts, kept women . . . But I never got over it. Love is a one-way ticket to the grave!"

And with that, the sound engineer emitted a sorrowful sigh, setting a seal on the sadness of his story.

Something like a cloud of depression wafted over the guests.

But, just at that instant, Op Oloop spoke softly, soothingly:

> Doutez, si vous voulez, de l'être qui vous aime
> D'une femme ou d'un chien, mas non de l'Amour même.
> L'amour est tout: la vie et le soleil.
> Qu'importe le flacon pourvu qu'on aie l'ivresse!
> Faites-vous de ce monde un songe sans reveil.

Silence wedged itself beneath the guests' crania.

There were so many routes open to reflection that their thoughts were paralyzed by the possibilities.

When no one thought it prudent to embark on any road at all, Robín Sureda suddenly spoke up. His words were met with outrage:

"Allow me to brag that I'm the youngest man at the banquet. I'm twenty-eight years old, and as long as my father continues to wire me three hundred pesos a month, I'll be a Student forever. This is the life! What I mean is, I know women. They're a product every man needs. I'm not interested in love. I follow the advice of an author who was once a classmate of mine and is still a good friend:

> *If you don't want to suffer*
> *Then make your love concrete;*
> *For when it comes to women*
> *It's your coming that's the treat.*

Quite so. For me, women are essentially holes, slots, slits. If you want the world to be rosy, stick twenty cents in the slot—slip it in the slit. Women are like those machines you find at amusement parks. And their slots, or slits . . ."

"Think of your mother, you swine!"

". . . their slots, or slits, require coins. If I'm wrong, I beg your pardon. But I've had a lot of women: single, married, widows. They're all the same. None are sublime. I agree with Slatter and his ilk, Op Oloop. Five years ago I fell in love with a girl from Tucumán. She was from a good family, but all she wanted was cock. Cock, cock, cock. Oh, and presents! Lots of presents! Now she's like a cane: she'll hang off any man's arm. She's such a whore she dies her Venus mound to match the hair-color of her man of the moment!"

"Will you watch your language! It's indefensible!"

"Oh, don't be such a cretin. This is how a real student talks, one who disdains the exaltation of his degree. We don't use doctoral falsetto. Men like you really piss me off, you know, watching what you say all the time, never using an obscene word. All that verbal hygiene would seem to indicate that your soul must be a septic tank. To have a clean conscience, you have to expel corrosive words and concepts—it's absolutely necessary. You defecate through language, as it were. So you can lecture me all you want. But you should know that my breath is fresh, and my mind is modern and not filled with the fecal matter of false modesty and prejudice."

"Don't get so worked up, Robín. Please, continue," they begged him.

"No. I can't now. You cut me off mid-flow."

A new silence. Uncomfortable. Several eyes flashed. And just when a storm threatened, there came a gentle breeze: it was Op Oloop, susurrating another poem in French.

The Maquereau, on hearing him, overflowed with tenderness. He watched him affectionately, observing his glorious detachment. And full of sympathy for his friend, he spoke:

"It's impossible to sing a *laudatio funebris* to our good Op Oloop, thunderstruck as he is by love. If there's one thing that merits no pity, it's love. And we already know that such poetic inspiration is likely to vibrate all the more when picked with the sensational syncopation of pity's plectrum! It's true that there are some truly incontrovertible grounds for suicide out there. Pain and sickness, for example, which, according to Lucretius, are the unparalleled architects of death. But not love, which is neither pain nor disease. Neither the mind nor the body is afflicted by it. Love is art. It quivers with emotion. And it burns with the flames of a blind, fervent spirit that knows nothing of the serene idiosyncrasies of the soul. With divine, impetuous freedom, love erects itself, dresses itself in the flesh of instinct. It creates a sophisticated duality. It doesn't reason: it declares its only *raison* to be the irrepressible fury of sex. And thus it lives, quenching its thirst, which is desire, with no motive other than the satisfaction of its egotism. Love is art. Sensibility is a sylph that must be clothed in the seamless tunic of spiritual doctrine. That's why whoever loves must, as an aesthete, also tame his impulses and train his secret desires to accept the hard, sweet reality of partnership. In order to love, one needs a bit of class, a bit of style. A lover's skill resides in capturing the soul of instinct in the same way a painter might penetrate a landscape. Pure lyricism! Thus the mysteries of passion will be unveiled. And love, like a masterpiece, will blaze in our hearts in all its glory. Let us deplore, dear friends, Op Oloop's love, for it is already a failure. His tragedy lies in numbers: in being all method and no style. His *esprit de geometrie* forces a square peg into a round hole, as it were. He wants to chart and graph it all! But the sentimental beings who inhabit our souls can't be organized into numerical series, coordinates, formulas. We've heard his heart explode. Perfection, shot to pieces! But let us not burden his rubble with the weight of an unnecessary pardon. He himself was solely to blame. Or perhaps it was his destiny to be ruined thus. Maurice Barrès has said as much: '*La vie des êtres sensibles est chose somptueuse et triste.*'"

The crude aggression that had reigned moments ago dissolved entirely.

An ineffable banality settled over all of the diners, disposing them to further chitchat and drivel.

Op Oloop, semi-submerged in the rolling waves of his reverie, hadn't missed a single word. He might have replied wittily. But cushioned as he was by the warmth of friendly phrases, he simply reclined upon his pillows like a sensual, abulic sultan wallowing in affections and perfume.

The waiters refilled their glasses.

As they were drinking, the clock struck.

1:30 A.M. "One o'clock already!"

"No, one thirty."

"*Caramba*! I'd better be off . . ."

"You, Ivar, aren't going anywhere. This isn't some Rotary Club dinner where we all wear silly hats and sing the 'Star-Spangled Banner' and all that gibberish. There's no taximeter running here. This isn't a parodic brotherhood meeting and you can't simply bang a gavel and adjourn the soirée. The significance of this banquet lies entirely in good conversation and mutual friendship. So you stay put."

"But I have to be in the studio by seven! I have to finish the Lunfardo soundtrack for a movie Fonofilm is shooting. I tell you, it's torture! Creole actors are as bad as Spaniards—they're animals. All pomposity and no elegance—all airs and no graces. Well, you know that already. And by the way, they're unbelievably unoriginal when it comes to love scenes. Side-splitting stuff, really. The ladies, all Marlene'd up, growl rather than speak. And the heartthrobs are all dolled up like Pina Menichelli and Francesca Bertini. They make their eyes bulge out and recite their lines with hoarse, gravelly voices—it's repulsive. Frankly, I have to ask, just what the hell do *you* lot think love is?"

"Liturgy."

"Chancres . . . *hic*."

"Taboo."

"Business."

"Romanticism."

"Shit!"

"Love is heroism. Hero comes from Eros."

"That's a lie! It's not heroic—it's despicable. Love = orgasm + organism. Love = tits + wits. Love = her bed + my head."

"Love fulfills man and sublimates his personality."

"Bah! It's venal and coercive. Proof enough right here. I had a woman once.

> *At first I loved her more than wine*
> *But then I failed to see the sign*
> *She'd be laughing while I'd pine!*
> *Now she isn't even mine."*

"Therein lies your error. Love and partnership should not be confused. Who belongs to whom is not a question of love."

"Yes, it is. Get married, you'll see. When you first get a wife, you pinch her derrière. After a month, it's just like pinching your own . . ."

"That's precisely why film stars all get divorced so soon after they get married."

"You deprecate a sacrament. Matrimony sanctifies and sculpts a woman's body."

"Yes, and that's the advantage of adultery: you get to reap the benefit of another man's efforts—let him sculpt away and then swoop in . . ."

"Nonsense . . ."

"Nonsense? The success of marriage comes down to three lies: she lies to him; he lies to her; and the four of them lie to the rest of the world."

"I once had a woman who was quite 'duplicable.'"

"Duplicable?"

"Yes: both her husband and her lover found her quite lickable. But all she wanted was to have a child. She would cross herself before coitus. She sprinkled holy water on the bed, in her bush, on me. And right in the middle of an orgasm, she'd gaze up in fear and fascination, as if she were watching a swarm of locusts."

"She was probably saying a prayer, poor thing!"

"Nothing unusual about that. Just a mystical form of erotomania. Love can take many forms."

"It can take on as many forms as you like, but what I like is the dormitive virtue of coitus."

"The dormitive virtue of coitus?"

"Yes. Allow me to explain."

Op Oloop, distant and present, gestured distractedly. His guests sat motionless in anticipation.

"'*Charme de l'amour qui pourrait vous peindre?*' the purest lover asked. And his question still resonates. Constant did not manage it with the serene effusion of his Adolphe. Goethe deliquesced and lost the way in Werther's labyrinth. Stendhal hardly even began to paint it with his red and black brushes. Proust was nothing but an exquisitely morbid soothsayer. Freud plumbed the unknown depths of the subconscious attempting to contract it. '*Charme de l'amour qui pourrait vous peindre?*'"

"No one. Love cannot be captured, in reality. It rebels against all logic and is aloof from guiding principles," Peñaranda proclaimed.

"And yet, ignorance attempts to subjugate it, regulate it, channel it into law, turn it into dogma! Folly. Love is the fire, water, and air of our private lives, and it will persevere, spreading freedom to the last two souls in agony . . ."

Gastón Marietti cleared his throat, hinting at his incredulity. He knocked back a bit of Grand Marnier. And then refuted.

"All well and good, Op Oloop. But the human species has returned to the days of bisexuality. It has turned the corner of the evolutionary parable. We are now in a neutral age in which, soon—in, say, *X-*

hundred years—there will be no men and no women but only men-women. Hermaphrodites are becoming more and more common. An English surgeon studied this phenomenon and published his results in *The Lancet*: he postulates the more or less imminent absorption of different genetic forces by a single person. The 'individual'—a fallacious term, by the way—will then recover its primitive quality of '*in diviso*,' making the old, absurd idea of '*amour propre*' into a transcendent and vital necessity in the erotic domain. In addition, the proliferation of so-called artificial insemination—particularly in well-off countries—reveals that heterosexual love is not particularly persuasive or even attractive, given that once the biological question has been overcome, the matter of your 'souls' becomes irrelevant. And as a corollary: the delayed nuptial predisposition, deferred nowadays from puberty to adulthood, means that love as a sexual commitment is also postponed. This essentially indicates that sex is stifled in the collective consciousness. All of which proves that the existing sources of life are drying up. And that once we've transmuted back into what we once were, 'being' will entail enjoying the deific privilege of giving birth to ourselves, killing ourselves, and thus possessing our own posterity."

This statement induced a serious stupor.

Op Oloop was reduced to a state of shock.

"Gastón, this vision of things to come is simply terrifying!"

Erik Joensun, as usual, couldn't control his outrage:

"So based on your predictions, masturbation will become irrelevant, ha ha. One would get oneself pregnant and give birth to oneself, ha ha . . ."

"That's right."

"And you, a maquereau of all people, put forward this hypothesis!"

"That's right."

"Well, you've got a fine future ahead of you, at this rate!"

Gastón Marietti's face flooded with pity.

"Don't lose any sleep on my behalf. As long as our contemporary morality continues to consider love taboo, as long as it repudiates our instincts—which nonetheless awaken and attempt to satisfy themselves—then we white slavers will continue to play our messianic role . . ."

"You, a messiah! Ha!"

"Yes, Captain. A messiah. Within every harlot lives a disillusioned woman. She sells herself simply because her pure love has gone unrequited. Maquereaux always trade on the disillusionment of disenchanted women. And they love us for it. They love us Magdalenically, as it were. Jesus, in a way, was our precursor . . ."

Giddy, burlesque, the host decided to frolick through the increasing ire of his naval compatriot. In an attempt to irk him further, he added, "Yes, Erik. Jesus was Gastón's precursor. Yes, Gastón, the sly Corsican educated in the streets of Marseille, right on La Canebière, along with *Henri-le-musicien* and *Coco-le-coiffeur* . . . Magdalenically, thousands of disillusioned women blocked his way, and he, in order to redeem them, shipped them out to Cairo, Bangkok, Djibouti, and Batavia. His apostles: sharks, traffickers, pimps. They did the rest, channeling the women's pain and suffering into voluptuous, lucrative resignation. Yes, Gastón, the very man here before you, guided by the hand of destiny, paved the road to Buenos Aires. Did you know that? He's an international sensation. Why, he's the inverse of our own ancestors the Vikings, who spread their crude Puritanism wherever they went. He brought to the pampas— an enormous wasteland of straw and thirst—the feminine wiles of France. Magdalenes from Dunkirk, with water-colored eyes for the parched masses of San Luis; Magdalenes from Lourdes, sweet and succulent, for the windy wild peoples of Patagonia; Magdalenes from Lille, lissome and bellicose, for the disheveled denizens of La Rioja—etcetera. And for the stalled motorists of Buenos Aires: the sensual magneto of Paris. Thus, thanks to his initiative, thousands have taken pleasure, and still do, in the proximity of a woman who, by contrast, is lost in a nostalgic world of her own. And even the most clay-brained idiots can turn their fantasies into reality, taking comfort in what would otherwise be an all-but-inaccessible delight. I hereby pay him tribute. The tariffed love that this great sex merchant put within my reach has been a veritable Venus flytrap of pleasure. Let us toast to Gastón, egregious benefactor of our nation!"

The toast, however, was thwarted.

"I don't think," argued the Commissioner of Air Traffic Control, "that celebrating a motive of that sort is really plausible. Prostitution is the gangrenous . . ."

"What about Madame Noélie Maynard? *Hic.* And her Maison de Massage-Curiosités? *Hic.* What about our orgies at Confort Moderne? Hic. *Hic*-oprite."

". . . is a gangrenous infection eating away at love. If it weren't for prostitution, we wouldn't have a seventy-percent failure rate on the medical exams required of our youth when they turn up for military service . . ."

"Fabulous! Even there it's beneficial! Prostitution discourages war by decreasing the number of men fit for duty. A country is never more pacific than when it's weak!"

"Your words sicken me, Op Oloop. How could you prefer a weak nation to a proud one?"

"Quite easily. Oh, quite, quite easily! Sickness is far easier to endure. It brings wise, kind-hearted friends calling to pamper and console! Pride, on the other hand, awakens hatred and invites attempts at annihilation . . ."

"You're really pissing me off, now. You venerate vice like a common criminal! Where's your honor?"

"I had a little doggie once named Honor."

The Student's interjection, uttered solely out of a desire to contribute something—anything at all—to the conversation was all the more humorous for being so unexpected. Each man laughed to himself and feted the statement in his own way.

"I once had a little doggie named Honor!"

"I once had a little doggie, *hic*, named Honor!"

"I once had a little doggie named Honor that used to urinate in the doorway to the Cathedral and the Casa Rosada and even the Jockey Club and the Banco de la Nación."

"I'm sorry, Op Oloop, but I've never once seen you at the Jockey Club."

"True. I had forgotten you were a member."

"You! A maquereau, a member of the Jockey Club!"

"Yes, Erik. Mitigate your stupor. I have as much right as anyone. My professional line doesn't differ from any other. We're all the same. I'm just another spoke in the wheel of . . . providence that includes banking, politics, and bribery. Venal fornication is not a crime: it's a business. White slavery, according to the League of Nations' official definition, is customarily a question of *élevage*. My own statistics indicate that forty percent of hookers come from lowly professions: servants, seamstresses, chorus girls—and they aspire to climb the social ladder by associating with gallant, cultured men, enjoying the hygienic amity of toiletries and dressing tables, and wallowing in luxury and pleasure. And so, my friend, the same benefits that my friends at the club reap by importing fine mares, I myself reap by importing fine fillies . . ."

"It's true. There really is no difference between *cafishing* horses and women!"

"*Cafishing*? What's that, Robín?" Ivar Kittilä demanded, desperate not to lose the thread of the argument.

"*Cafishing*? Exploiting, being a *cafisho*."

"True," Op Oloop interrupted. "*Cafisho* actually comes from pidgin Spanish: 'cat-fish.' Some immigrant grocer probably just hurled a new insult one day . . ."

"You're right! Perhaps it came about the same way as *flâneur*, which derives from 'flannel.' Maybe one day a French lady used it to abuse a reluctant client. Lunfardo is a very curious dialect. Now I am wondering if *cafiolo*, another word for 'pimp,' might not have a similar etymology. It could be a pejorative term for one of those habitués you see at brothels who do nothing but drink *café au lait* all day."

"Very likely indeed, Gastón. You must have heard the song sung here:

> *Mambrú went off to war*
> *I don't know when he'll return . . .*

Which is just a bastardization of the children's song you and I know:

> *Marlborough s'en va-t-en guerre*
> *Il pleut, il pleut, bergère . . .*"

"Indeed."

"Good. Well, these arrogant appropriations combined with such curt reductions of other languages will take Buenos Aires Lunfardo to unprecedented heights of lexicographical expression."

"That's precisely why I like it. In this country, flooded with immigrants, Lunfardo's self-assurance allows it to engage all languages, exploit them, and turn solemn expressions into sharp-tongued insults, all with a hint of burlesque. Why, I myself have experienced the bastardization of *maquereau*. That's why here in Argentina people say *macrof*. I've often wondered about it. *Maquereau*, clearly, means 'mackerel.' But is the original etymology olfactory? Or is it that hookers hang out on piers?"

"But doesn't it originally come from *makros*, the Greek word for long, big, tall?"

Silence.

"Superb! So you're going to manage to find a way for our Maquereau to have noble origins!" Erik grunted.

"Hello! I've got it! It comes from 'macrophage,' macroph-age! You can't deny that the meaning is well-suited to the job. You people do eat well!"

"Come now, Op Oloop! Based on that line of thinking I could just as easily claim that maquereau comes from the Latin *macheros*, machete, cutlass. And I don't even use a penknife!"

"Oh my. This is getting good, *hic*."

"This isn't the Royal Academy of Language."

"No need to get upset, gentlemen. I have a duty to know my profession's provenance and the semantics of the underbelly of the universe. If they used the same terms here as in France it would be easier. *Souteneur, tôlier, tenancier*. But there is yet to be a local Émile Chautard to write the Lunfardo version of *La vie étrange de l'argot*. Once someone does, I'll be satisfied with just the particle 'mac,' the arrival of my weekly giros, and my daily Picon grenadine."

The waiters, working noisily though discretely, cleared the table of the fabulous dessert spread and thereby induced an inevitable hiatus in the conversation.

Slatter used the interruption to go to the lavatory.

Erik, ever shinier and more rosy-cheeked, was speaking in hushed tones with Ivar, whose round, shaved head now seemed pale by comparison. They must have been speaking of Op Oloop as, when he lit a cigarette, they both diligently observed the way he contemplated the match's flame, stock still, with tired eyes that gazed out from distant, internal horizons.

There do exist some perfect creatures who take pleasure—perhaps in an attempt to thwart their very perfection—in seeking out the friendship of teratological individuals. Is this an affective phenomenon, or compensation for their over-noble temperaments? This is what they were pondering and discussing. Gastón Marietti's personality had perturbed them greatly. His ineluctable logic in subjects that should have been illogical and his implacable loyalty to absurd perversions seemed to them to be exerting a negative influence over their friend. The naked beauty of their easy, simple morality did not allow for such complexities, for the trappings of such paradoxes and dissociations. In the noticeable concern they extended to their compatriot, one could glean a certain element of anguish and alarm. Rebellion and blasphemy are easier for a timid man than an audacious one to stomach. Of this they were unaware. And on recalling the youthful Op Oloop, meticulous and concentrated, as compared with the figure before them, they fell back paternalistically onto the rationalization of the Maquereau's 'bad company,' believing his mindset must have been transmitted like a contagious disease.

Gastón Marietti instantly intuited the iniquity of their reasoning. He wanted to vomit forth his suspicions, but contained himself. The contractions that would've been required by such an effort made him sigh. And, vexed and determined to break up their little tête-à-tête, he held out an English silver ashtray to the whispering, finicky Finns. The almost-searching look they gave him in response confirmed the antagonism he felt for them both. And in an attempt to conceal it, he simply made an announcement:

"They're bringing round the cigars."

And he wiped the sour look from his face.

With feigned deference, the maitre offered the first cigar to the Student, thereby expunging the ire Robín had felt earlier on in the evening. Slatter, on returning, snatched up the second. And each man, with the exceptions of Op Oloop and Gastón, broke cigar bands, seals, and stamps to extract enormous Havanas from their glass hangars and pop them directly into their mouths.

The air filled with aromas of cordovan and cinnamon; sandalwood and coffee vapors wafted over the table. The curtain of smoke—now that the rest of the dining-room lights had been turned off—took on a tulle tinge in the semi-penumbra. And the contrast that the luminous cones projected onto the screen of the tablecloth created a magical stage with five crimson spotlights. Op Oloop, whose tired eyes were, as before, seeing the world from across his vast internal landscapes, took pleasure in the emergence of this illusory landscape, on which he saw the intricately embroidered silk cloth as a cluster of vines and the transparent bottle as a diminutive pond.

He decided, imaginatively, to enter the scene. And facing the Maquereau, the only unilluminated figure, he spoke to himself without hearing himself, which is the best way to ensure that everyone listens and no one understands:

"Franzi? . . . Yes, with me . . . . Oh, Franzi! . . . . Very bad . . . . Who could have guessed? . . . . Lost . . . . Completely lost . . . . You don't think so? . . . Yes . . . And the key is in the bite . . . . In the bite! . . . . What arms you have! . . . . Succulent . . . Like succulent pears . . . . Oh no! . . . . Not at all . . . . No flattery . . . . I like you just the way you are . . . . Height: 162 centimeters; neck: 32.4 centimeters; bust: 82 centimeters; waist: 58 centimeters; hips: 86.4 centimeters; thighs: 44.4 centimeters; calves: 28.8 centimeters; ankles: 18 centimeters. Ahh! . . . .

. . . . Yes, by heart . . . . The perfect measurements . . . . The pluperfect . . . . of a Venus not yet disinterred from her dreams . . . . Yes, of course . . . . . But better still when you sport your lovely nudity just for me . . . . Pshah! . . . . Never! . . . . That's because you haven't seen my shadow . . . . Shattered . . . . Mended! . . . . Oh, my shhhhha-dow! . . . . Wounded by terrible crocodile bites . . . . . I swear it isn't so . . . . . It seems the same, but it's different . . . . I'll patch it with chamois . . . . It pulls me, it demands my attention, it jumps like a chimpanzee . . . . Never! . . . . . It's horrific! . . . . I don't want to mar your shadow, which shines like a diamond in the water . . . . I don't want to . . . . Your shadow will suffer . . . . Because shadows suffer, you know . . . . Your insinuation pains me, physically . . . . My shadow is fading now in a wave of failure . . . . . . No! . . . . Leave me! . . . . I must weep . . . . I, too, console myself by preaching from a pleasurable pulpit . . . . But it's futile . . . . Feee. . . yuuuuu. . . . . tiiiile! . . . . . I'm doomed, a miserable minister . . . . Owwwww! . . . . . . bitten by relentless teeth . . . . Never mind, never mind! . . . I need to nourish myself with silence . . . . With the nourishing silence of death . . . . Yes, Franzi, my baby . . . . . . *ma cherie* . . . . . . because your arrogant innocence is worse than perversity . . . . And biting myself . . . . Owwww! . . . . A logical demon from a logical hell . . . . Owwww! . . . . like a reversible hyena . . . . An image straight out of literature . . . . Owwwwwww! . . . . Owwwwwwwwwwwwwww! . . . . Rising up to chew on my soul for ever and ever . . . . Ah! . . ."

Bewilderment paralyzed eyelids in mid-blink and dropped jaws on the spot. The guests' cigars—some had gone out—sat between slack fingers.

No one dared utter a word.

Op Oloop's psyche had once again begun to flow directly to his epidermis. While it was busy stage-managing the dream world he inhabited within, delirious numina from his nether regions tormented his countenance with a sordid, less-than-surreptitious pandemonium of masks, ululations, and whimpers. His soul was elsewhere, so the humiliation of his lapse was engraved upon his physiognomy for all to see. He was overcome by an urge to weep. And, as no tears came, his malaise turned ever more poisonous. He took on a victimized air, the look of an animal being preyed upon. His consciousness was occluded. It was a crippled mass, in search of the path of reason, stumbling and lurching amongst the ruins of his character.

His guests' quiescence was in fact a considered act of tact. Any utterance at all would have reverberated in the now empty vault of Op Oloop's corporeality. And perhaps led to a complete intuition or comprehension of his own unconsciousness, in which case, on realizing his helplessness, this perception of his delicate state would have led to tears and other acts of desperation. A sad fact—more pathos-inducing than the irony of his not even finding himself insane.

Yes, the flow of his spirit was flooding his flesh. But now his vaguely iridescent eyes—which had been revealing the darkest fragments of his soul: misty, enigmatic riverbeds inhabited by sentimental fauna; underworldly, immoral dreams whose symbolism was not readily identifiable; macabre, impulsive suburbs teeming with dandified emotions, all professing the exquisite snobbery of discretion—focused once more on the propinquities of life and men.

Blithely: "What's this? Not smoking? Please, smoke. I can assure you that these are the most excellent cigars in all of Buenos Aires. They come from an exceptional manufacturer, supplier of all the

Chiefs of Protocol of the greatest nations in the world. While I was in Cuba, Enrique José Varona, a noted connoisseur of meadows and springs, well-versed in the secrets of the production and maturation of cigars, recommended this brand to me as an exquisite favor."

"And what about you? Why aren't you smoking?" ventured Robín, striking a match to his butt once more.

"I smoke two cigarettes a day: that is enough for me. And I am faithful to the Egyptian blends—Dimitrinos, Matoussian, Senoussi—made from Macedonian tobacco."

As he spoke these words in the most natural manner, and as he was so calm, everyone became convinced that Op Oloop had freed himself, and rather gracefully, from his momentary mental mishap. Everyone but Gastón. On noting that time had not passed for his friend while he was "away," he realized that Op Oloop's recovery was in fact a sign of the true gravity of this anomaly, since it's always those defects that the mechanics of a subject's mind are incapable of registering that end up engendering the most egregious catastrophes . . .

The sagacious pimp intended, therefore, to stir up some chatter with the charitable aim of decentering his stricken friend. But Ivar attacked first, hurling himself headlong into the uneasy silence.

"So, you've been to Cuba! What a great country, eh? From My-ah-mee, in Florida . . ."

"From *Mee*-ah-mee . . . 'Miami' is a Spanish word so say it in Spanish."

". . . I've flown to the island three times to do location work."

"I myself have only been to *La Habana*. And only passing through. I was coming from New York—well, actually from Washington, because my work at the American Graves Registration Service directory led to an incident that provoked me to resign, to take a stand in defense of my ideals and my dignity. That's when the civil servant of sadness, the macabre strategist, finally abandoned his fallen army!"

"Why must you keep whining on like a little girl about the ten or twelve million killed in the war? Why, I wish we could have another one, so we could raise the price of wheat!"

"Erik!"

"By chance I met up with the same Kentucky tobacco grower whose son had died of *delirium tremens* after celebrating the armistice so indefatigably. He got me a job working in the auditing department for the Chadbourne Plan, which was aimed at regulating the sugar industry so shareholders could see bigger profits. I lasted three days. Just long enough to disprove the saying 'Cuba is like cork: it always stays afloat.' The Yanks—Root, Morrow, Rockefeller, Guggenheim, etc.—have plundered the Pearl of the Caribbean with their avarice. They have taken away the country's land and liberty. The Platt Amendment and all the trusts have made a mockery of Martí's ideals. There's no end to their attempts to increase their dividends. They'll happily exile organized natives to the back of beyond, and import blacks from Haiti and Jamaica to harvest the sugarcane. Meanwhile, Cuban citizens starve to death as they dither between paralytic siestas and frenetic rumbas . . . I lasted three days. And then I left. I have never put my science at the service of infamy. If I ever endured despotism, it was only to anathematize it, classify its disorder, crime, and injustice."

"Yes, right. That's grand. I know your tactics. Insult the foreman to befriend the worker . . ."

"Erik, please!"

"Then, once I had joined the Kemmerer Mission as their statistician I had the opportunity to get the figures on all the levying, squandering, and fraudulent shipping taking place in various South

American nations—to compare the financial iniquities and abuses of dictatorships vis-à-vis free states—and as a prophylactic corollary, to numerically forecast the social revolution that would occur the moment the people became conscious of the putrefaction all around them."

The Captain's irritation was unmanageable by this point. He spluttered rabidly, "*So*-cial re-vo-*lu*-tion! Well, that's quite a phrase! And then what?"

Op Oloop, tolerating the interpolation tranquilly, simply whispered in reply, "Then nothing. Just a verse from Robert Louis Stevenson:

> *I have trod the upward and the downward slope;*
> *I have endured and done in days before;*
> *I have longed for all, and bid farewell to hope;*
> *And I have lived and loved, and closed the door.*"

The last line was barely audible.

An invisible *charme* of painful beatitude perfumed Op Oloop's words. Speckled with sorrow, they concluded with a sigh that seemed to come from his now-closed eyelids more than from his mouth.

Empathy—showing compassion and entering into another's feelings—was not one of Erik's fortes. His interruptions—the roughest turbulence in the serenity of the banquet—were now so numerous that the host could no longer remember how many there had been. He knew that his compatriot's amity was loyal, if acidic. And that was enough for him. An internal friendship—one that strove sadistically to exasperate all ears in hearing with the aim of concealing the pure emotions that had taken root within! Thus, the Captain mimicked Op Oloop, mincing:

"*I have lived and loved, and closed the door.* Huh, huh, huh! You've never loved in your life . . ."

"Well, I'm sure that . . ."

"If you'd loved as one should, you wouldn't now be in the throes of such idiocy and heartache."

"Let me speak," insisted Ivar. "I'm quite sure that Op Oloop was indeed in love with Minna Uusikirkko, the daughter of the literature teacher at the Uleaborg Academy. I was his confidant. He would read me his poems and rant and rave to me. Isn't that so?"

The tobacco tulle enshrouded a smile.

"Precisely."

Now was his chance. Gastón Marietti's voice slipped in, silky smooth:

"I, too, am sure. Op Oloop has been and still is one of the finest connoisseurs of the products those of my profession import. His certificate of expertise must certainly sport many interesting annotations. Is that not so, friend?"

The curtain of smoke shimmered shamelessly.

"Precisely."

"That's not love. Love doesn't pitch its tent in a whorehouse. But I suppose you people don't understand that."

"How ignorant you are, Captain! Love is ubiquitous and pantheistic. It can be found in everything, everywhere. You confuse brothels with urinals. Your criteria mystify me. You're crippled by pharisaical morality, always looking out at others while your own internal censors corrode with filth. Houses of tolerance harbor more love, tenderness, and affection than many 'respectable' homes full of hypocritical licentiousness and secret lasciviousness. The collection of women at a *bagnio* loves infinitely more than those stationed at a missile factory or in a Mercedarian convent. For them, passion—which is generosity—isn't forced to produce the horror of death nor obliged to awaken the horror of life. Rather, it is freed, opened up, an offering to the thirst of men. Open vice is in fact virtue, and a virtue that is sorely lacking in the sanctimonious swines who masturbate in secret. That is all."

"I think you got the wrong end of the stick," Peñaranda remarked. "Trafficking in women will eventually annihilate the species by spreading diseases that lead to biological mutations."

"Not at all. Don't mix your anger and your hangar. More people die as a result of air traffic than amour traffic."

"I would tend to agree. I'm part of a syphilographic study at a syphilis-control dispensary. According to their statistics, syphilis wreaks more havoc in abolitionist countries than in those that have regulated prostitution."

"Bravo, Robín! Your figures electrify me!" Op Oloop interrupted. "They coincide exactly with my own personal thesis. Prostitution is impudicity, not offense. As such, seen as a movement that relaxes the soul, it can be distilled and even converted—by changing the object of erotic inclination—into a force that modifies and controls the sexual apathy growing ever more common in our society. Our management of love is abysmal. The Greeks structured their citizens' sexual lives into three distinct yet parallel categories. They had wives in the *gyneceum*, for procreation; *hetaeras* at their symposia, for spiritual relaxation; and *dicteriades* in the *lupanar*, to delight their instincts. I believe in this triphasic love. Our current attempt to deal with the problem is risible at best. Prostitution, as one of its facets, merits a study of its endogenetic and exogenetic causes, as well as its cultural and social transcendence. The Soviets, by attempting to suppress it, are simply making matters worse. What is to be done? Reeducate cocottes and sanctify them by virtue of maternity! Vaginal derision would thus be redeemed through nativity. I have never seen mothers more concerned about their children's virtuousness than prostitutes."

"Oh, wonderful! Then we can shout, 'The whore that bore you!' and not get our faces smashed in. Fabulous, fantastic! *Hic.*"

The Commissioner of Air Traffic Control was indignant.

"I am stunned, Op Oloop, by your heterodoxy."

"Heterodoxy? It's uterodoxy!"

"For shame!"

"I fail to see why, Erik. Today is a great day for me. Today, of all days, I am commemorating a near millenary experience with regard to love. From August 7, 1924, when I first set foot in America, to today, I have had assiduous, systematic contact—twice a week, on Wednesdays and Sundays—with Aphrodite, the people's Venus—a hooker, if you will. I say 'near millenary' because . . ."

"Get to the point, will you?"

". . . there have been nine hundred ninety-nine . . ."

"What? You can't possibly mean to say that the whole

> *Honorable Ivar: I would be most grateful if you would lend my spirit your services by joining me at the cloth I shall lay tonight, at 9:30 P.M., at the Plaza Grill.*

business was intended to celebrate your nine hundred and ninety-ninth fuck with a whore?"

Silence.

More silence.

"No. To celebrate the thousandth. You see, tonight is my night . . ."

"That's a hell of a motive!"

"Unbelievable!"

"It's a decent and valiant motive. The human condition imposes ineludible obligations which it is necessary to fulfill so as not to fall into psycho-moral trauma. Our endocrinological make-up cannot be fulfilled by dogma or counsel. It demands love. And it must be gratified. It's like an abscess that must be popped in order to cure the ulcers of the soul draining away the body's humors. That's why I've never taken the least notice of Paul the Apostle, who said, '*bonum est homini mulierem non tangere.*' Given a choice between the Jewish convert from Tarsus who brokered Christianity in the Mare Nostrum and any modern sage like Kretschmer, Jung, or Pende, who spread their scientific psalms the world over, I'll stick with the latter. That's why I've chosen to sadden the saint and stroke as many strumpets as possible . . ."

"Nine hundred and ninety-nine! What a stupendous accomplishment!"

"That all depends how you look at it. The accomplishment might reside in overcoming tedium. An unsatisfied libido has a vivacious imagination. It gets channeled into Koranic dreams of promiscuous houris and exhausting intercourse with armies of exquisite succubae. Inversely, when thirst is quenched methodically it suppresses desire. Satiation becomes mechanical. And interrupted. I myself have proven as much. Detailed, circumspect, from the very beginning, my desire was impeded by my numerical vocation. I decided to systematize male love, which is innately forgetful, into a permanent memory. A calamitous catastrophe! I did precisely the opposite of your compatriot Don Juan . . ."

"Don Juan was a Corsican?"

"Yes. Don't trouble yourself. Just read the life of Don Miguel de Mañara."

". . . who seduced and forgot. So my erotic punctuality became an imperative mathematical desire. I possessed women so that I might possess their statistics. I don't know what strange allure I found by assimilating sex and numbers, whereby the displaced pleasure of copulation was recovered in the joy of computation. I won't burden you with all the details of this long voyage through tariffed love.

But suffice it to say that I docked at every port with my bowsprit erect . . ."

"Hurrah! Long live Op Oloop's bowsprit! *Hic!*"

". . . and I set sail again feeling withdrawn."

"That's all masculine love is, anyway. You withdraw after the orgasm and then become withdrawn in the unction of your own nostalgia . . ."

"Magnificent, Robín! Alcohol obviously hones your phraseology . . . So I kept an extravagant log of my affections—in which volume the truth of my exploits is both poetic and licentious. It is the only thing of beauty I have produced in my entire career. I have it here. Go ahead, read it."

"You read it."

"I'd be delighted. The first entry coincides with my arrival in America: August 7, 1924. I won't bother reading the column headings."

> BIRDIE, 17 years old. Blonde, *cheveux de lin*. Chorus girl from Ziegfeld. Unbelievable tits! My hands are still cupped.
>
> SOLANGE, 38. Brunette. French. Thin. Four sisters, all prostitutes. *Chiqueteuse*. Fifteen dollars!
>
> MERKEL, 26. Lithuanian. Almost albino. Scar from a caesarian. Pudgy. Foul-smelling perspiration. Repulsive.
>
> DOLORES, 15. Andalusian. Olive-skinned. The beauty of a Murillo, with a dark background . . . worthy of a Valdés Leal.
>
> MARITZA, 42. Viennese. Gray-haired. Friend of Strauss, "*An der schönen blauen Donau*." Seven abortions. And the waltz played on . . .
>
> FAY, 18. Japanese father and Mexican mother. Silky black hair, parted in the middle. Bronze bibelot. Cuddles and cruelty.

KLYMENE, 31. Greek. Titian blonde. Skinny as a rail. In the game for nineteen years. Wit and coitus both adroit.

SHEILAH, 22. Moroccan from the Oran Kasbah. Copper-colored. Sandy skin. Coy. Self-centered.

TANKA, 14. Indian from Cuzco. Sallow. Impenetrable. Sharp, distrustful look, like the sun streaming through a crack.

GWILY, 29. Yank. Celtic blonde. Ex-secretary of the Legation in Quito. Alkaloids. Certain papers . . .

COMUMBA, 16. Honduran. Black. Tropical shell. Serpentine spasms. Fetid.

DENDERAH, 25. Egyptian. Long hair like Nefertiti. Kohl and exophthalmia. Shaved cunt.

LUDMILA, 38. Russian. Brown. Ballerina from Nijinsky's troupe. Enormous ass. Hips swung like gondolas.

BEBA, 23. Argentine mestiza. Shiny hair. *Bois de rose* complexion. Very smug, but phenomenal!

"*Basta, basta*! Your 'statistics' are sickening."

"It's true, Op Oloop. Enough."

Sullen, diabolical, nodding at the submarine Captain and the Commissioner of Air Traffic Control, the host stopped reading.

"Forgive me. I can understand your outrage. After all, these things are so far beneath *you*, and so far above *you*. From the clouds, love must seem like something immaterial, since altitude makes everything look small and insignificant. And from the depths of the sea, it must be monstrous, since all that water deforms the images shining down. Please accept my apologies. But since the rest of us are right here on street level, allow me a few words of elucidation. My ledger is a work of experience, not of pleasure. It is not a *guide rose* for procurers nor a chivalrous manual for young Turks. The thousand harlots whom I have physically and erotically certified have supplied me with the material necessary for innumerable analyses and deductions. With this data I could give you a rundown on the most prostituted races, regions, and nations on the planet, in the blink of an eye. I could give you indices on the age of defloration, length of time in the profession, and stages of disillusionment reached by its victims. I could give you statistics on the hygienic and correlative ethical-social issues involved; or the percentages of known motivating factors: poverty, salary, desire for luxury, lack of role models, lethargy, etc; a synoptic chart of biological factors: defects, heredity, deterioration; the average earnings of madams, pimps, and whores; the differences between 'the road to Buenos Aires' and 'the road to Shanghai'; the international standards of living for hookers; even the way the market influences girls' choice of names and nicknames."

"Christ, *che*, you're amazing!"

"Truly extraordinary!"

"Didn't I tell you he could give us indices on the universal exchange of crab lice?"

The Head of Sanitation had stopped hiccoughing.

"Well, could you give me the numbers of Lulus, Margots, and Toscas to be found in Argentine bordellos? I've never been to a single one that didn't have several of them."

Op Oloop began to rummage through his files. He positively radiated pleasure. His passion for the task produced an immediate and effervescent euphoria that freed him of all preoccupation. His sublime contemplation had reached zenithal heights. It was easy to see his old addiction to records once more—that method was the critical counselor of his consciousness. All else disappeared for him in these moments. Even the love that plagued the innermost depths of his self!

His joy irked Erik and Ivar. They bent their heads together in confidence. And they began a furtive, hurtful whispering campaign in which sarcasm, hand gestures, and evil looks all flew back and forth. The Maquereau, sensing that he was being disparaged, resolved to slip back into the conversation. And, without diminishing his dignity with any inappropriate behavior, he spoke.

"My dear Op Oloop, your compatriots' interest appears to be waning. I felt I should warn you about this, as they might get up and walk out while you're still delving into your data."

This barb stung them to the core and roused new imprecations.

"Stop meddling and mind your own business!"

"There's no reason to misrepresent our intentions."

"I neither meddle nor misrepresent. I simply affirm."

"You affirm what? Come on, tell us!"

This short squabble stymied the Statistician. He surrendered both the inherent satisfaction of Slatter's question and the no-less-satisfying scientific satisfaction of showing off how well suited he was to answer it. So, forsaking himself to himself, arms dangling, he fell back into his chair. His face distorted, he seemed to be submitting to the Captain's intransigence.

"Come on, tell us!"

Gastón, unnerved, didn't say a word.

There came that calm that precedes certain phenomena, both meteorological and spiritual. That disorientation that clears the air of birds and the soul of ephemeral ideas. That paralysis that stores the perversity of man in the atelier of his impulses, and his nature in a corner of the sky.

The Maquereau, not looking up, instead looking inside himself, felt both the warm glances of good will and the fingernails of ill will burning his cheeks. He wanted to shout, to release his feral fury, give free rein to the rage that he was stifling; but he did not. He still possessed the fortitude to surmount this desire and defer to his phlegmatic side. His secret war rampaged through him. He sniffed. He snorted. And then he bared his soul, breathlessly.

"Allow me to lie upon the beach like a shipwrecked man. I've just been tossed about in a terrible squall. If, gentlemen, you'd known the turbulence of the internal sea on which I tried my luck—as heretics often do—you'd have made the sign of the cross in fear. As for myself, well, you can see for yourselves. I was born in Corsica, the island home of two of the world's greatest volcanoes: Napoleon and, apparently, Don Juan. That should give you an idea of my burning, smoldering passion. Because it does burn, gentlemen—I'm talking to you two—it burns as insatiably, as voraciously as theirs did. Please don't brag and say that you silenced me with your invective. It's in my interest to be quiet. I'm the only one who can repress and defeat myself. And therein lies my triumph. If I couldn't temper my passion and force it below the surface—the way you do with your submarine so as to launch torpedoes at close range—my career would be a complete failure. My success lies in having tamed the flames of passion so that they burn others, not me, as when you train a dog to attack others for your own safety. We maquereaux of noble lineage possess perfect strategies of self-control. What would I have gained by admonishing your disloyalty to Op Oloop and your unmannered behavior towards me? Nothing. The preposterousness of a campfire in the mid-summer heat. But now, on the other hand, you've grown attentive—and in doing so, you damage only yourselves."

"What are you talking about?"

Silence.

"I never put the cart before the horse. Just as gangsters and smugglers struggled to keep the Volstead Act intact because they earned their living during the 'dry' season, we maquereaux of noble lineage . . ."

"There is no such thing as a maquereau of noble lineage!"

". . . are happy to endure the derision of contemporary society. We know that in a state of perfect moral and economic harmony there would be no traffickers, no pimps. We, therefore, would be forced to suffer the effrontery of obtaining other employment. The mere idea instills terror amongst our ranks. It trains us to be astutely conformist. It obliges us to be cautiously correct. And it induces us to support politicians and other authorities, thanks to which our business thrives and prospers. There's no such thing as a radical maquereau—there's no such thing as a volatile maquereau. My orthodoxy takes great pleasure in manifesting these beliefs, albeit in muted fashion, to truly educated people who are able to exclude obvious truths from their evident cynicism. I have, however, been known to be wrong. Especially when those people lack the necessary insight, and confuse understanding with prejudice. Here, for instance. These gentlemen deem my presence pernicious to Op Oloop's spirit and even assume, most disgracefully, that I have somehow contaminated his soul."

"No one said that!"

"Why, you're just making that up!"

"I don't need the evidence of your words—it hardly matters whether you actually said it. I've borne the weight of your assumptions, and that's enough. Some judgments are so bloated that they seep into the eyes—I've seen yours, engorged with shock, with false modesty. While you've been whispering away, the exertion of transmitting your ideas made you clench your teeth like women in labor. And as you let your insults fly, you flailed and then failed to recover your balance. I wasn't born yesterday, gentlemen. If my company offends you, do me the favor of taking your leave. I myself am quite comfortable with my eccentricity."

"As am I."

"Captain, you didn't want coffee anyway, did you?"

"Fucking hell, would you all shut up! I don't give a monkey's ass about this so-called gentleman, or his sermon. We'd already agreed to leave, but now, to spite him, we'll have the satisfaction of staying."

Op Oloop bounded up euphorically from his lassitude.

"At last, Erik, at last! That shameless sentence vindicates you! Utter nakedness, whether elegant or repulsive, is what we want! Ideological nudism! I said earlier that we were seven variations on a cynical, central theme. And now this has been proven. You were determined to disguise yourself, to be what you seem and not what you are. But on casting off that guise, you old killjoy, you've shown the genuineness in you that the daily grind can never castrate!"

"Huh. If we always said what we thought . . ."

"It's worse to think and not say—it infects and corrodes the spirit."

"I understand that. But really, I'm so venomous that I have to uphold the purest principles in order not to contaminate others . . ."

"And right you are to do so—but not here. To those of us who watch life from behind the scenes, the naiveté of fools is repulsive. You've been acting quite contrary to your true nature. It was all for show: confess it now."

"Well . . . all right, I confess . . . you're right."

"You don't know how relieved I am to hear it. You've just risen in my estimation. I knew that you were a timid, I mean, dangerous fellow, clear sighted, someone who always protects himself. But now you've let your guard down. We timid people carry our melancholy with us like a portable phonograph . . . but when we hear it playing inside another man's friendship, the song sounds crude, harsh. You'll have time yet to play your records for us. But first, you should learn your lesson. Gastón was just advocating the convenience of not dissenting to anything so as to take advantage of everything."

"Indeed. I never dissent. And if you two wish to please me presently, please persist with your displeasing presence."

The felicitous turn of phrase caused resounding hilarity.

While the guests' faces were all smiles, Ivar Kittilä shook the Maquereau's hand.

"*Pardon-moi*. I take back what I thought."

"And I, what I said."

"*E viva! Tutti siami amici.*"

The host clapped his hands violently several times.

The maitre came running and stood at attention.

"Why have the champagne glasses not been refilled?"

"*Vite, vite: Cordon Rouge Monopole!*"

"I beg you, my friends, to overlook the flaws of this evening's dinner. Those who have honored me at other soirées know how I strive to ensure that the menu and wine selection are faultless."

"It's true," the Student corroborated. "I've already been present, by my calculation, at the earlier commemorations of Op Oloop's having reached seven hundred, eight hundred, and nine hundred fucks, respectively. And the food was better without so many snobby sauces and other ostentatious special effects. Really now: rose petals in our cocktails? Soon they'll be bringing us host wafers in Chantilly cream, butterfly wing steaks, and lily compote."

"You see, this is what I mean!"

"Don't worry. I, too, have hosted banquets. And I can vouch for the Jesuit expression, 'A friend is someone who eats like a horse and cleans like a pig.'"

"Erik!"

"Bravo, Erik!"

Gastón Marietti held his hand out ceremoniously to the Captain.

"My hearty congratulations. There are those who have sagging bellies. Robín appears to have a sagging heart. I commend you for having made his shame sag as well!"

"Very amusing. But wait till the wind gets knocked out of *your* sails," Robín threatened, jokingly.

Op Oloop stood. His gangly physique took on a wary, frenzied look. Alcohol had opened his guests' ears, and they all waited anxiously for the balsam of the Statistician's discourse. He lifted his overflowing cup and spoke solemnly:

"To your health."

And he downed it in one.

Everyone's expectancy was colored with pity. This untimely display of gravity, just when lightheartedness had begun to take hold once more, turned their eagerness into resentment. Having at first been prepared to listen, they now struggled to respond.

Robín Sureda, as audacious as ever, was unanimously chosen as their spokesman. And he used their earlier insults as a jumping-off point:

"Gentlemen, I know perfectly well that friends, like cigarette lighters, tend to fail just when you need them most. Why, my own uselessness is notorious. Unless it's for a bash or a brawl! Then I'm quite capable. I've helped squander the fortunes of several gentlemen now living on the streets with no capital—unless you count Buenos Aires—and no gold—unless you count their fillings. I only occasionally show up to my exams, but never miss a workers' strike or university party. I can box, so I like to piss people off. See, if it weren't for my jibes, I'd never use my jabs. So the touching thing about my friendship with Op Oloop is the mutual indifference that unites us. I don't care about statistics, and he has no interest in who I punch. That being said, what I wouldn't give tonight to be able to reach out and touch his heart, saying, 'I offer you my solidarity, both in tough times and joyous ones!' I can't explain the strange forces that oppress him or set him free, what hidden spirits lead him to make either sublime proclamations or idiotic ones. I'm a tough nut to crack, I've got a hard shell, but inside I'm sensitive. Forgive the fanfare. I've seen how troubled he is and it pains me not to be able to share his pain. So I propose a toast, before we retire, to clean the stain of his sorrow."

"Fine. Now let Peñaranda say something."

"No, no. A few words each, and it's only fitting that a compatriot go next."

Op Oloop's eyebrows—two wings soaring across his forehead—knotted up in a frown. The resultant mass of wrinkles made him squint, and he looked so austere as to be nearly cross-eyed. In fact, more than looking, he seemed to be spying.

Such fragile pleasures! The feast had been so full of temperamental fluctuations and sudden fits of ferocity. Op Oloop tried to orient himself, searching cautiously for a way out. Such fragile pleasures!

Erik elbowed Ivar, and the host's ex-classmate stood.

"If I were Chaplin perhaps I could do a decent job miming the sentiments required by the present circumstance, since I worry words alone won't do: Op Oloop is one of those people not often described in human nomenclature. A profoundly tragic figure, describing him requires some new, bizarre terminology—and this peculiar jargon would be the only language that could come even remotely near to making any sense of his austerity, via sarcasm. Ever since he was a child he was always different—he was delicate, silent, tender: highly estimable qualities, qualities of true men. To we other, grubby children, spending all our time playing, so much deliberation seemed unreal. Children find children who act like adults comical, just as adults find adults who behave like children risible. We were hurt by his behavior—which has now been inverted. We made fun of him, played endless tricks on him. But he survived! Time has shown me that he hasn't changed, in essence. He simply has a different focus now. The man-child was convex; the child-man is concave. In the former, everything flowed outward—now it all flows inward. If the human soul were a sound booth and one could verify the phonic register of passion, the auditory range of instinct, the sound waves broadcast by our consciousness, I could come up with the coefficients and statistics required for a technical solution to the anxiety that afflicts you, Op Oloop. But that's impossible—science has yet to reach such heights. You'll have to suffer through it. Your isolation has been shattered. Your soul is cracked. And we can hear wild animals howling through the fissures—their cries polluting your mental atmosphere and shouting down the song of your melodic heart."

Words were absorbed, ideas circulated.

"Enough! Enough dissection!" Op Oloop clamored. "You're all alarmed for no reason at all. You overreact. I'm not a boat adrift in the sea. I can still govern myself!"

"No, Op Oloop. Your government is toppling. You'll never again enjoy the bourgeois peace you once did. A radical is on the loose. A radical, calling for revolution and plotting a coup. A radical: love!"

"Enough about love! Love, for me, is order, computation, records, numbers."

"Yes, up to one thousand. But once you get to one thousand one . . . when you get to Franzi . . ."

"No, No, NO!"

Op Oloop's vehemence progressively increased the circumference of his mouth and the volume of his voice. A torrential flow of bile was being released, requiring him to open his oral orifice as wide as possible to discharge it.

"No, no, no," he repeated, now calmly and evenly. "How wrong you are, my friend. Those first thousand were units of flesh. This is a union of the soul."

He was pale, perspiring.

"Forgive me. I didn't know."

"Well, then I'll tell you. Franziska: twenty-two years old, baby-face, five languages, smooth skin, expert in consular finance, mother dead, father Quintín Hoerée, arms like the flesh of pears: the only woman on the face of the earth!"

"What? The daughter of Quintín Hoerée, the plywood importer? You fell in love with *her*?"

"We're engaged to be married."

"En-*gaged*-to-be-*mar*-ried? But you're twice her age and twice her height!"

"That may very well be. But she's the only woman in my world who's ever been unattainable. Once I possess her, I'll possess the key, the secret to an eternal algebra . . ."

His misery, until that moment soft and languorous, suddenly hardened. His feverish eyes glared aggressively.

Everyone opted to remain silent. In such circumstances, even the slightest digression would have been tactless. Just as spectators at a circus hold their breath at the most climactic moment, their silence sustaining the acrobat in mid-air, Op Oloop was thus suspended by six strands of silence.

Though not for long.

A stronger impulse pulled him down. And when he hit the ground, he shattered into a discursive, malicious rage.

"There's nothing objectionable about it. Contempt only serves its own contemptibility. But it's a false, empty gesture, like that of the Gallic dandy who challenged a rogue to a duel for having insulted the Virgin, not out of religiosity but out of gentility—since the virgin is a woman and therefore weak . . . *(Challenging look all round.)* So, Franziska, *me voici.* Ridiculousness and somberness have united in the suspicion that you're simply another statistic, that you've already joyfully partaken of my most intimate and passionate performances, that you've trampled the ethics of cohabitation, brandishing the secular insignias of ardor and impudence. *(Sidelong glance at Peñaranda.)* Although you tasted Rousseau's *Confessions* as tentatively as plastic fruit, I know that if you were here you'd devour this diatribe with real relish, like a bonbon. You, more than anyone, know the profound satisfaction of picking up on others' idiocy. That delightful inanity that puts on airs to hide its lack of perspicacity, seeking to bury its shame under sermons of hate. *(Spiteful sneer at Erik.)* People here, Franzi, are always condescending to Don Juan's stratum. They praise and extol him hollowly. They belong in his lowly spiritual community. That's why, in the secret boudoir of their minds, amid anguish and impotence, they replicate the depraved path of his lewd sensuality. *(Nausea aimed at Sureda.)* They don't know that working backwards from his particular fate, I've organized a new aesthetics of love, vastly different from the instinctual mechanics that gentleman exhibited. People don't realize that the 'Tenorio Theory' comprises an equation that simple psychiatry can resolve. They don't see that Don Juan was a rabbit of a man, baleful and sickly, who never really loved *(Sarcastic allusion to Cipriano.)* We thirsty men who can never quench our desire will always have nostalgia to liven up the monotony of our twilight years. But those who sipped from the chalice and then urinated into it, those who drank without first being parched, they won't see a woman's arms holding a heart aloft on Charon's ferry to console them when they cross over. *(Harsh criticism of Ivar Kittilä.)* Like a modest faun, I'll live in the memory of the roses I once picked. A devotee of Ronsard, the prince of poets, I sat in every garden to compile the *grand de luxe* catalogue of love. My insides embalmed with numbers, I take rapturous delight in carnal metaphors, just as perfume in a bottle can be enjoyed as a metaphorical flowerbed. *(Gesture of ill will to Gastón.)* Hedonists, crude shepherds of the flock of pleasure, will never understand me. Though Casanova and I are the same height, I was never so low. They'd place me with the filthy Aretino, scourge of princes, on the same shelf as Ovid and Martial. But I perfect my persuasive proficiency to stimulate the spirit and not the mucous membranes. Even if that sublime and yet wasted effort leaves me spent!" *(Final look of pity cast on all.)*

He was still pale and perspiring.

His plunge into introspection had drawn the tendons and the blood in his face downward, thinning it out. This matte-finish oval showed the *V* of his furrowed brow, the inverted *T* of his nose, and the prominent, wide *U* of his chin. Above this abbreviated alphabetical series, his hair had fluffed into a feverish crest of chestnut-colored curls.

The guests took advantage of his temporary absence by peeking—like nosy neighbors spying over the garden wall—behind his closed doors and into otherwise inaccessible regions. They could make nothing out. A thick fog enshrouded Op Oloop. One guest held an index finger to his lips, signaling silence. There followed pitying glances, the nodding of heads, and a tacit consensus to allow the animosity of his onslaught go unremarked upon.

Only the Commissioner of Air Traffic Control condemned this approach.

"I have no reason to keep quiet. I didn't insult him—far from it. Why, I was defending him. I won't tolerate this effrontery. It's vilipendatious!"

The Maquereau sensed a mix of dignity and alcoholic obstinacy in the Comissioner's resentment and made up his mind to intervene.

"Psst! Have a bit of patience. When an introvert leaves the light of his cell, the world looks so somber that he sees traps set for him everywhere. The most casual allusions—like yours, Peñaranda—although entirely devoid of malice, take on totally disproportionate significance. Accustomed to measuring logical microns, when such personalities fly the coop, their standard susceptibility becomes morose, since the models they carry for measuring inner and exterior life are entirely out of balance with the rest of the world's. Delirium is just a corollary. Because delirium is always just that: the adoption of a personal truth—or falsehood—that flies in the face of the established truth—or falsehood—accepted by the general public."

"All right. But it's still vilipendatious!"

". . . I confess I've often heard paranoiacs express such perfectly sensible ideas that we might want to consider that the possibility that Op Oloop's anomaly, which happened to be focused on us, was simply one of sustaining pure ideas in so debased an atmosphere that their very properness caused us to reject them. To recapitulate, his diatribe might seem despicable to us only because we've lost all sense of sensibleness, since we've grown used to using spurious appearances as our guide. So, not a word!"

"Whatever you say. But it's still vilipendatious!"

The word swung back and forth like a pendulum in Peñaranda's brain.

Over the course of the banquet, the guests had changed positions without changing places. Such movements often occur without one's knowing. The hinge on which our senses swing, the hinge that sets the mind in motion, eludes the vigilant id. Most of the diners were now presenting other faces to one another than those they'd begun the meal with, and displaying differing degrees of urbanity. Erik was now sweet and Peñaranda, bitter. Only the Maquereau remained stable. Though lightly tinged by ire, he was as tranquil and serene as ever.

Such circumstances expand and warp the airspace that our bodies occupy. And when a crazed astral body is flung from its foundation, it rattles ectoplasmically within the once-perfect shell of its body. It doesn't take a particularly lucid clairvoyant to see that the soul is the body's internal suit of clothes. A suit subject to the intellectual fashions and temperamental climes we unwittingly exhibit. A suit that becomes threadbare, gets mended, and even disintegrates. A suit that silences our affectations and tolerates our misery, as required by the four seasons: love, hate, disdain, complacence.

The Commissioner of Air Traffic Control was tattered and trembling. He was feeling the chill of his peers' reproach. And he insisted once more, icily:

"I won't accept that! It's vilipendatious!"

Op Oloop, who in just a few hours had dressed and undressed himself many times, dragging out the vast contents of his psychological armoire, now found himself nude, in the solitude of introspection. Finally, the commissioner's neologism reverberated therein. And, once the barrier was broken, Op Oloop threw on an old robe to attend to the goings on outside. He opened one eye first. Then, using his hand, he smoothed the wrinkles from his forehead. Once he was haloed in serenity, the two wings that were his eyebrows glided across his forehead once more. Caution steadied his posture. And he spoke.

"*Vilipendatious* . . . Have you stopped to consider the beauty of the word? Vi-li-pen-da-tious. Who said it? So euphonic, so tonic! So glorious a word, one could almost be tempted to vilipend!"

Peñaranda bit his lip. Brusque and highly strung, he flushed a crimson wave of shame. He then put on an expression of compassionate fury, swallowing the torrent of abuse he'd been prepared to unleash.

Gastón Marietti quietly applauded his self-restraint.

"Well done, my friend. Holding back your spitefulness helps Op Oloop liberate his soul. Look at him. It's simply sublime. You try to insult him and he turns it around so innocently. Only someone in the throes of delirium, tormented by the wreckage of civilization and bonhomie, could manage such a feat."

In the interim, the Statistician had taken out a fountain pen. Stricken by a graphical mania, he began to sketch a series of charts and formulas, delighting secretively in their esoteric meaning.

"Vilipendatious! What an extraordinary word. It could come in very handy indeed. Crossword puzzles, logogriphs, extraordinarily difficult numerical cribs! To whom did it occur to use it?"

"To me," ventured the man in question, apprehensively.

"My hearty congratulations, old friend! You know, just as there are master sommeliers, there are also master wordsmiths. The word is a divine emanation: a *sephira*. You clearly have a handle on such things. I knew I said you were terribly well educated for a reason. To come out with something of such spiritual substance as *vilipendatious*!"

Standing noisily, someone collided with Op Oloop's enthusiasm: Robín.

"Pardon me for a moment," requested another guest almost instantly: Erik.

The host, frowning as he watched them walk off, suddenly felt the sharp stabbing discomfort of something ominous looming ahead. He jumped up so brusquely as to alarm the others. And taking great strides, he lumbered off after the pair.

The maitre bowed as he passed. Op Oloop registered the man's deference, though he didn't go so far as to recognize the man himself.

Once through the door he turned and shouted, "Bring the bill."

The others quickly huddled together to examine Op Oloop's graphics.

"What an exceptional human being! He both recalls and forgets everything!"

"Indeed. Especially forgets. Everything in him tends towards oblivion. That's why he remembers so much!"

Ivar, moved, nodded along with the Maquereau's summation.

"He's always been that way. At school we called him the Cyclops because he was so big and tall. He hasn't changed a bit. He still has that same poise without being impertinent, still the same melancholy wisdom. And yet tonight . . ."

"Yes. Tonight he's absent . . ."

"Perhaps he . . ."

Silence.

No one dared to say it. There was something noble about their wordlessness. Each man opted to smolder in silence and purify himself with pain rather than express the fears sequestrating his spirits.

When the others returned, their expressions remained as grave as the guests' suspicions. They feigned otherwise, glancing casually at the papers on the table.

"Do you see?"

"Not at all."

"If they were blueprints for sanitation works . . ."

"Well, gentlemen: vilipendatious! Peñaranda's word, concealed by enigmas and spectralized by numerals . . ."

The maitre had slipped the bill onto a silver tray and deposited it beside the returned Op Oloop.

The string of figures seduced him insuperably.

He instinctively summed any sequence of addenda the same way that country bumpkins can't help but count the number of stories on a skyscraper. Once he'd verified the accuracy of the maitre's addition, he realized that the slip of paper was indeed the bill. Consequently he went over it once more, item by item. Once it had been certified, he stared off into space, recollecting the dinner.

He was unable to relinquish control. It was a constant obsession. Without raising his eyes, he reviewed their consumption, compared brands, consented to the prices. More than anything, professional zeal was what urged him on. On straightening up and seeing the maitre standing beside him, he smirked at him as though he were an infuriating inferior.

"Fine. It's all fine: two hundred ninety-eight fifty."

He was beaming.

Had he been poor, eating above his station—one of those who affect the haughty indolence of millionaires in such circumstances—he would simply have paid up without a word; men like that are such cretins that they let themselves be robbed, all the while awaiting restitution.

Op Oloop, on the other hand, was generous but strict.

He withdrew his wallet and his pen. He calculated a ten percent tip and deposited three hundreds, two tens, a five, and three ones onto the tray.

Then came a somewhat sobering faux pas. Seeing that Op Oloop was putting away his billfold and his pen, the maitre took the tray.

"Wait!" the Statistician cried, more distressed than authoritarian. "It's not all there yet."

And he pulled out his coin purse.

He had only thirty cents. Which he added to the tray. And then he extracted a small notebook from the inside pocket of his jacket. He rummaged diligently therein. And finally, joyfully, he placed a little red five-cent stamp atop the three hundred-peso bills.

"Now you may take it," he announced. "The tip is included."

By this point no one was surprised. The guests, chatting among themselves, surveyed the scene with cool detachment. What was one more eccentricity, when things had already gone so far?

But Op Oloop's composure was further shattered by his guests' overall half-heartedness. Ivar yawned. Slatter cracked his knuckles. The Statistician was annoyed. The harmony of the table—so carefully orchestrated in a concert of words and manners—had, to his mind, been ruined. It was as if a Jean Antoine Watteau canvas had come to life, only for its subjects to adopt plebeian poses. And so, in a show of sophistication, Op Oloop sidelined his censure and spoke sparingly instead.

2:50 A.M. "My dear friends, it is now ten to three. The time has come for us to take our leave. I will always cherish tonight's dinner and hold it high in my esteem, along with other proceedings of great pomp and passion that have ennobled my affections. Thank you. Thank you all."

And he stood with somber sophistication.

Everyone followed him and no one said a word.

While they were all collecting their coats, affinity united Erik and Ivar, Slatter and Peñaranda, the Student and the Maquereau. Standing alone, tugging on his gloves with gentlemanly severity, the Statistician watched his shadow sway.

They departed. The stillness of the night was bliss. The Parque de Retiro's moonlit ramps were so inviting, gleaming like silver-plated sleds. The river breeze made the grass shiver and sifted the sparrows' sleep from the trees.

"Let's go for a walk," Gastón suggested.

"We've got to be going. It's late. I have to be on the Fonofilm set at seven. Great party, though."

"Good night, gentlemen. By the way, I need to speak to you about personal matters: I shall come by to see you on Wednesday."

"Why not sooner?"

"Perhaps . . ."

Turning the corner, they headed towards Recova. They'd already made their arrangements. They'd head down to the Scandinavian bars and *boîtes*, where smoked herring, old gin, and salted butter inspire Nordic merrymaking . . . where songs of fjords and forests blend seamlessly with the buttocks of obese barmaids from Oslo and porcelain hetaeras from the Royal House of Denmark.

Immersed in insouciance, Op Oloop watched them wander off.

"What jerk-offs. If that's what they call friendship, then my ass is a geranium," Robín announced, affronted.

Happily, that absurd good-bye was more than made up for by the next.

The Head of Sanitation and the Commissioner of Air Traffic Control shook their friend from his marasmus. And their effusion made him smile a smile that shook under the force of their bear hugs. It was a smile illuminated by four pupils, two of which were tearful.

On hugging him for the last time, Peñaranda said, "Thank you. Everything was superb. I just hope my wife doesn't yell at me!"

And he scurried off reluctantly.

This incidental mention of conjugality made the subject swiftly ascend the pecking order of Op Oloop's sensibilities. When celibacy grows tiresome, the soul longs for the serenity of a nuptial scene. He'd always dreamed of it. And just when he thought he had it within reach, bam!—disaster. He knew that the untainted love of a spouse was the sun and the air that he so required. Bathed in her presence, immersed in her effluvia, his spirit would have formed calm, deep pools—free of Freudian frippery—and shone like a new constellation.

Immersed in insouciance, he grew misty-eyed.

"It's obvious. I'll never get to enjoy the slippereal pleasures of domestic bliss. Wife and pipe! Tenderness and science! Great Dane and '*la vie parisienne*!'"

"Bah, forget that stuff!" the Student said, trying to cheer him up. "There's no reason to think about that nonsense. You have too many obsessions, no wonder you're so upset. Just say to hell with all that shit! Can't you see it's pointless?"

"Oh, if only!"

Then something strange happened. Still phlebitic, he experienced a sudden and crushing return of determination.

"Yes! You're right! I can see it! I want to say it! I will! To hell with all that shit! I'll be freer than free. Purer than pure! Truer than true!"

"That's the spirit!"

They had drifted, in their silence. They were now walking along a raised platform dotted with flowerbeds, overlooking the hollow, the illuminated gardens, the plaza, and Puerto Nuevo.

The cyclopean eye on the English Tower winked loudly.

3:15 A.M. Three fifteen. He was the Cyclops. But his view was hazy now, as he attempted to re-bolt his inner doors and enjoy life by escaping from himself. He paid no attention to the time. When he returned to his friends, his vision was soaked in joyous delectation. The stillness of the night was bliss, because night is sensual and feminine and belongs to women, while day is male and it is man who must toil through it. And the star-studded indigo sky rhymed with the blue of Op Oloop's spleen, streaked with lecherous filth.

Sporting a deliberately roguish smile, he pulled Gastón aside.

"What's new?"

The Maquereau attempted to change the subject. He knew what Op Oloop was getting at. He tried to dissuade him, in homage to the emotions that had been expressed earlier that day.

"No, no, Gastón," Op Oloop impugned. "No subterfuge. Be loyal. What's new? Where? Quick!"

Hot blood infused his demands with a braying agitation.

Gastón amended his response.

"Calm yourself, my friend. I suggest you calm yourself. Your nervous system is all out of kilter. What do you want with more excitement?"

"Calm. Yes, calm! Someone spoke of the dormitive virtue of coitus. That's what I need. Sleep, SLEEP, SLEEP."

"All right. If you insist. My agents informed me that we got a few in yesterday: three São Paolans via Salto, four Uruguayans from Paysandú, two French ticklers via Cologne and Tigre, and, straight from Southampton, a Swede . . ."

"A Swede! A Swede? Where, Gastón, where?"

"Over on Santa Fe, a block and a half from Callao. You know the place."

It was a rash, adolescent departure. The spiritual chains and the padlocks of Op Oloop's will lay ineffectually at his feet. He ran to the Student. Before hugging him, he slapped him on his stevedore's back and pinched his swarthy cheeks. Then, with a tad more restraint, he bade farewell to the Maquereau. A disjointed farewell, with abrupt gestures and truncated words, like a man about to miss his boat. And he ran off. The ground was flat, but his anxiousness caused him to lean as if over a gangway. There was a taxi approaching. He climbed in, wheezing exhaustedly, and let himself be carried away. He waved repeatedly from the window as though it were a cabin porthole. The car sailed swiftly round Plaza San Martín. When it could no longer be seen, both companions felt as if a captainless boat were drifting away, into the rough seas of love.

But they were still not disengaged.

In his retinas, Op Oloop had the images of Gastón and Robín in bas relief, like a couple of cameos. And they, baffled, still held his image pressed against their chests: a negative of his face.

They continued conversing, telepathically.

Out of the entire cast of friends, the Student—impudent master of insults—and the Maquereau—ever-poised pessimist—represented the two opposite poles of Op Oloop's own outlook, an outlook that he—melancholy Cyclops—magnified by the formidable alchemic lens of his learning. To them, the Statistician was the *summum* of analytical ability, the genius that linked antinomies, the numina that could find water in the desert.

They kept conversing.

When the automobile screeched to a halt before the designated door, they, in the park, sighed a final farewell. Their conversation ceased. And just at the precise moment when Op Oloop—now disconnected—was ascending the stairs to the apartment, Sureda and Marietti—severed from his presence—were descending the worn ramps.

3:30 A.M. It was three thirty.

Impatient yet dignified, Op Oloop rapped on the door with his knuckles. When it didn't open immediately, he knocked again. There was something complicit, something forbidden about his insistence that made him hold his breath. But something, too, that made him feel romantic. When he heard footsteps approach in the semi-darkness and then saw the ray of light stream out from the door and onto his chest, he was overcome with elation. He spoke his name through the crack. As he waited to be let in, he composed himself. And once the way was cleared for his entry, the hallway filled with his frame and with the warm smile of the *madame* who'd come to receive him.

"You? At this hour?"

"Yes! What's the matter with that?"

She didn't respond. Instead she made a face he couldn't interpret and, in a sickly sweet voice, asked him in.

These days, that was all Madame Blondel did: smile at new arrivals and show them to the main hall. That, and request a tip for the maid, of course. She was working the door, in the final stages of a long career, spending her spare time dreaming innocently of a little house on the Breton beach of her childhood. Meanwhile, all her memories clotted together in her heart like so many aneurisms; all her tears lay buried beneath her desperate *maquillage*; and all the jewels given to her by her "sweethearts" were pinned to her black taffeta dress, suitably buttoned up to the neck. Her jowls were flaccid and her breasts sagged idly. Flesh doesn't lie. She was still attentive and kind, but with a certain maternal acrimony, though she had never been a mother. Perhaps it was the invincible yearning for motherhood.

A client was just leaving.

Since Op Oloop knew the relevant routines and reverences, he intercepted the *madame*. And he asked his question, almost overbearingly, in French:

"*Madame Blondel, où est la suédoise?*"

"*Maintenant elle est occupée.*"

An expression of absolute, authentic exasperation was emblazoned across his face. Ever since the Maquereau had given him the data, the image of the Swede had come to life in his mind like a little Galatea. So he pictured her at will, placing her in his preferred positions, and giving her the voice, face, and manners of people who— either out of excessive self-regard or excessive imagination—ended up quite resembling himself. This eclipsing of his own reality irritated him exceedingly. He gritted his teeth. He grumbled. Though he'd never laid eyes on her, he considered her an adulteress for having ruined his fantasy. He couldn't accept that she, so present in his spirit, might disappoint him just when his senses were about to certify her existence . . .

The *madame*, having concluded her bows and curtsies, returned and sat down beside him.

"How about we have a little whisky, Op Oloop?"

"Have what you like. I'll pay."

Her greed won out over her pride. She wrote off his sharp tone. And, calculating the greatest possible gain, she called over the maid.

"Ramona, two Canadian Clubs with tonic."

When she turned back to face him, she found herself unable to meet his eyes. The Statistician's face intimidated her. He'd again adopted the stance of his ancestors when they were going through tough times. The stance of Soren Oloop in the Van Ostade painting. The stance of defense, of buttressing, the one that closes off each entry and affirms the supremacy of silence. Perched stiffly on the edge of the divan, he thrust his left elbow down onto the armrest. Wedged his cupped hand under the tip of his chin. Stretched his index finger the length of his nose, so as to be pointing at his baleful eyes. Barred—with the triple lock of his remaining fingers—the embrasure of his mouth. And placed his thumb beneath his jaw as if he were withholding terrible secrets. He remained thus for quite some time. Immobile.

He was such a compact block of silence that the *madame* sagely ended up ignoring him. On her long odyssey of brothels and bordellos she'd seen men of every ilk: indifferent and ardent, unfathomable and unrestrained. There was no sense in getting upset over the mysterious behavior of one more man. She poured the whisky.

Holding a glass out to him, she said, "Drink. You'll see the Swede soon enough."

"The Swwww-ede!"

Op Oloop didn't seem to speak. These sounds filtered disparagingly through the fingers covering his mouth. His disdain was gelid. He didn't take the glass from the woman's outstretched hand. He didn't move at all.

His indolence piqued Madame Blondel.

"Come now. Take your drink. Forget your cares. You'll see the Swede soon enough," she repeated.

His impromptu spasm was paroxysmal. It was as if a statue had come to life, gesticulating erratically. The classic posture of the Statistician's ancestors came undone. Not even Op Oloop himself knew what dramatic typhoons had lashed through him. He stood. He shook. He was stricken by convulsive gusts until he finally sat down once more. Then he took the glass. And, staring at the whisky the way one stares into a crystal ball, he spluttered the same words, this time with his voice tight, as though spitting out some insult.

"The Swede!"

He sweated.

Disgust made him mutter obscure imprecations.

Just then, a jubilant cry drowned out his drivel: "Look! Here she is! The Swede!"

He trembled in stupefaction.

Madame Blondel took his glass so he could stand, more to avoid having him spill whisky on the carpet than out of any sense of courtesy.

Op Oloop was now immobile, his maw drooping, his face a wooden effigy.

Gawping wide-eyed at the young woman who approached, he found himself delving determinedly into the banks of his memory. Something vibrated within him. His mind flashed like a camera, and he captured the image of her entire body. Her appearance was not what he'd imagined, though it was similar or analogous to one he'd stored back in the multitudinous arcades of his mind. Febrile, he rummaged through them, as if on the verge of identification. Suddenly he became overexcited.

"What! Can it be?"

He observed identical characteristics, a familial resemblance, the same mannerisms as another woman to whom he had once been devoted. And then his interest cleared his vision. In fact, it became sharp and perverse. And while the Swede asked the *madame* to change a fifty-peso note, the Statistician's bewilderment turned analytical. Shamelessly, crudely analytical.

His suspicions must have been manifold. They settled into insolence.

"You're no Swede," he spat in Swedish.

The girl's shock shook her limp, spent, depoeticized flesh.

"You're no Swede!" he reiterated violently. "Why do you lie? What's your name?"

Turning her head indifferently, the girl gazed at him in silence. She was suffering this onslaught of factuality without a sound. It had worked many times before—suffocating the embers of truth with the solid ash of silence. She said not a word. Not a word. She took the money Madame Blondel held out to her and left the room.

Op Oloop stared at her from behind, retaining the image of her body in his eyes. He was thereby able to extract the methodology of her gait, the willowy ease of her canter, the swing of her hips. There were multiple coincidental features. Turning back to the *madame* he made an inquiry.

"What is her name?"

"Kustaa."

"Kustaa? What did I tell you? She's no Swede! She's a compatriot of mine! She's Finnish!"

His elation gasified into a sort of affected giggle. And his breath, sheathed in his smiling glances, floated around the waiting room. Two harlots approached him. Madame Blondel handed him his whisky back.

"Fine. Let's drink to the health of your compatriot."

Having been just on the verge of downing it, he now lowered the glass from his lips in slow motion. And his face clouded over to such a degree that he almost couldn't be seen through the haze. He was trapped in a miasma of fear and anguish.

Some people place their passions above their principles. Op Oloop was not one of those. His mental phalanx always came first. The word "compatriot" had sprung from his lips quite naturally as a geographical expression, but when the *madame* repeated it teasingly, it resonated uneasily. He had no *patria*. He didn't believe in the well-intentioned exclusivity that enclosed the borders of each state—only in the ill intentions of every individual that had yet to be purified by the sacred fire and gleaming waters of revolution. And given that he accepted the universality of sex without restricting it to any particular region, the scruples that guarded his conscience rose up in revolt, demanding a modification of that patriotic faith. His inner battle became progressively more chaotic. It took him over entirely. He felt his old platoon of ideas begin to march to the bugle of irony. He suffered the scorn of knowing his error. But he overcame it. His patriotism was a synthetic substance that only surfaced after he'd decanted his great universal love. He recalled having ruminated on exactly this subject on a number of occasions. And he repeated this verdict, dispelling the opprobrium that clouded his face *comme par magique*.

He stood.

He took two slow sips of his whisky.

He was impassive.

A statuesque *porteña* stuffed into a skintight silver lamé dress discerned that, having recovered his senses, Op Oloop had become approachable. In a cunning attempt to commandeer his attentions, she exaggerated her usual display of lasciviousness. She sauntered over slinkily. Her *parfum de boudoir* almost oiled the Statistician's nose. Stroking her gauzy gullet in voluptuous enticement, she made her intentions clear. She awaited his command impatiently.

But it never came.

Op Oloop classified her particular lack of class almost instantly, the moment he noticed her maneuvers: she was a rustic Venus, embellished by the endearments of a few choice idiots. He hated the type of harlot who prided herself solely on coming in a pretty package. Stupidity camouflages itself in beauty. And without knowing why, he turned away from her radiantly fatuous little head.

Regrettable.

His sorrow subsequently swelled. His eyes virtually collided with the darkened doorway of Kustaa's room, where the lights had just been turned off.

The sight of the emerging gallant disturbed him superlatively. Hatred and disgust. A small, angular man, buttoning up his vest. His sallow skin still shone with sensual sweat. And his eyes gleamed with satisfaction! Op Oloop followed his every step, almost confiscating his actions. He was no longer interested in his "compatriot," dumped in a corner, her blonde hair hanging loose, half covering her face and cleavage. He was no longer thinking of her. He was thinking of him. Or, rather, he was trepanning this stranger's brain, striving to discover the degree of his delectation, the cause of his congenial smile, the force with which he had swung his triumphant plunger . . . but Op Oloop's diligence didn't pay off. The only thing he was able to ascertain was that the most competent lovers are often those who are seemingly the least endowed by Mother Nature. So certifying said skill in this man's puny body, Op Oloop sunk his chin to his chest to scrutinize himself and sum up his own sorrows.

A fluty voice turned his head.

"Fine. See you soon, *madame*."

And as soon as the gentleman swung into the corridor, Op Oloop felt so inhibited that he stood stock still, blinded, like a conscript who falls asleep while standing night watch.

He was plainly in pain. Overwhelmed by an ache that turned everything to sadness, the persistence of his hopeless trajectory finally got the better of him. His eyebrows and lips both drooped downwards. Pessimist expression. His matte-white face seemed to have been whittled away to mist.

The incessant darting of his eyeballs could be seen under his closed lids. Again looking inward. Perhaps he was poring over the paradox of his prior passion for Kustaa and his consequent catastrophic realization that she was in the arms of another. Perhaps he was probing the enigma of why men fall in love with their dreams, which are then so destroyed by harsh realities that their dreamers become cuckolded by their own illusions. Perhaps . . .

4:00 A.M. "I thought you wanted to see your compatriot. Come, she's free now. Hurry up, it's four o'clock."

Op Oloop's eyelids fluttered with gusto. On opening them, his eyes were misty.

"Yes. Yes, of course. But tell me, who was that man that was with her just now?"

"Don Jacinto Funes. Good man. Spanish. Upstanding. Playing-card manufacturer."

Op Oloop's mind was still reeling. Hatred and disgust. He couldn't cast them off in so short a stretch of time. The idea of adultery obsessed him. He'd concocted a kind of wedlock with the Swede out of his anticipation. And without ever having heard her voice, he was already suffering from her infidelity!

Suddenly, against all expectations, an irrepressible force impelled him towards Kustaa after all. She was still in the corner. Vanquished, silent flesh. Brusquely, he placed his hand beneath her chin and tilted her head up.

"Kustaa!" he shouted.

And, thrusting his face towards hers, he planted a kiss on her. A stentorian kiss, styled to be sadistically sensual.

"Kustaa! I am your fellow countryman. I'm from Finland."

Squeezing her bare arms, he lifted her up off the ground. He raised her to his own height. He snarled, "Come on. Get going!"

Op Oloop was so overbearing now that his tone alarmed all the women present. He had a fabulous reputation for his gentility and culture, so no one could explain this boorish outburst. Still, the fictions we inhabit frequently change course when these narratives become interpersonal. Women of the night know this perfectly well. That's why they're docile and allow destiny or fortune to cast them this way and that, much as they cast their own shadows.

Kustaa hardly even raised her eyebrows. She fixed her gray pupils on Op Oloop. And she wrote off his rudeness with all the formidable forgiveness of the frail and undefended.

They entered the bedroom.

She turned on the light.

He slammed the door shut.

There was no tenderness or delicacy. Op Oloop was frenetic. There was a pirate aboard the ship of his character, and the first thing he threw overboard was urbanity. Next, choleric, Op Oloop embarked on satisfying his instincts: he ripped off the woman's red sequined dress in one go. He tore the bows and ribbons and lace off her bodice—what a terrible assault upon those bastions of modesty! What a fanatical ripping away of pins, sequins, bows! Like a bud surrounded by withered petals, her bust emerged, inglorious, sullied by slobber and anxiety. He ambushed her breasts, bruising them as he bit.

A demonic wind whistled through his teeth, born of *bisous* and plumbing the depths of his soul. While pleasure howled, reason spoke blearily in choked Finnish:

"Kustaa . . . I've seen you before . . . I don't know where . . . I don't know when . . . But I know you . . . Helsinki? . . . Uleaborg? . . . Aabo? . . . You're mine . . . You belong to me . . . Ever since we were children . . . You're engraved in my adolescence . . . My whole youth bloomed in the sun of your memory . . . Kustaa . . ."

Op Oloop's hands—usually so intuitive and sensitive—became brutal in his rapture. They ran up and down Kustaa's body tirelessly. They encircled her waist and neck. They stroked her thighs and stomach. They were now the slimy hands of a satyr . . .

"Kustaa . . . Do you hear me? . . . You've been mine since childhood . . . In forests of firs and poplars . . . like little bear cubs . . . we played in the snow . . . sleds . . . woodcutter's taverns . . . grog . . . Do you remember grog, Kustaa? . . . Kustaa? . . . Why don't you speak?"

The girl, hardened by resignation, hardly responded. Her native language cut through her like a knife, but she sat still, bendable as a blade of grass, tottering between Op Oloop's tenderness and his fury. She sat unspeaking, in a silence that whimpered through her eyes, as though she were dead, as though only the dregs of her soul still flickered within her. Her limp, spent, depoeticized flesh! Flesh serving as a proving ground for so many vilipenders! Vanquished, silent flesh!

Mulier sui corporis potestatem no habet: sed vir . . . What a tortuous truth! She had never been mistress of her own body. From her father, who tainted her with the terror of incest, to the compatriot who was now so deliriously devouring her, her flesh had never obeyed her own desires but only those of others. She recalled the days of boarding school, when her aunt and uncle had tried, uselessly, to screen her from the appetites of the other students. She ran through the brutish abuses of her first boyfriend, the abortion she was forced to have, and then the many depravations inflicted on her by her succeeding lovers. And reeling off this list of hardships, she recalled the rough treatment she'd received from the *souteneur* who brought her to Buenos Aires, and then the derision she'd endured in that very apartment. Never, never had she been mistress of her own body! Victim of outrages and ignominies, of brutality and ferocity, of kicks and slaps, she'd learned to expect nothing from men. So, lost in this bedlam of sin, her mind raced back to what should have been. She understood the lure of love and hated never having felt the exaltation of its idyll, the sublimity of a swoon. Her thoughts growing loftier still, she abhorred not having triumphed in the face of adversity, blissfully overcoming all her hardships by finding a good man who could be hers and hers alone. So, on summarizing her sacrifices—degrading, venal, naïve, extortionate—she kept silent so as not to sob.

Suddenly the Statistician's zeal abated. He lowered his eyes and hands both.

"Forgive me, Kustaa . . . I behaved badly . . ."

His contrition wounded her. She was so sleepy and exhausted she'd turned sallow, having decided—as on other, identical occasions when clients had lost control—that she would become a flesh and blood bibelot. A mere libidinal trinket. But now she changed tactics. Her initially dour disdain had evolved into sympathetic scorn. And she replied in Finnish, in a hoarse, hollow voice.

"Don't worry about it, sir. That's what we're here for."

Op Oloop was flabbergasted.

Something immutable, an overwhelming conviction, made his mouth go slack and his eyes shut tight.

"The same voice!" he murmured.

And hastily, chastely, he fumbled with her, attempting to cover her up with her torn dress. He had the uneasy impression that he'd profaned a venerated memory.

"Oh, no! That's not what you're here for. No one is here to be anyone else's rag. I behaved abominably. I don't know what's come over me tonight. I'm not myself. Forgive me, I beg you."

"I grant you my forgiveness. You have no reason to beg."

This made Op Oloop even more anxious. He flushed at his fiasco and found himself so mortified that, sitting on the edge of the bed, he was unable to look Kustaa in the eye.

She placed the palm of her hand under his chin—repeating sweetly the same gesture that he himself had made imperiously. And when their eyes met, their glances froze for a moment, as though they'd been down this particular path together before.

"Those eyes! . . . Your voice! . . . I've seen them before! Like my own flesh and blood!" Op Oloop babbled, growing desperate at not being able to locate her features in his memory.

"Impossible. We just met."

"That's not true. Everything about you is familiar to me . . . Where are you from?"

"Uleaborg."

"Uleaborg! Can it be? Are you telling me the truth?"

"I have papers to prove it. I was born the year of the war."

"Kustaa . . . Kustaa what? What is your family name?"

"Iisakki. Kustaa Iisakki."

"Iisakki? Hm. That rings no bells. Maybe I don't know you? But there's something inside me that makes me feel certain. Something that tells me that you've been mine since before you were born."

"Really! Calm yourself! You are far too excitable. It's as though you aren't even Finnish. Just a moment ago I was yours since childhood, now it's since before I was born. You must think I was quite precocious!"

When she spoke that way, her lips—rich in amorous nutrients—drew close to Op Oloop's. And they met in a soft, slow kiss.

Curiosity and cunning proscribed sleep. Naturally astute, Kustaa resolved to probe the secret passions and passionate secrets of her client. They had enough in common for her to be intrigued by him. Besides, she could often comfort herself after finding such things out about a client. Nothing consoles one's own disillusionment like others'. If all the victims of love banded together, the solidarity of their failure would change the face of the earth. She was vaguely aware of this. Besides, she had no patience for those phlegmatic men who always hid their pain—nor for the inapprehensible sorts who turned love into a simple pastime.

"I suppose you're married, just like all the others . . ."

"No."

"Good. Don't ever marry. Marriage is a tax on bachelorhood."

Silence.

"Don't be so shocked. I know because of all the tributes men pay us. Those of us who speculate in sexual contraband know all about the difficulties of love when it becomes subject to duties and obligations. Love requires freedom, or else it asphyxiates. Oh! Why do you look so ashamed?"

"Well, you see, I'm in love . . ."

Kustaa fell silent. The Statistician had put so much unction into his confession that she cherished its honesty, as though it had been an offering to her. Women are quite perceptive when it comes to assessing a man's romantic nature. They feel the pulsations of his desires, the flimsiness of his fantasies, as well as his vast potentiality. So, belittled by Op Oloop's greatness, Kustaa waited for him to speak next.

"Have you ever been in love?" he asked.

"Yes."

"Then why are you blushing?"

"Because no one's ever been in love with me!"

She cast her eyes down into the violet nimbus of the bags hanging beneath them. She shivered slightly. And when a sob bubbled up to the surface, Op Oloop pulled her to him.

"Poor thing. You poor, poor thing!"

In the time that had passed since he left Helsingfors, he had learned to quiet his instincts, domesticate them, tame them. The discipline of numbers, in part, and the steely control of his emotions, had made him unruly in his treatment of women. He'd never held them high enough in his esteem, since they—overwhelmed by solicitations, the constant demands of men—couldn't satisfy their urges selectively and then frame themselves in perfect morality, utterly composed, as men do. That's why his frequenting them was tangential: it served only to safeguard the status of Op Oloop's virility. He simply patronized them, taking their bait but refusing to enter their complicated labyrinths. That is, he sipped their nepenthes without being conned into concubinage. He tipped them, and, without criticism or pity, noted a name, a figure, and a few notes in his logbook. That was all. From time to time, in truly exceptional circumstances, when he trespassed into forbidden terrain and found a potentially interesting mate, or else some old mummy with an interesting past, he lingered on. For no logical reason, as he was consoling Kustaa, he thought of Paul Allard, the French intellectual put in charge of setting up a brothel for military use during the war. He wondered what could have become of him. And Hildebranda, the Italian countess who, according to her companions, had moved up in the world and was now known as "the camel," not because she had a hunchback but because of the frequency and ease with which she got down on all fours to allow men to climb on. And then he began to coo again.

"Poor baby! What a life you must lead!"

Kustaa, still teary, disentangled herself from Op Oloop's arms. She watched him stroke her with paternal tenderness. And, not knowing how else to show her gratitude, she stretched out, naked, atop the bed's violet coverlet.

The chromatic contrast favored her complexion. The reflections from the brocade enlivened her limp, spent, depoeticized flesh, making it shimmer vivaciously.

Op Oloop began to undress.

He was no puritan. Puritans are cynics possessed of a ludicrously stifled urbanity. He, by contrast, faced the vicissitudes of life with all the openness that life itself bestows upon the strong and healthy. Some believe that morality is intelligence, or rather, shrewdness; for Op Oloop, morality was strained determination, or rather, a vital rhythm. And that was why, at this juncture, he abandoned all his scruples and naturally decided to quench his thirst.

On seeing himself half-naked, however, a feeling of hostility caused him to shrivel. The sexual act, the *act* par excellence, disconcerted him immensely because it was so lacking in grace. Fervid, appallingly unaesthetic, its fleeting fury and subsequent groaning orgasm repulsed him unfailingly. He would have preferred it if nature had instilled the act of copulation with all the graces of equilibrium and ecstasy. And as if to underline its hideousness, when he lay down beside Kustaa, the disproportion of their statures stressed the supremacy of platonic love over the absurd plasticity of carnal love.

But her touch had already excited him. And he spoke, almost ruefully:

"Love is the only thing that makes a hypocrite of me."

Just as he was gripping her breasts in excitement, he heard the telephone ring stridently in the next room. Madame Blondel attended to the call. Marietti and Van Saal were on the line, asking for him. Op Oloop flattened himself against the lavender coverlet, all ears. An unjustified panic was crushing him. He heard her reply, almost peremptory: "No. He's not here. He already left."

And then, validating the lie, the same voice, derisive this time: "Sure! No problem! Like I'd really interrupt him *now!*"

Though they turned back to their amorous games, Op Oloop wasn't the same. He'd clouded up again. It was as though every grief and sorrow known to man had congregated on his face. He was awash with imprecision. His heart was wrenched by a vile vacuity.

Kustaa couldn't make sense of this change. She slipped from beneath him and sat up slightly to look at him directly. The Statistician turned his head away and in the process his lips collided with a dangling nipple. An impulsive, melancholic pleasure overcame him with new delights and fears. And, losing all control, he began to verbalize.

"Oh, baby . . . Oh, my little girl! . . . Who would have thought, eh? . . . We're lost . . . completely done for! . . . You see? . . . Our souls are in torment . . . torment! . . . They've been bitten by crocodiles . . . We only have thirty-four percent of our souls! . . . Let's cross that corridor . . . carpeted with creatures' buttocks . . . Follow me! . . . No . . . I don't want to enter those vaginal grottoes . . . Ivar . . . Do you know Ivar? Ivar Kittilä? . . . He's the one who told me . . . He says that on the other side of the sea of love lives death . . . This way . . . Tell me, are your arms lianas or venomous vipers? . . . Now you must salute . . . Now! . . . The captain of this army of penises is the sovereign of silence . . . Of the nutritious silence of death! . . ."

Befuddled and alarmed, Kustaa became increasingly desperate. It was this muffled, groaning desperation that led her first to curl up into a ball and then to jump out of bed, and finally to slap Op Oloop's hands and cheeks in the naïve hope that he would return to his senses. It was a miracle! His babbling ceased. Soothed slightly, she placed a cold compress moistened with cologne on his forehead, and then Op Oloop's paroxysmal drivel finally died down. As if emerging from a trance, he ruffled his hair, opened his eyes, and once more inspired trust and friendship.

"Please, don't be afraid . . . It was just a fleeting fit . . . I've been drinking . . . I just came from a banquet with friends . . . Overdid it, you know . . . I thought that the feast would be a tonic, would help me forget . . . But alas . . . Forgetting doesn't cure love . . . That's the truth, Kustaa . . ."

"Yes, I understand. But you scared me! You said such grotesque things! If my mother . . ."

"You have a mother?" he asked languidly, in a vague attempt to change the subject.

"Yes."

"Where?"

"In an insane asylum, in Helsingfors."

"In-an-in-sane-a-sy-lum?"

"Yes. After she divorced my father, the shame and sorrow drove her mad."

"Shame? Why was she ashamed?"

"Because of what he did to me."

Op Oloop, sweetly, beckoned her to his side. She accepted, albeit faintheartedly. Her eyebrows, generally raised in disdain, were now curved in bitterness. She lay down, resting her head beneath his right armpit. He ran his fingers through her hair.

"Well?"

"He raped me. I was twelve. It was quite brutal. There was a terrible scandal. It was unbearable. My grandfather, the literature teacher at Uleaborg Academy . . ."

"What? WHAT?"

". . . died during the trial."

"So you . . ."

"And my mother resol—"

". . . are Minna's daughter!"

"—ved to divorce him."

"Minnna Uusikirkko . . ."

". . . and once she had, she lost her mind."

". . . my childhood sweetheart!"

Without realizing how, they both found themselves standing in the middle of the room.

"You? The boyfriend that my mo . . . ?"

"So that's why you seemed so familiar! So that's why!"

They were both exhausted, panting, united in wonder.

The scene had been both compelling and pathetic. Each of them spurred on by who knows what hidden needs, they had dived head-first into that volley of revelations. Their words tumbled out, colliding with each other. It was an onslaught, and each of them raced full-throttle towards the other's old anguish. And, reciprocally, they achieved the immediate aim of being heard, as well as the lifelong goal of being understood.

Double victory and double defeat.

There opened before them, now, a vast and sinister expanse.

Reticent nostalgia and concerted rage. The vertigo of a spirit braced in by refinement, and the languor of a soul sickened by abandonment. An unfathomable moral anguish, striving in vain to share its guilt, and managing only to murmur . . .

"It's all because of me. If I had married Minna . . ."

And then came the calamitous tears that condensed all the heartlessness of the present moment into two words:

"My mother! My mother!"

There was a long pause. Anxious and oppressive.

Kustaa reacted first. Benignly—a naked Antigone—she led Op Oloop to the bed. Her tenderness was legitimate, chaste. But her words didn't translate into consolation. They were desolate, heartrending. They seemed more like lamentations.

Creeping ever more timidly, Op Oloop's subjectivity had entered the innermost jungles of the self. In his dejected resignation, even his flesh felt old. He retired to a supporting role. He let the deadweight of his head—an empty factory—loll to and fro like an idiot's.

Then he stood. His vision was blurry. His legs were jelly. He tried his best to dress.

"You're forgetting your vest," Kustaa said.

A poor choice of words. By association, Op Oloop recalled the Spanish playing-card manufacturer who had so offensively buttoned his up after gloating over his conquest. And all the Statistician's fury came to the fore.

"Out! . . . Out! . . . I will never allow it! . . . You're my daughter! . . . Minna . . . Good God! . . . I won't allow it! . . . Quickly! . . . Get dressed! . . . What are you waiting for, Kustaa? . . . You're my daughter! . . . The daughter of our dreams! . . . Minna and I dreamed of having . . . a daughter like her! . . . and a son like me! . . . You're just like her! . . . Where's my son? . . . Tell me! . . . I demand that you tell me! . . . What? . . . You think you can't conceive a child in dreams? . . . That you can't give birth in dreams? . . . Kustaa: come with me this instant! . . . I'll take you . . . You'll go with Franziska . . . With Franziska! . . . Do you know who Franziska is? . . . Oh, Franziska! . . . Fran . . . zis . . . ka . . ."

Kustaa's high-pitched shrieks pierced Op Oloop's gruff shouting and made their way to the hall.

Madame Blondel and the two other whores came running.

When they began to bang on the door, Op Oloop froze, petrified. His pupils were dilated. His mouth was sneering, his lips shone with spit.

The door opened. Instantly, the *madame* took charge, casting a domineering look all round. She knew that in situations like this, it paid not to talk. She slipped over to where Kustaa stood. She covered her fragile, faded body with a robe. And she exhorted her to speak:

"Tell me, quickly now! What's going on here?"

"He wants to take me away. He says I'm his daughter. The daughter of his dreams. He's acting crazy."

"Nonsense. Has he paid you?"

"No."

"Well, collect your dues."

And with that she stood back, prudently, in wait like a vulture.

Kustaa didn't know what to do. Some form of reverence kept her from interrupting Op Oloop's spellbound, hieratic trance. He was no longer just a "client" to her. He was the man who knew her mother. And through that alone, regardless of whether his other assertions were true, she felt a connection that put her in his debt, and made her disinclined to take money from him. She protected him in her pity. But the *madame*, inflexible, urged her on, winking. So Kustaa approached him. Pretending to whisper into his ear, she rummaged in the pockets of his vest, which still hung on the back of a chair. She felt bills. Exactly forty pesos. Bittersweet elation flooded her face.

"Here."

"Good. Now go. Leave him to me."

Op Oloop was still disorientated. Madame Blondel's outburst had produced further emotional distress. Trauma seemed to have overtaken modesty entirely. Stupefied, his mind was paralyzed. Organic unease inhibited the flow of his usual ideas and behavior. He dove, attempting to latch onto something, but was unable.

The *madame* took him by the arm.

"Come. Let's finish our whisky."

He rejected her deference. He strode out into the foyer, through the door that Kustaa had left open.

His sensibilities were entirely disordered: timid and audacious, fearful and irascible, all at once. His usual aplomb had turned to distrust. His customary good nature, which had led girls at houses of ill repute throughout the Republic to have such a soft spot for him, had vanished without a trace. Grim and pigheaded, he glared at them now, feeling besieged from all sides, hounded by a attack that had turned his soul inside out, showing it to be no more than the dirty interior of a glove. His moral sense had contorted in irritation. He, so measured, so meticulous, so well mannered, realized that he was being perceived in a different way. It was an accusatory perception, one that ascribed faults, slights, and misdeeds to him that he knew he would never commit. In that depressive pandemonium, his surging blood—overexcited by the great encephalitic workload required—provoked a choleric explosion . . . a gesticulatory choler, at first, full of ferocious tics intended to annihilate phantasms and goblins. A violent choler, afterwards, that turned sharply on Madame Blondel, as though she were the very embodiment of the force undermining his purity.

"You can't throw me out! . . . Why, I'm Kustaa's father . . . Not the father that raped her as a child, of course . . . I'm only guilty of not having materialized my dreams . . . with Minnna . . ."

"OK, OK. Just do me a favor and sit down, please."

"Never! . . . I don't want to! . . . You're trying to trick me . . . To punish me by forcing me to peek through the keyhole and see all of Kustaa's depravations . . . Never! . . . I know you, you old harpy! . . . Kustaa is coming with me . . . She'll live with Franziska . . . With Franziska! . . . Do you know who Franziska is? . . . Oh, Franziska! . . . Fran . . . zis . . . ka . . ."

"Yes, yes."

"*Yeeeessss.*"

It was a piercing cry, an upright, vertical cry rising up over the prone lassitude into which his earlier words had fallen. A shriek that alarmed the *madame* and led her to employ all of her cunning in an attempt to rid herself of Op Oloop.

"Yes . . . I'll dream her all over again . . . I'll transport her from this ludibriousness . . . Because Kustaa is mine . . . Mine! . . . Never again will she be had by some Spanish playing-card manufacturer . . . I won't allow it . . . Do you understand? . . . Come on, Mr. Playing Card, if you think you're man enough! I dare you to button up that vest again!"

On extending this challenge, unhinged, Op Oloop ran towards the room he'd just exited. He stopped just in front of the door. And, violently, wildly, he began to punch at his own hallucination. Then, flushed, impetuous, as though his illusory rival were attempting to flee, he followed him from one side of the room to the other, accosting him, tackling him, still screaming.

"Come on, if you think you're man enough! I dare you to button up that vest again!"

Finally the physical fatigue and neuropathic excitation exhausted him entirely. Images were superimposed, winnowing. Lights flashed, noises rang in his ears. There was the stink of magnesium, clownish giggling, explosions. He'd taken leave of his senses and at last entered the true chaos of sensorial insanity.

Madame Blondel was no fool. She was entirely ignorant of Op Oloop's secret logic. For her it was utterly incomprehensible. But she knew she had to get him out of there. She ordered the maid to find a taxi.

Meanwhile, she called Kustaa.

"You were right. He's out of his mind. Distract him. You're the only one who can do it. Then we'll get him in a taxi and end of story."

The soul is a dark room. In slowly learning to differentiate between his feelings, man illuminates it, little by little, and thereby manages to see inside himself perfectly. That perfection, however, startles him. And the radiance of the illumination dazzles him! But soon the intensity of this light becomes insufficient. Exasperated individualism becomes more and more exigent, demanding an ever more brilliant glow. Man wants the light to reach to the walls of his own flesh. And that desire isolates him and, by burnishing himself ceaselessly to achieve this new transparency, he becomes debilitated, damaged. And that's when calamity strikes. Terror turns his transparency opaque. The walls of the room tremble, buffeted by gales. And the soul slowly dims and reverts to what it once was: a dark room.

Kustaa approached Op Oloop. She called out to him. She sensed the doubt and disorder within. And there was a lone, low voice in the dark:

"Who are you: angel or devil?"

The Statistician came to his senses. His eyes looked out on the world once more, seeing without spying, without hallucinating. On recognizing Kustaa, he kissed her. Her kiss still tasted of insult. She kissed him back. His kiss still tasted of entreaty.

When Ramona returned to announce that the taxi was waiting, Op Oloop seemed calm—*furor brevis*—his ire now mollified, his fêted composure reigning once more. His blood flowed meekly through the delicate channels of his brain. His old eccentricity, transformed into a torrent during his fit, was a tranquil stream once more. His moral sense still reverberated, but now rather like the distant echo of a concert that's just ended. He had almost entirely forgotten the whole episode. Amnesia, in cases such as this, is a blessing from above. The ability to forget, subsequent to certain psychoneuroses, is like a providential cloak that comes to cover up all the misery that's been revealed.

Coyly, circuitously, the *madame* encouraged him to leave.

4:40 A.M.

"Kustaa, it's four-forty already. You got carried away tonight. Come now: it's late. I have to go and prepare your tonic. Say goodnight to the gentleman."

The Statistician watched both women forlornly as he formulated a question he couldn't translate into words. His inner voice was sluggish. After an attack, intellectual inflection often lacks fluidity. The wheels of his mind spun, but the friction they produced as they rubbed up against his nerves was excruciating.

Kustaa deduced his defeat by his docility, and it made her all the more devoted. She knew that under her compatriot's dark expression shone the bright spotlight—profound and true—of a goodness so pure it verged on inanity. And she wanted desperately to reach it. But she was impeded by *tristesse*. The simple, straightforward *tristesse* of a beast being led to the slaughter. And she leaned silently against his chest, offering the nape of her neck to the surrender of one final kiss.

And indeed, Op Oloop bent his head. Or rather, he let it hang *à la* Christ on the cross. He was spent. The touch of her skin and hair did not arouse him in the slightest. In fact, *au contraire*, it caused him to sob imperceptibly. And when they were about to separate, the Statistician encircled her waist only lightly. He hadn't the strength to hold her, to take her away. He tried to persuade her of his redemptive aims. But as Unamuno once said, to persuade one needs both right and reason. So how could he convince her? The shame of his failure sought solace in her hair. There was a moving pause, after which Op Oloop was again overcome by an intense urge to speak. But he had nothing to say. He searched his heart. It was full of deferred tenderness. What indescribable joy! Bringing it to his lips, he at last succeeded in pouring it into her ears so lovingly that when they separated, both were weeping.

Madame Blondel sent Kustaa to her room. But she returned immediately, holding Op Oloop's vest. The *madame* snatched it from her hands.

"Go back to your room this instant!"

When she tried to hand it to him, Op Oloop's eyes narrowed down to two prickly points. He ground his teeth, attempting to vocalize a diatribe that was strangled in a grunt. The *madame* was unable to interpret his disgust as being in some way related to his basic decency. Thus, she tried again, holding his vest out to him.

He snatched it from her and hurled it to the floor.

"Get that out of here—it's a disgrace! Again with the Spanish playing-card manufacturer? That miserable shit! Where is he? If I get my hands on him he'll never button another vest as long as he lives!"

Madame Blondel's eyes lit up. All through her wanton life she'd taken advantage of man's weaknesses. Whenever she was faced with their faults—inebriation, amorous frenzy, erotic perversion—she'd always managed to turn them to her advantage. Their weaknesses made her strong, contented, smug. Seeing his choler recrudesce, she advanced.

"He went this way. Come. Don't you see him? It's Don Jacinto Funes: he went this way. Follow me!"

The Statistician followed her footsteps, fists and teeth clenched. He was lacking even a child's basic distrust. By the time they reached the street, his inner turmoil had made him gaunt. He was feverish, sweaty, deranged; he was entirely in her power. She pushed him into the waiting car.

"There he goes!" she said. "In that cab! Straight down Santa Fe! You must catch him!"

She slammed the door shut and leaned forward to speak to the driver.

"Take him home. He lives on Larrea, the seven-hundred block."

Once back inside, slouching on the sofa, she downed Op Oloop's whisky like someone celebrating a narrow escape.

Beneath the canopy of heaven, the car slipped off into the night like a beetle.

4:50 A.M. Not ten minutes had passed when there came a knocking. Judging by the sound, the tapping of a key on the door, Madame Blondel immediately assumed it was either the Commissioner or some other assiduous client.

Her surprise turned to wonder when she saw Gastón Marietti—none other than Gastón Marietti!—come walking down the hall with two other gentlemen, one a nice-looking fellow with curly hair, olive skin, and built like a stevedore; the other somewhat older, frowning, pointy-faced, steel-chested, and rather resembling a javelin thrower. For her, this unimaginable scene was so great an honor, she had a hard time coming to terms with the sight. It was as if the Foreign Minister had shown up unannounced at some third-rate consulate. What a look Gastón had! And how he grinned as he savored each of his words!

"First of all, Madame, allow me to introduce my friends: Robín Sureda . . ."

"At your service."

". . . Creole through and through, and Piet Van Saal . . ."

"My pleasure, Madame."

". . . Finnish."

"Finnish? What a coincidence! We just had another Finn here a minute ago!"

"Op Oloop!"

"Exactly."

"That's why we're here. Would you mind telling us, Madame . . ."

"Please, have a seat. Ramona, bring us four Johnny Walkers."

"Though perhaps it may appear inappropriate, the reason we've come at this hour is because . . ."

"Oh, Monsieur Marietti, you know that my house is your house. I'm entirely at your disposal, no matter what the hour."

"Thank you. As I was saying, the reason we've come is to find out whether anything untoward has happened to Op Oloop. If he behaved normally while he was here. That's our chief concern. He's a good friend whom we all esteem greatly, and over the course of the day his health appears to have deteriorated due to a series of incidents I shan't enumerate. But, Madame, I beg you, if . . ."

"Well, let me tell you. Monsieur Op Oloop is always very proper. And we all know he's exceedingly intelligent, not just because of what he knows, but by the good-natured way he always converses with us in our spare time. It's only the real assholes who bother putting on airs in here."

"Did he tell you if he was going home?" Van Saal interrupted anxiously.

"Well, let me tell you. Monsieur Op Oloop arrived very late, which is not at all like him. He seemed on edge. He asked me to introduce him to a young Swede we have. The moment he saw her he was completely enraptured. The moment he heard her name he said she was actually Finnish. Then, even more on edge, he went off with Kustaa—that's her name, you see . . ."

"Forgive me, Madame. This is quite urgent. Do you know whether he went home?"

"Well, let me tell you. I was the one who put him into the taxi, after all."

"What! And was he inebriated?"

"Worse than that. Much worse, I'm afraid. When he was inside, in the bedroom, he acted very strangely. He ranted and raved—really lost his head. He said the girl was the daughter of his dreams. Of his dreams! Can you imagine? Do you want to speak to Kustaa? I'll call her. Anyway, then he had a couple of fits, just because another client buttoned up his vest in front of him . . ."

"Did he, by chance, do this other client any harm?"

"No. He attacked him . . . how can I put this? . . . in a dream. The client had already left. Then Monsieur Oloop insulted me just because I handed him his vest. He hates vests now, it seems. This one right here is his, actually. At any rate, then he asked me if I knew some girl named Francisca. The very name seemed to mesmerize him. I've never seen him like that, never seen him act so strange, so . . . how can I put it?"

". . . crazy."

His friends, nodding their heads, saved her from having to say the word. Each one said it to himself. Robín Sureda advised Van Saal to carry on his pursuit. The *madame*'s tale was now showing signs of having lost all perspective. Becoming increasingly perturbed, Piet attempted to bring it to a close.

"So then, Madame, you led him to the taxi. Did you hear him give the driver an address? Was he able?"

"No. I did it myself: Larrea, the seven-hundred block. Not far from here."

A devastating blow.

"Damn it! He moved quite some time ago! He lives in Palermo now, on Avenida Alvear," said the Student contritely.

"Come on! We haven't got a moment to lose."

"Maybe he's already home!"

Piet and Robín took their leave. The Maquereau, with a mixture of deference and urgency, spoke to her alone for another moment.

"So, Madame, work leaves you plenty of spare time? To what do you attribute such a drop off in business?"

"To vulgarity. Buenos Aires women used to be so demure, so honorable. And that meant that they were hard to pick up—there was more demand for our kind of service. Nowadays there's as much sleaze here as in any civilized city. Everyone's opening their legs! We ought to do away with vulgarity. Monsier Gastón, perhaps you could do something about it, since you have so much influence . . ."

A benevolent smile played on his lips.

"Yes, you're right. The truth is, the country has made a lot of progress since I started the 'road to Buenos Aires.' '*Nella raffinatezza dell vizio c'e la civilitá d'un popolo.*' But it's true. So much progress, so much civilization."

"It's not good for us. Do you remember the Centenary? Those were the days! It was such a pleasure . . ."

"Yes. Such a pleasure to see how virtuous all the women in Buenos Aires were!"

"We're waiting, Marietti," insisted Van Saal, plainly distressed.

"I must be off, Madame Blondel. At your service."

He bowed ceremoniously before joining his friends.

He would not for anything in the world want to seem unobliging. He was perfectly aware of the fanatical concern and support that Piet Van Saal felt for his friend Op Oloop in the present circumstances. And he wanted to honor this, offering all of the services and favors he possibly could.

They climbed back into the cab that had brought them there.

"Take us to Avenida Alvear," said Robín.

Certain people have a particular genius for friendship, shying away from the gaudy satisfaction of their instincts in order to dedicate themselves instead to the genuine recreation of intelligent camaraderie. Van Saal, for one. Ever since the Statistician had surreptitiously escaped from the Consul's home, he had been terribly worried, imagining the worst. True to his heart, loyal to his brain, he had embarked on a search, in an attempt to keep Op Oloop out of harm's way. He hadn't had a moment's peace. He had traipsed across the city several times already, running himself ragged in order to interrogate Op Oloop's acquaintances; telephoning the Statistician's home and the police station incessantly; taking the officer who had intervened in the traffic accident to all of his friend's favorite haunts . . . all for nothing. Not a single soul gave had given Van Saal a single encouraging clue. The more off-course he drifted, the stronger his desire to succeed. He knew his duty, in this time of emergency, and he didn't hesitate to chase down every last possible lead in trying to ascertain Op Oloop's whereabouts. Late that night he had returned from the Tigre River—where he'd gone in order to determine whether Op Oloop might have gone out alone on the Consul's yacht—and began to scour the *boîtes* popular with the Nordic crowd. Nothing doing. He returned to his friend's home. He waited until three in the morning. He was sure, by that time, that something terrible must have occurred. The Statistician, after all, was precision personified. In need of consolation, like many a man who's given up all hope, he returned to the precincts of pleasure. Perplexed, in a Scandinavian bar in Recova, his eyes suddenly widened. Ivar Kittilä and Erik Joensun were just walking in, somewhat unsteadily. He pounced and began to interrogate them.

"Well, what a coincidence! We've just come from the Plaza Grill, from one of Op Oloop's banquets."

He rejected their words. He couldn't believe his ears.

"Impossible. I telephoned the Grill. I telephoned the Grill!"

"Yes, I know. But he told the maitre to say he'd just stepped out. I remember quite well."

"He wouldn't do that to me! Not to me!"

"You could tell it really pained him to do it. You should have seen him! He was a real mess! Op Oloop is headed for deep waters, Piet. He's really losing the plot!"

Van Saal's dejection diminished. His *paisanos* sat down to explain further. Their walk over to the bar had aroused the demons of alcohol. That being the case, their explanations took on the fastidious attention to detail peculiar to certain drunks. Van Saal was therefore made painstakingly aware of each of the Statistician's inconsistencies, outbursts, and outlandish hypotheses. Even more heavyhearted than he'd started, then, he urged the pair to accompany him on his search. They flatly refused. Their flimsy excuses enraged him. He could stand no more. He gathered up their indispensable information and left.

The cab sped swiftly down the street.

The extended silence of Piet, Robín, and Gastón for a good part of the journey was the sum of three severe but silent soliloquies. Van Saal, the most distressed of the trio, finally burst out with his most recent conclusions:

"As far as I'm concerned, from this moment on, Erik and Ivar no longer exist—they're dead to me. I would never have suspected them of being so disloyal. Friendship is the most noble thing life has to offer. It supercedes love: its roots are deeper, its blooms more beautiful."

"And it supercedes death, since it is born not of material instincts but of a sublime stirring of the soul. Death eternalizes and immortalizes it."

"Precisely, Gastón. Erik and Ivar disgust me."

"Don't even mention their names! I don't know what the fuck they were thinking! And they had the nerve to subject us to their moronic reflections all through the meal . . ."

"And after the meal, too. They seem especially taken with you, Gastón. For some reason they seem to blame you for Op Oloop's moral and ideological deviations."

"That doesn't surprise me in the least. Those cretins don't dare insult their compatriot's genius. Op Oloop clearly deflated them with his dialectics. A few sophisms were enough to put their noses out of joint. But, as it turns out, they were depraved enough to take in literal terms what he clearly had set forth as paradox. Just imagine what would've happened had our friend actually been up to his usual standard! You know how well he conceals his superiority at a banquet—how he has the ability to erase any intellectual distance, lowering himself to the level of his friends' banality, their common chitchat. Well, tonight he was lugubrious, absent—in his own dream world, always afflicted and often dejected. And those two insignificant idiots spoiled everything, every step of the way, and all over nothing, without even taking into consideration the implications of the tragedy that we were attempting to preclude by humoring him . . ."

"What do you expect from a couple of jerk-offs like that? They spend all night acting chaste and modest, but as soon as they leave, Piet here finds them in some club, getting up to who knows what. As far as I'm concerned, the Sound Engineer is . . ."

". . . the sort who spreads his balls out on a table like a Spanish cape, as Rabelais would say, and then launches right into some tactless liturgy. Am I right?"

"You're right. And the Captain is a . . ."

". . . passive pederast. Don't you think?"

"Well, actually, that hadn't occurred to me. But I bow to your superior knowledge. I realize you're both perceptive and an authority on the subject. I just imagined he was so decrepit that he'd developed rheumatism of the prick."

They'd neared Op Oloop's house.

The moment the car stopped, Op Oloop's manservant, who'd been forewarned of their imminent arrival, popped his head out of the fifth-floor window.

"Is he here?" shouted Van Saal from the sidewalk.

"No."

The word fell like a cornice stone.

Op Oloop's friends were crushed beneath it, staring at each other in silence. They were too worried now to speak.

5:10 A.M. Piet's next proclamation impeded the progress of their ominous presentiments. He glanced down at his wristwatch: 5:10 A.M.!

"Come on. We'll go to police headquarters. The Inspector has arranged for the cooperation of every station in the capital. If there's any news of Op Oloop, they'll have heard. Let's go. This officer is very interested in the case. He's the one who was there at the crash on Avenida Callao and attended to the proceedings when the Consul whacked Op Oloop with his cane."

"That Consul's a real pig himself, while we're on the subject . . ."

"Don't remind me! He didn't even react when I slapped him in the face. A coward. It seems all my compatriots are showing their true colors tonight. One's craven, another a criminal. Still, I suppose that's life. Aren't the two of you tired, by the way?"

"Not at all! Nightlife is just training for students of medicine like myself. This way, when the hospital calls me in the wee hours of the night to perform some operation, I'll be fresh as a daisy."

"Something tells me those days could be a long way off . . ."

"Depends. I should have graduated four years ago, true. But I'm in no rush. Since I'm always in training, I'll always be prepared. Anyway, I've always worked at night: assistant at the syphilis dispensary, nurse at municipal health services . . ."

"I, too, prefer the night, for readily comprehensible personal reasons. What's more, it gives me great joy to see that other men do, too. As many as possible, as far as I'm concerned. The sun upsets me. I haven't seen it for ages. When I first began my career, this arrangement brought me no end of inconvenience, of course. Since I didn't have my company registered at the time, several checks actually expired before I was able to cash them."

"What a state of affairs!"

"You, Robín, know that I am epicurean. The hustle and bustle of the city, its daily drudgeries, all that makes my skin crawl. Just a plethora of machines, miseries, ambitions. Night, on the other hand, is fragrant, opulent. The city withdraws into itself, it retracts, it rests. And relishes itself. I prefer the pleasures of repose to those of movement. Stasis over kinesis. The maestro said as much: better to rest your legs under the shade of an olive tree than wear them out in the stadium."

The car pulled to a stop outside police headquarters.

"Piet, you go on in. We'll wait for you here."

"Scared?"

"Robín, I'm offended! It's simply a question of tact and tactics. The only thing I have to fear from the police are higher kickbacks. The Commissioner is a bit hostile, you see. In need of a little more sweetener."

Van Saal returned shortly.

"No news. I don't know what else to do! I can't stand not knowing! It seems so unfair to want to help so badly and yet have fate deny me the opportunity. Because I'm sure that Op Oloop is in need of assistance. I know it—I can feel it. I have a terrible premonition. And I can't do a thing!"

"Calm yourself, Piet. We're all almost as anxious as you are. But there's no need to lose our heads. Go back in. Insist that they check all the precinct houses. Robín and I will wait here."

5:12 A.M. Op Oloop arrived home just as his friends departed.

From Madame Blondel's place to the seven-hundred block of Larrea, the Statistician's journey had been paralytic. Balled up in a corner of the back seat, every curve and turn was torment, making him wobble and sway like some amorphous globule. There was no conscious tension in him to maintain his material order. No human element to restore dignity to the hierarchy of his life.

On nearing his passenger's old home, the driver, believing him asleep, shouted, "Here we are, sir!"

But he was not asleep. The driver ascertained that Op Oloop was watching him, albeit without focusing, and that his passenger's brain was functioning, albeit so slowly that driver could only assume that he was on drugs. He reached out and jiggled the globule back and forth.

"Here we are: Larrea, seven-hundred block."

The miraculous power of numbers! Mechanically, Op Oloop replied:

"I no longer live at Larrea 721. Take me to Belgrano, the corner of Cabildo and José Hernández. What are you waiting for? I need to complete my thousandth entry! Why are you looking at me like that? I've suffered a defalcation. A sexual defalcation. Do you mind? Hurry up! Hurry up, I say!"

When they arrived, his friend the "manicurist" had already closed her "shop."

Rabid, he began to shriek, "Home! Avenida Alvear. Get a move on!"

He had never been so difficult. But just this once, he took pleasure in treating someone unjustly.

Muttering, he fell back against the seat once more.

Op Oloop's cranium was a nebulous, dark black sky. From the back of his intellect, a bilious light just barely projected the vortices of his personality. The crackling, dry leaves of his deeds and the dust storm of his passions rustled and stirred in this great void. His delirium sizzled and spluttered in a maelstrom of dreams. Everything buzzed. And a mournful howl pierced his soul, unbalanced his heart, and demented his pulse. A howl born of chaos, emitted by the miserable creature within him, attempting to prune away the aching branches of his nerves, to smash his emotional looking glass.

He bowed his head disconsolately. He'd broken out into both a hot and cold sweat. He tried desperately to make himself feel again. All in vain. His resolve lay in ruins. Noble goals reduced to rubble. Walking among them, he felt wounded by the awareness of his own helplessness. Feelings of failure, of fear, swarmed around the crumbling columns of his valor, whose shafts still showed traces of nobility and pride. And in the antiques market frequented by his old inclinations, he found that hesitation, distrust, abulia, and negligence had plotted his definitive downfall. He tried again to modify his mindset and to feel—but was unable. An enormous owl, in command of his interior landscape, occluded the horizon with its wings.

The taxi was now on Avenida Alvear. Op Oloop rolled down the window. The river wind rushed in and a thousand tiny, wholesome jets of air penetrated his pores. This manifold booster shot helped him cast off his melancholic panorama. And the tenuous, bilious light within him, channeled now into a fury of gusts and flames growing stronger and more forceful, swept through his eyes in a whirlwind that surged from the inside out. Only four reluctant petals, hangers-on, remained: Freedom. Toil. Education. Love. Four petals of a flower that would never again bloom in Op Oloop. He sighed. And then they fluttered out as well.

Op Oloop was empty now. He realized at last what utter desolation was. All that was good and bad, all that was future and all that was past, had left his being: the excellence of egotism; the Pythagorean delights of numeracy and methodology; the pomps of art and caprice; the extravagance of ecstasy; the consolation of vice. Hovering in that void, he intuited his state. And summoning all of his strength—like a man with an incurable illness, on the verge of giving up hope—he overcame this depressive bout and managed, briefly, to appear to return to his senses, to a state of tranquility.

"Stop here. Second building on the right."

On entering his apartment, he found his manservant waiting.

"Sir, what is it? Are you ill? Have you been hurt? The police have been asking for you quite insistently. Monsieur Van Saal has stopped by several times. He was here with some other gentlemen not two minutes ago. Can I be of some assistance? I'm at your service, sir."

Op Oloop handed him his hat and gloves.

"What? Something stuck in my teeth? What are you staring at?"

"Nothing, sir."

"Good. Then go to bed. Oh! One moment. Franziska . . . Mademoiselle Franziska Hoerée. Did she call for me?"

"No, sir."

"*No sir*," Op Oloop mimicked the man, in his thoughts, as though pointing out an unforgivable omission. "No, sir—no, sir! Of course not. Why would she? All the same. Whores, every one of them. Fickle. Not fit for the heroism of love! Why would she call? Of course not."

He crossed the room sullenly. He locked the door of the study behind him. And as he paced inside it, he picked up the thread once more.

"But that isn't right. It's not possible. Franziska is different. She's the faultless fiancée. Her perfect tiara protects and illuminates me. Her veil of sighs could never conceal disloyalty. No, no, no! Franziska knows that our love reigns supreme over all that opposes it. This is her father's fault. The Consul! Implacable hyenas. Poor Franzi! All for being faithful to me. But no! They won't win. Our love is paroxysmal, yet we needn't go up in the flames of desire nor smolder in possession. We've already found our place in the blue meadows of death . . ."

5:15 A.M. The clock struck quarter past five. The reverberations of the gong floated in Op Oloop's words. He hung suspended, pursuing its chimera.

Then, though he couldn't say why, the open door beckoned him out onto the balcony. The vertigo was appalling! A macabre whirlwind of notions made his head spin. He attempted to regain his balance and another whirlwind made the buildings, trees, and automobiles spin in a demoniacal pandemonium. Caught in the midst of these two types of chaos, he windmilled frenetically in and out of himself. Like a shipwreck, he felt himsef smashed up against the railing. Havoc whipped ferociously through him. When he dared to open his eyes, the street was upended. The asphalt turned to rubber and stuck to his eyelids. It yanked and pulled him so forcefully that he staggered and stumbled, nearly giving in. Just when vertigo was on the verge of wrenching him free, Op Oloop shut his eyes, guillotining its magnetic pull.

Perspiring, he rapidly reversed back into the study. He sat. Amid all this mental mayhem a great beam of bright light shone through.

"The blue meadows of death!"

And in these meadows—glorious frieze—the fine, fragile image of Franziska, refracted ad infinitum, each icon reflecting new beauties, each image comforting him anew.

But he was unable to lose himself in this wonder.

On recovering, his study—full of bookshelves, adding machines, and diagrams—filled him with disgust. He who had filled his days with data and knowledge now saw the negative side of this vanity. It was all so insufferable! It had all been for nothing. He felt no pain, only scorn and derision at seeing Time wag its empty wineskin at him, offering advice:

"Idiot! Next time, fill it with love!"

Writhing in his chair, stricken by sharp spiritual pangs, he put his hand to his chest and felt his notebook. Intoxicated by a sudden obsession, he impulsively turned to the pages of his libidinous statistics. In the section assigned to Number One Thousand, he began to write.

> KUSTAA IISAKKI, 21. Finnish. Blonde, secretive. Daughter of Minna Uusikirkko. Nearly my daughter . . . Daughter of my dreams! *Coitus interruptus.*   0 0 0 0 . . .
>
> OP OLOOP

As he printed his row of zeros, a lump formed in his throat, and he whimpered:

"Is that love, Minna? Is that happiness, Kustaa? Is that what awaits me, Franzi?"

He blushed. The answers—quite obvious—made his affective aberration all the more apparent. No emotion seemed agreeable to him at this stage. His gloom grew from feelings of futility. When he concluded his statistics of sensuality with his signature, the four Os of his first and last names aligned with the four zeros of the row above. He found it to be distressingly, depressingly symbolic. And on closer scrutiny, he interpreted the four zeros as destiny's judgment of the four cardinal aspirations of his life: freedom, toil, education, love. And his waning passion for life took on a crepuscular hue.

The art and science of everything resides in knowing how to deal with one's destiny. As an adolescent reading Daudet, Op Oloop had gleaned that truth, which guided his steps at many crossroads. But on that night, every *fatum* and *ananke* had gathered in the cavern of his cranium. He could not shake them off. The tricks of the trade that he'd used for twenty years to raise himself, refine himself, lionize himself, all failed. They were mere mirages, lavish *burladeros* where he'd hidden from his predetermined fate. So predetermined that it glinted in the four nullities of his name!

The Statistician submerged himself now in a placid pool of tranquility. He quickly tallied his life's trajectory. He had missed the mark. He scrutinized the possibility of charting another course. He was afraid. He submitted, then, to his fate, his impotence and his sterility. And he accepted that he was the incarnation of an absurd theorem.

Seeing the envelope for Van Saal that he'd neglected to finish addressing that morning, he touched it with his fingertips. The solitude of the *S* rudely indicted him. As redress, he resolved to write to Piet first. The numen channeling his spirit's last energies focused his lucidity so spectacularly that, rather than write, it seemed as if he merely transcribed:

Dear Piet,

Silence! As long as life can be endured in dignity, it is our duty to live it. But when one has proven the fallaciousness of his guiding principles, living is cowardice. Do not judge me. Only death can judge life. This is my decision.

Silence! Let your compassionate smile be a delicate flower. Let the tiny sun that dances in the pupils of your eyes be the sun that shines into the chasm of my rest. The sun that slides down in your tears.

Silence! Why should I exalt you in some sterile recollection? Reminisce with me. You, too, are the product of remembrances. Never allow them to be actualized by love! It would bring back the memory of the false future that you'd forged in your fantasies. And that is fatal.

Silence! You know that in my egotism I have contradicted as many assumptions as I could, and that now I contradict the supreme principle wherein duty resides. You know that as I descend into euthanasia I am mocking God. Well, deal with it.

Silence! Do not drape your pity like a blanket over my body. Do not set an example with some phony philosophy. We are all examples already: of the futility of the lives free of paradox that we lead in our deepest selves . . .

Silence! A tragic, contorted silence. My breath returns to the air, my fire to the sun, my shadow to the earth. And all of my joy to the indispensable muteness of the world. Not a word. You'd run a terrible risk. You might hear yourself . . .

Silence! I am a soul full of death. This makes me proud. Death is the only fortune worth possessing. From a posthumous distance I'll seek your amity, which was the greatest blessing in my life. We'll chat on the path of mystery.

Hosanna, Piet!

OP OLOOP

He quickly read back over the letter, unfeeling. He was simply effecting a plan that must have hatched in his subconscious, now bringing it to lazy fruition. He took another sheet of paper and wrote.

Gastón,

Kustaa Iisakki, the "Swede" you told me about, happens to be the daughter of my psyche. Though in fact I did not make my dream material, I am still responsible for her reality. Due to the love I had for her mother—Minna Uusikirkko, daughter of that Uleaborg Academy literature professor—I beg you to cooperate with Piet and Franziska in the noble task of redeeming her soul.

I am confident that I can count on you, as I always have.

OP OLOOP

He smiled gravely as he blew the ink dry. His writing was neat, steady, sober. Immediately thereafter, without the slightest hesitation, he put something else into writing.

I, Optimus Oloop, bachelor, thirty-nine years of age, native of Uleaborg, Finland, do hereby declare in this holographic last will and testament:

First: That I have no compulsory heirs; Second: That I have no outstanding debts nor is anyone indebted to me; Third: That my patrimony consists of the furniture in this apartment and twenty-eight thousand pesos that are deposited in the Banco Anglo Sud Americano; Fourth: That I bequeath the furniture and all scientific instruments to the National Center of Statistics and the rest of my belongings to my manservant; Fifth: That I bequeath my money, in equal parts, to Minna Uusikirkko, Kustaa Iisakki, Piet Van Saal and Franziska Hoerée; Sixth: That as the first named party is hospitalized at the Helsingfors Women's Insane Asylum, Piet Van Saal will be authorized to administrate her sum to help her recover her senses; Seventh: That as the second named is a prostitute *chez* Madame Blondel, in this city, Franziska will be authorized to administer her sum to re-educate her; Eighth: That my body is to be cremated and my ashes scattered over the Río Plata by the Commissioner of Air Traffic Control, Don Luis Augusto Peñaranda, where the city's sewage pipes drain into the river; meanwhile, the Head of Sanitation, Don Cipriano Slatter, is to write the following epitaph on the beach:

HEAR LIES OP OLOOP.
FOR HIM, NOTHING WAS HARD
EXCEPT LOVE,
WHICH IS WHY HE LOVED
EASY WOMEN!

Ninth: That I name Don Gastón Marietti, faithful friend whose wealth and culture surpass good and evil, as executor of these provisions. In Buenos Aires, this twenty-third day of April, 1934.

OPTIMUS OLOOP

His indifference shattered as he signed the will. The contraction of Optimus he was used to employing had been decided upon when he was a young boy, during that ineluctable melancholic phase that accompanies life's first disappointments, when one despises everything, starting with oneself. From that time on, he only signed his full name on official documents. The letters, those final expressions of his soul, had not been invested with any particular significance for him. They were simply the last examples of his pulchritude—

nothing more. But having now signed the ultimate document, Op-timus regained the sense of superior decency implicit in his own etymology. And he, who had been so accustomed to concealing it in life, was proud to flaunt it in death.

He wrote Gastón's address on an envelope. And without stopping to consider the logic of his actions—guided only by the habit of leaving his correspondence on the desk for his manservant to dispatch in the morning—he placed the corresponding postage on the letter to Van Saal. Wishing to do the same with his will, he was pervaded by a sense of impatience on ascertaining that he had only one-centavo stamps left. But this did not detain him. As Marietti's envelope was adorned with a scarlet border occupying much of the blank space, and as the certified cost of the postage required far more one-centavo stamps than would fit on the front, Op Oloop meticulously affixed the rest to the flipside, adding this inscription on the obverse, just below the border:

"Postage continues on back."

The Statistician seemed to be under a spell, behaving like a mute android. His determination, perplexingly predetermined, precluded all verbal discourse.

He stood. He attempted to walk. But a gushing, fulsome agony welled up in his throat. He couldn't just leave this way. His eyes, moved by an unspeakable desire to weep, would not let him.

He sat again, and wrote:

> The devastation of love has ordained my death. Its miracle undertook the definitive sabotage of my soul.
>
> Don't be angry, Franzi.
>
> Men who love Love flee from women in search of Woman. My case exactly. But when I found you, my peace was shattered.
>
> Don't object, Franzi.

I am for all intents and purposes dying of love. What an odd experience! The perfection of love destroys the very happiness it engenders.

Don't repent, Franzi.

Life is a whole series of columns, bearing the weight of immeasurable death. The fall of one man is innocuous, as is removing one column from a structure. Removing one column does not bring the heavens above tumbling down.

Don't fret, Franzi.

Love is like a falling stone. If there was no ground to stop it, it would plunge perpetually into the soul.

Don't whimper, Franzi.

I'm going to the world of the dead in the hopes that I shall be with you; when you dream of my absence, you will wake by my side.

Don't worry, Franzi.

Forgive me. I who have overcome life's worst hardships simply cannot bear the purity of your love.

Don't cry, Franzi.

Only I have the right to cry . . .

OP OLOOP

A bitter flood of tears streamed down his cheeks. Shocked, he noted that he was unhappy. Then he saw two arms outstretched towards him, offering tearful, tender mercies.

"No. No. No. It's too late. Impossible!" he shouted, afraid he would succumb again to life.

He put the letter in his wallet and stood. He opened the balcony door slowly. And from the far side of the study, like a high diver trying to dissipate his fears by diving blindly into his destiny, he ran through the threshold and jumped into the abyss.

Isochronally stricken, in the midst of sleep, Franziska shrieked, her shrill cry piercing the air. For her insomniac family the sound was another sliver of pain in the silence. For Op Oloop, it was the soundtrack to his demise.

His leap was exact, mathematical. The initial arc—head tucked between taut arms that spread out gradually like wings—was as graceful as a swan dive.

But the speed of the impact smashed him to pieces. Op Oloop's body lay inert on the pavement, fragments flecking his tie. Having cracked his skull on the curb, his encephalic matter oozed out. His right arm was twisted grotesquely and his hand had come to rest atop a pile of dog droppings. His wristwatch appeared to be intact. But the clock—his life—and

5:49 A.M.

his life—always lived by clock—had both stopped ticking at 5:49 A.M.

From the fifth floor, Op Oloop's manservant heard the commotion made by the first passersby. Once he overcame his horror, he telephoned police headquarters.

When Piet, Gastón, and Robín arrived, the Inspector was already making his way through the onlookers gathered there. Swiftly, on his motorcycle, he had beaten them to the scene, not so much out of pride in his duty as police officer, but more because he was in a hurry to prove the accuracy of his earlier premonition.

He was glancing round, smugly. Having been correct, he was now arrogant.

As Van Saal approached, he froze in horror. His face ran the gamut of dismay and desperation. His friends attempted to lead him away, but he stood rooted to the spot. His persistence smacked of masochism, as though he were attempting to overcome his pain with sheer horror.

Just at that moment, a boisterous gang of night owls walked up. Doctor Daniel Orús (Junior) poked his head in. On seeing the Statistician's corpse, he called over his fellow merrymakers. And, as he nudged two bits of brain together with the tip of his cane, he spoke derisively.

"I know this guy! He likes to fake fainting spells. Well, he's certainly fucked this time. A catastrophe was in the cards."

Piet's nerves couldn't withstand this latest outrage. He charged, furiously. If the Inspector hadn't intervened, there might have been another corpse on the street.

Robín, gifted in the art of defusing enmity, spoke up.

"Allow me, Marietti. Take Piet home. I'll arrange for the body to be picked up."

As he climbed wearily into the car, Van Saal suddenly seemed decrepit. Broken by hardship, doubled over by tragedy, his face withered.

"Come, Piet, a bit of fortitude. At least let's show that there can be valor in resignation. Let your sympathy surpass your sorrow. Op Oloop would have wanted it that way. His life and death were doubly cursed by the philosophy and order of numbers. But now the ultimate tally has been taken. Fortitude!"

No reply. There was nothing that could console him. He could still see his stiff friend on the black screen of his mind. He rejected the evidence, instead mulling over the bygone splendor of Optimus Oloop.

Almost home, his voice subdued, he whispered to his ill-fated friend:

"I told you, Op Oloop, I told you. Love is light and darkness both. Blinding light when the spirit is empty, but when it is knowl-

edgeable and disciplined, it is dark . . . . dark . . . .
. . . . dark . . . ."

And the night, EMERGING FROM ITS DARK, SOMBER TOMB, MADE WAY FOR DAY.

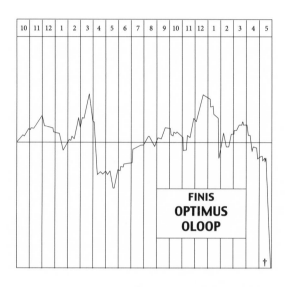

JUAN FILLOY was an excellent swimmer, dedicated boxing referee, and talented caricaturist; he spoke seven languages and he practiced as a judge in the small town of Río Cuarto, where he spent most of his life. He died in 2000 at the age of 106. A world-champion palindromist, he mined the entire dictionary for his books, coined new words, and used only seven letters in the titles of all his works.

LISA DILLMAN is the translator of over a half dozen book-length works of literature, history, and pedagogy. She is a professor in the department of Spanish and Portuguese at Emory University in Atlanta.

SELECTED DALKEY ARCHIVE PAPERBACKS

SELECTED DALKEY ARCHIVE PAPERBACKS

HARRY MATHEWS,
  The Case of the Persevering Maltese: Collected Essays.
  Cigarettes.
  The Conversions.
  The Human Country: New and Collected Stories.
  The Journalist.
  My Life in CIA.
  Singular Pleasures.
  The Sinking of the Odradek Stadium.
  Tlooth.
  20 Lines a Day.
ROBERT L. MCLAUGHLIN, ED.,
  Innovations: An Anthology of Modern &
    Contemporary Fiction.
HERMAN MELVILLE, *The Confidence-Man.*
AMANDA MICHALOPOULOU, *I'd Like.*
STEVEN MILLHAUSER, *The Barnum Museum.*
  In the Penny Arcade.
RALPH J. MILLS, JR., *Essays on Poetry.*
OLIVE MOORE, *Spleen.*
NICHOLAS MOSLEY, *Accident.*
  Assassins.
  Catastrophe Practice.
  Children of Darkness and Light.
  Experience and Religion.
  God's Hazard.
  The Hesperides Tree.
  Hopeful Monsters.
  Imago Bird.
  Impossible Object.
  Inventing God.
  Judith.
  Look at the Dark.
  Natalie Natalia.
  Paradoxes of Peace.
  Serpent.
  Time at War.
  The Uses of Slime Mould: Essays of Four Decades.
WARREN MOTTE,
  Fables of the Novel: French Fiction since 1990.
  Fiction Now: The French Novel in the 21st Century.
  Oulipo: A Primer of Potential Literature.
YVES NAVARRE, *Our Share of Time.*
  Sweet Tooth.
DOROTHY NELSON, *In Night's City.*
  Tar and Feathers.
WILFRIDO D. NOLLEDO, *But for the Lovers.*
FLANN O'BRIEN, *At Swim-Two-Birds.*
  At War.
  The Best of Myles.
  The Dalkey Archive.
  Further Cuttings.
  The Hard Life.
  The Poor Mouth.
  The Third Policeman.
CLAUDE OLLIER, *The Mise-en-Scène.*
PATRIK OUŘEDNÍK, *Europeana.*
FERNANDO DEL PASO, *News from the Empire.*
  Palinuro of Mexico.
ROBERT PINGET, *The Inquisitory.*
  Mahu or The Material.
  Trio.
MANUEL PUIG, *Betrayed by Rita Hayworth.*
RAYMOND QUENEAU, *The Last Days.*
  Odile.
  Pierrot Mon Ami.
  Saint Glinglin.
ANN QUIN, *Berg.*
  Passages.
  Three.
  Tripticks.
ISHMAEL REED, *The Free-Lance Pallbearers.*
  The Last Days of Louisiana Red.
  Reckless Eyeballing.
  The Terrible Threes.
  The Terrible Twos.
  Yellow Back Radio Broke-Down.
JEAN RICARDOU, *Place Names.*
RAINER MARIA RILKE,
  The Notebooks of Malte Laurids Brigge.
JULIÁN RÍOS, *Larva: A Midsummer Night's Babel.*
  Poundemonium.
AUGUSTO ROA BASTOS, *I the Supreme.*
OLIVIER ROLIN, *Hotel Crystal.*
JACQUES ROUBAUD, *The Form of a City Changes Faster,*
    Alas, Than the Human Heart.
  The Great Fire of London.
  Hortense in Exile.
  Hortense Is Abducted.
  The Loop.
  The Plurality of Worlds of Lewis.
  The Princess Hoppy.
  Some Thing Black.
LEON S. ROUDIEZ, *French Fiction Revisited.*

VEDRANA RUDAN, *Night.*
LYDIE SALVAYRE, *The Company of Ghosts.*
  Everyday Life.
  The Lecture.
  The Power of Flies.
LUIS RAFAEL SÁNCHEZ, *Macho Camacho's Beat.*
SEVERO SARDUY, *Cobra & Maitreya.*
NATHALIE SARRAUTE, *Do You Hear Them?*
  Martereau.
  The Planetarium.
ARN...

CHR...
GAI...
DAN...

JUN...

BER...

AU...
VIK...

JOS...

CLA...
GIL...

W. ...
GE...

PIO...
STI...

JEA...

  Monsieur.
  Television.
DUMITRU TSEPENEAG, *Pigeon Post.*
  The Necessary Marriage.
  Vain Art of the Fugue.
ESTHER TUSQUETS, *Stranded.*
DUBRAVKA UGRESIC, *Lend Me Your Character.*
  Thank You for Not Reading.
MATI UNT, *Brecht at Night*
  Diary of a Blood Donor.
  Things in the Night.
ÁLVARO URIBE AND OLIVIA SEARS, EDS.,
  The Best of Contemporary Mexican Fiction.
ELOY URROZ, *The Obstacles.*
LUISA VALENZUELA, *He Who Searches.*
PAUL VERHAEGHEN, *Omega Minor.*
MARJA-LIISA VARTIO, *The Parson's Widow.*
BORIS VIAN, *Heartsnatcher.*
AUSTRYN WAINHOUSE, *Hedyphagetica.*
PAUL WEST, *Words for a Deaf Daughter & Gala.*
CURTIS WHITE, *America's Magic Mountain.*
  The Idea of Home.
  Memories of My Father Watching TV.
  Monstrous Possibility: An Invitation to
    Literary Politics.
  Requiem.
DIANE WILLIAMS, *Excitability: Selected Stories.*
  Romancer Erector.
DOUGLAS WOOLF, *Wall to Wall.*
  Ya! & John-Juan.
JAY WRIGHT, *Polynomials and Pollen.*
  The Presentable Art of Reading Absence.
PHILIP WYLIE, *Generation of Vipers.*
MARGUERITE YOUNG, *Angel in the Forest.*
  Miss MacIntosh, My Darling.
REYOUNG, *Unbabbling.*
ZORAN ŽIVKOVIĆ, *Hidden Camera.*
LOUIS ZUKOFSKY, *Collected Fiction.*
SCOTT ZWIREN, *God Head.*

FOR A FULL LIST OF PUBLICATIONS, VISIT:
www.dalkeyarchive.com